DREAMS OF TIME AND SPACE

Jumpmaster Press
Birmingham, Alabama

Copyright

Dreams of Time and Space, by Various Authors

Copyright ©2022 all rights reserved. No part of this book may be used or reproduced by any means, graphic, electronic, or mechanical, including photocopying, recording, taping or by any information storage retrieval system without the written permission of Jumpmaster Press™, except in the case of brief quotations embodied in critical articles and reviews.

This stories in this anthology are works of fiction. The characters, incidents, and dialogue are drawn from the many author's imaginations and are not to be construed as real. Any resemblance to actual events or persons, alive or dead, is entirely coincidental. Registered trademarks and service marks are the property of their respective owners.

Cover Art copyright: Sébastien Decoret Image ID: 108605032

Library Cataloging Data
Names: Various
Title: *Dreams of Time and Space,* by Various Authors
5.5 in. × 8.5 in. (13.97 cm × 21.59 cm)

Description: Jumpmaster Press™ digital eBook edition | Jumpmaster Press™ paperback edition | Alabama: Jumpmaster Press™, 2018 - 2022. P.O Box 1774 Alabaster, AL 35007 info@jumpmasterpress.com

Summary: A collection of creative Science Fiction stories written by talented authors affiliated with Jumpmaster Press™.

ISBN-13: 978-1-958448-48-9 (eBook) | 978-1-958448-12-0 (print)

1. Science Fiction 2. Anthology 3. Stories 4. Creatives 5. Authors 6. Collection 7. Writers

Printed in the United States of America

DREAMS OF TIME AND SPACE

Table of Contents

Ice Breaker by Rick McVey	5
Zarwendi Attack by R. Kyle Hannah	45
The AIs are Revolting by MarkAdam Miller	57
Toleris Prime by Don Heron	67
Children of The Sky by Gustavo Bondoni	81
Savortha's Tavern by Dale Kesterson	97
The Human Museum by R. Kyle Hannah	131
Incident on Kappa-15 by Will Neely	145
The Reggae Poodle by Joseph Valorani	175
A Darrius Knightman Mystery: Murder across a Sea of Stardust by Jorge E. Ortiz Marti	189
Mustangs by Art Lasky	231
Big Dreams by Patricia Spradley	237

ICE BREAKER

Rick McVey

Xylo Fanata gritted his teeth and grimaced. Another massive slab of ice split from the cliff and slowly toppled into the gargantuan metal hopper. It crashed atop the tons of ice already gathered in the battered box, a cloud of frozen flakes of icy dust slowly rising and settling as the slab rocked still. Roughly rectangular but with rounded edges, the box was pocked with dents and long scratches. Spikey shards of ice stuck out of the open top, confirming that the box was full. Before the dusty ice particles settled, huge wheels rimmed with jagged teeth slowly rotated, biting into the ice floor of the canyon. The flat transport cart below the box lumbered from the towering cliffs of ice to the processing station that would seal the entire hopper and fling it into orbit.

Xylo took a deep breath and slowly exhaled. He had been an ice miner for almost half of his forty-three years. He stared down from his observation tower, a smile pulling at the corners of his mouth. It felt unreal; in just a few hours he would finally be leaving it behind forever. He reached into the pocket of his parka and rubbed the small, metallic disk that he'd kept close to him since receiving it two months ago. He thought of his cousin, Charn Ringle, and the smile grew.

The entire mining operation was automated: the tall, thin tower that inched along the cliff walls, the powerful splitters that ripped the wall into chunks, the giant metal hoppers that caught the chunks, the lid assembly, and the maglev rail that shot the sealed boxes into orbit around the icy moon, Estopel. Xylo was just the overseer. His title might have been Chief Miner, but he was mostly a robot babysitter.

Now he would put the baby to bed one last time. He tapped the console in front on him.

"Convoy, this is Fanata. The last one for this run is going to the rail. I'm clearing the booth and headed to the Bug."

"Roger, Fanata," a woman's voice replied. "We'll have the last load locked down before you get here."

"Thanks."

"We're as ready to go as you are," she said.

Fanata doubted that was possible. He took one last look at the endless white crags of ice.

"Thanks," was all he said.

ଔ   ୭

The tiny Bug holding Xylo and his one bag rocketed down the same maglev rail that had flung the ice crates into orbit. Acceleration pushed him deeper into the oversized chair that held him snugly in place. Xylo felt the familiar sense of disquiet present every time he had been flung into space in the Bug, a small craft that was both ship and suit.

Xylo looked out of the small viewport of the Bug as it closed in on his destination. Below him, the gleaming white surface of Estopel, his home for the last 20 years, sped by. The ringed world–Honor–that held the moon in its gravitic grasp, loomed over the horizon. He shook his head. Honor, a name whose origin was lost in the mists of mythology, had always seemed wrong to Xylo. He had never found anything about the planet honorable.

He stretched his neck and leaned to his right as much as he could to see the immense structure that was his immediate destination. The giant cargo ship was constructed of dozens of metal boxes identical to the one Xylo had just flung from his mining camp. The Train.

The Train had been assembled in orbit above Estopel by joining bundles of the boxes nose to tail, 135 tanks in all. The colossal structure stretched more than two kilometers.

Xylo's Bug floated along the length of the giant ship until it reached the lead bundle of the train. A ring of squat tubes - the Train's powerful T-Drive ion engines – surrounded the bundle. It also held the small crew cabin that would be his home for the next week.

He felt the gentle nudge of altitude jets automatically direct the Bug toward a bulging oval jutting out from the lead bundle. A few other pods similar to his were already attached to the docking oval. One larger craft with blocky protuberances of various lengths extending in odd angles mixed in with the smaller Bugs. Xylo assumed it was a survey ship or maybe a shuttle from Estopel's lone orbiting station, Chilton.

The Bug's automated guidance system steered the ship in a slow and steady approach. He barely felt the contact with the oval. The locking mechanism clanked, and a gentle hiss filled the cabin. Xylo sniffed the tang of the Train's atmosphere as it equalized with the Bug's. The hatch opened fully, and he squinted against the bright light of the docking chamber.

He checked his vest pocket one more time to be sure that the disk from his cousin hadn't floated out during the flight. He pried his body from the seat and made the temporary adjustment to microgravity. Wedging his body for leverage in the small hatch, he pulled his bag from the small storage bin behind the seat and pulled himself upward out of the cabin.

Out of the Bug, he found himself in the relative spaciousness of a short round tunnel. A few meters ahead, Xylo saw the tunnel bend, and he floated through the tube's turns until he came to a set of double doors. Large red letters stenciled out a warning.

Caution. Pseudo-gravity systems active beyond doors. Proceed with caution.

He waved his hand over a small sensor in the wall and the doors smoothly slid aside. Xylo carefully put one foot through the portal onto the deck and immediately felt the pull of the artificial gravity coils connect him to the deck. He eased the rest of his body into the small reception room.

No one else was there. No surprise. It was an automated system under continuous AI monitoring. Trains ran on notoriously sparse crews. They were not going to waste personnel on greeting some ice slub from Estopel.

"Convoy, it's Fanata," he said to the open room. No need to tap for attention when there was continuous monitoring. "Which cabin is mine for this run?"

"Welcome aboard, Xylo," a smooth feminine voice replied. It was different than the one he had talked with earlier. He suspected that it was the train's AI. "You will be in Cabin 4 D," the voice continued. "Do you need any assistance to find it?"

"No, thanks," Xylo replied. "Been on these runs before. Just to be sure, though, tell me, when I come out of this reception room, I'll be on C Deck, right?"

"Yes, that's correct," the voice said. "If you like, I can display directional arrows on displays along each passageway for guidance."

"Sure, why not," Xylo said. He had learned the hard way to be confident in his ability to be wrong.

A panel beside the door marked Exit lit up with Xylo's name.

"Thanks," Xylo said. "By the way, what do I call you? Convoy?"

"Megaleena," the voice replied, "but my friends call me Eena."

Friends? Xylo thought. AIs don't have friends. Clearly, I have good reason to have confidence in my ability to fail.

"So, can I call you Eena?" he asked.

"Depends," she replied, "on how friendly we get, doesn't it?"

"Alright," he said, raising his eyebrows slightly, "message received. I'll stick with Megaleen".

"Eena is fine. I'll give you the benefit of the doubt," she said with a hint of a smile in her tone. "For now."

☙ ❧

Xylo looked around his cabin and nodded his approval. Not a luxury suite on the Holiday Habitat around Capstone but spacious enough to keep me from feeling claustrophobic, he thought. Centuries of spaceflight had taught humans to keep passengers and crew peaceful and content by giving them space inside the ship in proportion to the time they were going to be there. The roughly one-billion-kilometer flight from Estopel to Mussiana would take just over seven days and Xylo felt fine about bunking here for the trip.

He stowed his bag in a locker and sat on the edge of the bed. He closed his eyes, listening to the almost imperceptible hum of the Train's life support systems. He let the quiet and the warmth of the cabin soak into him. It was bliss. Life on the ice moon had been hard, lonely, and dangerous. He had chosen it anyway.

For all of its hardship, being an ice miner on Estopel was one of the best paying occupations in the Alliance.

Few people lasted on Estopel for more than five years. That was usually enough income for a comfortable life three-times over elsewhere. Almost anyone who stayed longer than five years usually lived the rest of their lives there, however short they might be. Xylo, a relatively young man at 43, had thought himself a lifer after twenty years. The Estopel admins figured him to be back after he took this year-long sabbatical.

He smiled grimly and shook his head. They hadn't even asked.

Xylo fished around in his vest pocket and pulled out the scratched and dented metal disk. He self-consciously looked around the cabin. He knew any surveillance sensors would be impossible for him to find without an illegal privacy sniffer. Illegal, but easy to find if you knew who to ask.

He knew he didn't need to worry. The five-cm disk was innocuous and represented no more threat to the Council than anything else he had brought onboard. He rubbed the warm gunmetal gray disk between his thumb and forefingers and thought of Charn.

He and Charn had been nearly inseparable growing up together on Mussiana, closer than any brothers. Now he was the only remaining family Xylo had. He peered at the disk and thought of the many games of Flip that he and Charn had played with disks like this. But this one was special.

Unlike a standard Flip disk, this one had an almost imperceptible line running around the outer edge, easy to miss. Xylo recognized it as soon as he removed it from the box Charn had sent him. He took the disk in both hands, his thumbs and forefingers twisted each side of the disk in opposite directions until the disk split into two halves. There were shallow concave indentations on the inner surface of each half. Not large, but just large enough to hold a tiny piece of folded paper.

Xylo and Charn had thrilled each other with secrets they had passed back and forth inside the hollowed disk. They had been childish and silly and unimaginably important to those two young boys so long ago. He had been amused to find that Charn had again hidden a note inside the disk. He had assumed it would say "Happy Birthday!" or some other mundane greeting. It did not.

He reached in to remove the note, to read it once again, when an alarm chimed over the train's intercom.

"Attention. Attention please. Acceleration will begin in five minutes. Stow all loose items and prepare your acceleration couch. Again, acceleration will begin in five minutes."

The alarm rang again, and the message repeated.

Xylo stood and spoke to the air. "AI, transform the bed for acceleration."

"Yes, sir," a gentle female voice replied. This definitely is AI, Xylo thought.

The bed folded into an L-shape, the head sliding up the wall as the foot of the bed moved and bent to form the seat and leg supports. The sides turned inward to provide lateral cushioning. No wasted space on a Train.

He screwed the disk back together and tucked it back into his vest pocket. He did not take the time to read the note again. It didn't matter. He knew it by heart. He still didn't understand it better than the first time he'd read it.

"Hurry home, cousin," Charn had written in small, neat letters. "New world, old world. Don't call. Find me."

The journey from Honor to Mussiana was relatively uneventful. Other than one night when Xylo had had dinner– and too much to drink– with the Train's captain, nothing much had happened. The fact that Xylo had been unable to get anything more than a smile from the very real and very lovely Megaleena at dinner that night made the resulting hangover that much worse.

Xylo noticed an almost imperceptible change in the feel of the ship, and he realized that the powerful T-drive engines had fallen silent. They had been firing almost nonstop for the whole journey, first to accelerate and then reversed to decelerate. Xylo knew their silence meant the massive Train had settled into orbit around Mussiana.

The Train docked at Processing Station Five, an ice processing factory that covered a relatively large part of the surface of Chip, one of the two very small Mussian moons. The neighboring moon, called Dale, was the topic of much wonder and scrutiny. No one knew the origin of those names, but questions drew the occasional snicker from old pilots.

Almost immediately after they docked, he gathered his belongings and hurried to catch a shuttle to Haven, Mussiana's orbiting habitat, where he would transfer to a lander to the surface.

The moon was small enough, and the factory important enough, to be equipped with pseudo-grav generators, and Xylo's walk from the Train through the travel hub was all at one gee. The shuttle to the habitat, however, was not. Years of working in the on-again, off-again gravity environments of Estopel had given Xylo the ability to quickly adapt to pseudo-grav changes. He easily adjusted to microgravity as he floated into the cabin of the shuttle.

He found a window seat, pulled himself into it, and settled in. Out the window, a tanker caught his eye as it zipped away from the station. He assumed it was loaded with water for one of the many orbiting habitats scattered throughout the system.

He closed his eyes in hopes of a nap and had almost drifted to sleep when someone gave his shoulder a tap. He looked up to see an older man, blond with subtle streaks of silver in his hair, floating in the aisle.

"Mind if I take this one?" the man said with a nod toward the seat beside Xylo.

Xylo gave him a grunt and shrugged his shoulders. "Go ahead."

The man pulled himself into the seat and strapped in. Xylo closed his eyes but almost immediately the older man spoke again.

"Kiren Slassen," he said, holding out a hand. "I think we may have met before. At a safety conference. I'm a tech on Chilton."

Xylo tried to not let his annoyance show. Fanata had never been much of a social animal and even after twenty years living in his small apartment on Chilton he only knew a few other residents on the station by name. Over two thousand Estopel workers called Chilton home; Xylo was on a first-name basis with less than twenty.

"Maybe," Xylo curtly said.

"Fanata, right?" the older man said, pointing at Xylo, then snapping his fingers. "Ice slinger! You from Mussiana?"

"Yeah."

"Garrard's World for me, born and bred. But I got a sister and a couple of nephews in New Athens I haven't seen in a while."

Xylo realized he wasn't going to escape this conversation. He inwardly sighed and decided to make the best of it.

"You got kids?" Xylo asked.

"Yeah, a son," Slassen said, "but I don't see much of him. Or his mom for that matter. He's a captain on a deep space survey crew on the station around Gris. Doesn't come inward often. We stay in touch but," he smirked, "he's got his own life."

Something about the way Slassen had said the last sentence made Xylo feel that it may have been a very long time since Slassen had heard from his son.

"How about you? Married? Kids?" he asked.

"Oh, no," Xylo said, waving his free hand as if to ward off an evil spell. "No sane person would hook up with me for the long haul. Not as long as I was slinging ice. Maybe now–" He let the sentence hang.

Slassen cocked his head. "You not going back?" he asked, squinting a bit.

"No," Xylo said, "twenty years is enough."

"Moving to Mussiana?"

"Maybe short term," Xylo replied. "I was born there, got a cousin there I'm looking forward to seeing again."

"Got a new job lined up?"

"Not worried about it," Xylo said. "I'm pretty well set."

"Yeah, you ice slingers are rolling in it, aren't you? Twenty years? That's some serious credits."

"And some good investments," Xylo said.

"I'm thinking it may be about time for me to make a change myself," Slassen said. "I don't have anything close to twenty years, but I've never been one to stay in one place for long. It's a big system. Still some places I'd like to try before I pack it in."

"Twelve worlds, One System!" Xylo gave a half-hearted, mock salute to the official motto of the Alliance.

"Twelve," Slassen snorted. "When I was a kid it was just ten. They grant planet status like it was a popularity contest or something. Arturus isn't even a real planet. Just a big moon around Honor."

"It's bigger than Morgana. Bigger than Capstone and Escapia."

"But those are real planets that orbit a star," Slassen retorted with vehemence. "Sure, Arturus has a big habitat, but it's just a moon!"

Xylo had no desire to discuss politics. He shrugged and settled into his seat.

"I don't know why we keep pouring all our resources into this system anyway," Slassen said, leaning closer to Xylo and lowering his voice. "We ought to be working on developing new seed ships and heading out for a better place for humans to live. Even if it takes generations. We did it before. Except maybe this time we can find a system with a few decent places."

Xylo had heard the lunacy too many times. A decent place to live. Slassen meant some place like Earth. Xylo had heard all the stories when he was a kid on Mussiana. He knew all about the legends of rolling seas and huge continents teeming with every kind of life imaginable. The mythical birthplace of humanity was filled with fantastic stories no reasonable adult would believe.

Earth, if it ever existed at all, is long gone now, Xylo thought. Slassen was right about one thing; humanity had done it before. The seed ship that had brought humans to the Lux system was proof. It still silently orbited Mussiana, a frozen monument to the system's earliest explorers.

He'd never been on the derelict. Like most students on Mussiana, he had been on sightseeing trips that took him close enough to see the ship at a distance. It has been strictly forbidden to actually tour it. By law it had remained untouched, a sacred reminder of the sacrifices that his ancestors had made to spread humanity to the stars.

No one really knew just how long ago the seed ship had left Earth, how many centuries it had sailed through the vast stretches between stars or even how long ago it reached Lux. Xylo believed it to be many millennia. The T-Drives that drove every interplanetary craft in the Alliance were fast, but they traveled at a fraction of the speed of light. He did not know for sure, but Xylo doubted that the seed ship would have had anything faster than T-Drives. Travelling between the stars would have taken many generations. The fact that they had made it even here was just short of a miracle.

And now this old man was saying humanity ought to roll the dice again.

"I think I'd just as soon spend my retirement in less demanding ways," Xylo said.

"Retirement?" Slassen asked. "How old are you? Fifty?"

"Forty-three," Xylo replied flatly. Life on Estopel must have been even harder on him than he figured.

"Forty-three and retired," Slassen said with a chuckle. "You are going to be so bored."

"Nah," Xylo said, looking out the shuttle window, "I don't think so."

ଔ   ୭

Xylo easily found his way from his arrival gate to the departure lounge on Haven.

He saw from the readout of departure times that his lander would not leave for the surface for a couple of hours, so Xylo ordered a drink and sat in the bar nearest his gate.

He watched the people passing by and Xylo was struck by the odd feeling that things seemed different from how he remembered the station in the past. It took him a moment, but as he watched he realized that hardly anyone looked happy. To the contrary, almost everyone he saw walked by with their heads cast slightly downward, faces either expressionless or vaguely angry. No one made eye contact with him or with any of the other passersby. The station was not as bustling as he remembered it. The few people there listlessly moved, without any energy. The platform is just as well-lit as ever, he thought, but it feels–darker.

Xylo shook his head to clear it. It must be me, he thought. He took another sip and sat his still half-full bourbon on the bar, picked up his bag, and made his way to the boarding gate. He was surprised to see a human attendant at the gate rather than the usual automated check-in kiosk. The attendant, a sour-looking man, held up his hand.

"Stop," he curtly said. "Name?" A large square panel where Xylo stood faintly glowed.

"Xylo Fanata," Xylo said, reaching into his vest pocket to pull out his palm pc. "From Estopel."

The attendant looked Xylo up and down with suspicion. He tapped something Xylo couldn't see on the top of the podium.

"Maybe you outward slugs don't know, but more civilized citizens of the Alliance use implants for ID now," the man said without looking up.

"Yeah, thanks," Xylo said. "We know. It's just not a priority."

The man looked sharply at Xylo. "Make it one," he said. "I've sent instructions and markers to direct you to nearby implant clinics. Check your pad." Xylo clearly heard his disdain. "If you plan on staying on Mussiana for more than a week you'll be expected to schedule an implant procedure. After a week you'll be expected to have the implant or leave. Otherwise, you'll be forcibly deported."

"I thought implants were just a convenience," Xylo said.

"It's the law."

"It's required?" Xylo asked, stunned.

"Oh, it's still voluntary," the man said with a smug smile. "But if you don't have one, you can't stay. The only reason I'm letting you down to the planet this time is that we can read your ID and itinerary on that lump of metal you're carrying. Next time you won't be so lucky."

The man gestured to the lighted square where Xylo stood, and the glow died.

"We have what we need," the man said brusquely. "Enjoy your visit."

CR   SO

Xylo looked out the window of the lander as it slowly approached the clear dome that covered the large transportation hub for New Athens. A series of larger domes stretched away from it toward the dim setting sun. The land around and between the domes was mottled with low vegetation of green and purple growth, a testament to the ongoing effort to transform Mussiana into an environment that would eventually be more friendly to human beings.

The lander gently touched down beside the smaller dome. Gentle vibrations shook the ship and both pad and lander sank below the surface of Mussiana. Xylo looked through the viewport. Overhead a panel slid closed, sealing the chamber from the outside.

Mussiana's gravity was light compared to the one gee of pseudo-grav in the orbiting habitats where Xylo had lived most of his adult life. He easily made his way from the lander down the disembarkation tunnel and into the main New Athens transport hub.

The station was crowded. A few passengers were clearly family members being met by relatives, but the bulk of the others simply left the tunnel and disappeared into the crowd. Xylo stood for a moment, hoping that one of those people would be Charn. He still had gotten no message from his cousin other than the cryptic note in the disk.

He wandered further into the large open area in the center of the dome. Tram stations ringed the outer rim, clearly marked with destinations. Most of the destinations were local; regular runs that took travelers on several different routes the city proper and the suburbs of New Athens. A few were express trains to other cities in Mussiana's northern hemisphere, some as far away as four-hundred-kilometers.

He scanned the crowd. Still no Charn. He shrugged and shifted his gaze to the multitude of digital displays of arrivals and departures. There it is, he thought. Chicago.

If Charn wasn't in New Athens, Xylo's next best guess was their hometown of Chicago. It was small and familiar. Presumably it would be easier to find Charn there. The memory of the many places the two had played as children made him smile and he started across the dome.

He jostled his way through the crowd and was halfway to the station when strong hands grabbed him just above the right elbow. A sharp sting shot through his shoulder. He tried to turn but failed.

To his surprise, his body continued walking toward the Chicago station. He felt his feet contact the floor. He saw the people around him, heard the murmur of their voices, could even smell the aromas from kiosks of the food vendors. But each sensation was just information without context. He knew they all existed but felt completely separated from them.

There was no pain. He felt no euphoria. He remained fully conscious. He knew he should be alarmed, terrified even. But he felt no emotion. He had become merely a passenger in his own body.

Am I dead? he thought, but then realized, Dead people don't walk, Xylo.

The hands led him just past the Chicago tram station. He tried to focus on the readout above the kiosk. Interesting, he thought. I know those words. But I can't read them.

He tried to turn his head to look as they passed but failed. He and his handlers quickly slipped through a narrow portal that appeared in the wall behind the kiosk. It closed quickly behind them.

This is a long, narrow room. No, not a room. A corridor.

Xylo continued walking, the hands still on his arm. But he felt the grip loosen.

I hear too many footsteps for just two people. I wish I could see them.

They walked for what felt to Xylo for a very long time, occasionally turning left and right through doors and corridors. They came to a room.

Well, this is different, he thought. There's a table and some chairs and a cot. They're leading me to the bed. Are they putting me to bed? Am I tired?

He sat on the bed, still failing to see the faces of his handlers. They gently eased him onto his back, and he lay flat. A face suddenly blocked his view of the ceiling.

It is a woman. She is pretty but she is looking at me in an odd way. She seems sad. For me? She is speaking but I don't know what she's saying.

Her hair tickles my cheek. It is not very long but she is very close. She smells good. She has blue eyes. Her hand is touching my cheek. I wish I knew what she was saying.

Then she was gone, and all Xylo could see was the blank ceiling. The lights dimmed.

I guess I am tired. I feel really slee…

Then he felt nothing.

ଓ   ଓ

Xylo woke in a remarkably calm state of mind. He blinked as his eyes adjusted to the gentle glow of the ceiling. He turned his head slightly to the right to take in the small room when he realized that he had control again. He jerked his head straight and put his hands in front of his face. He sat up so quickly that he nearly rose off the bed.

Right, he thought, this is Mussiana. Less gravity. Even though he hadn't called the planet home for two decades, muscle memory from his youth helped him rapidly adjust. He glanced around the room.

He was on a simple metal frame cot. A half-dozen metal chairs, facing inward around a metal table, sat before him. There were no markings on the walls and the room's soft, warm white light came from the ceiling panel overhead. The whole panel glowed, making the entire room well-lit without any sort of glare. There was one door, directly across the room from his cot.

He stood quietly and made his way toward the door, careful to be as quiet as he could. He didn't know who had abducted him, but he frankly didn't care. He didn't like the idea no matter who had done it.

He made it less than halfway across the room when the door swung open and the woman from before entered. She stopped inside the door and gave him a soft, nearly apologetic smile. She certainly didn't seem threatening and, as he looked at her clearly for the first time, Xylo re-evaluated his blanket condemnation of his abduction. If you're going to be nabbed, he thought, there are worse-looking kidnappers. He stopped that line of thought.

Don't be stupid, he nearly said aloud. He started to speak but she beat him to it.

"Mr. Fanata, I'm very sorry about last night. We had to move quickly and as unobtrusively as we could. Taking the time to talk to you in public was not an option," she firmly said. Something about the cadence of her voice and her overall bearing convinced him that she was used to command.

"Well, I'm assuming we can talk now, can't we?" Xylo asked, the sarcasm clear in his voice. "Wherever we are seems to be pretty deep in New Athens. I doubt anyone is going to hear us here."

"Wrong about that one, cousin," came a sardonic male voice from the corridor. Xylo glanced past the woman's left shoulder to see Charn Ringle step into the room. Even for a Mussian, Charn was a tall man. His shaved head towered over both Xylo and the woman, and he moved with an ease and grace that accentuated his tough, athletic frame.

In no time at all Charn had crossed the room and wrapped Xylo in a strong embrace. Xylo laughed with relief as he returned Charn's hug.

"Cousin!" Xylo exclaimed, pounding Charn's back as they broke from the welcome. "I don't think I've ever been happier to see you!"

"Xylo, I'm sorry we had to grab you the way we did but it really was necessary," Charn said. He motioned toward the woman. "I'm sure you haven't had the opportunity to properly meet. Xylo, this is Rawna Sardasian."

She extended her hand to Xylo.

"Pleasure," Xylo said and shook her firm grip.

"Rawna is Chief of Security for our little band," Charn said.

"Band?" Xylo asked, raising his eyebrows as he looked from the woman back to his cousin.

"I know you've got questions," Charn said, "and we'll get to them soon enough. But first things first, what would you like to eat? We don't have gourmet options here by any means but hopefully there's enough variety to suit you. How about a protein patty and fries?"

"That'd be great," Xylo said.

"You've got it. Rawna, if you don't mind, would you tell Skeed? I'd like to stay here to talk with Xylo."

"Certainly," she said, nodding to both men before leaving the room.

"Sit," Charn said as he pulled a seat toward the table.

"Charn," Xylo said pulling his own chair, "what is this? I've been trying to get in touch with you for months."

"Well, I told you not to call. As far as anyone knows, Charn Ringle is still missing after a vacation trip to the Rippled Highlands a couple of months ago," Charn said, leaning back in his chair and putting an elbow on the table.

Xylo looked at him with disbelief. "Missing? I don't get it. Are you in some kind of trouble? I don't remember much about last night, but the way I was led around it seems like we're pretty much in hiding."

"You're right about that," Charn said. "We are in hiding. As far as me being in trouble, well–no. Not yet."

Xylo waited for his cousin to continue. When Charn didn't offer any more, Xylo reached into his vest pocket. "And what's this?" Xylo asked, tossing the Flip coin onto the table. "Some kind of joke?"

"It's not a joke," Charn said, sitting up in the chair. "I knew it would pique your interest. And it had the added benefit of seeming completely innocent if anyone else found it."

"Alright, not a joke," Xylo replied. "A game, then."

"No," Charn said, leaning so far forward in the chair that his elbows rested on his knees. "Not a game either."

Charn looked at his cousin for a long moment. took a deep breath and stood. Xylo leaned back in his chair to look at the taller man.

"Xylo, what I'm about to tell you is going to sound crazy, but you have to believe me when I tell you that it's not. And after I tell you, you need to make the call as to whether you're in or not. I don't want to commit you to something there may not be a way out of. But once you're in, you're in. There's no turning back."

"What's that supposed to mean?" Xylo asked, chuckling. "Like some sort of blood pact? You going to take my first-born child?"

"I told you," Charn said so softly that Xylo could hardly hear him, "this is no joke. It's entirely conceivable that the end result could be death or permanent exile; for me and everybody else in our organization."

Xylo stared at him. He realized that his cousin was as serious as he had ever known him to be. "Okay, fine. Can I ask a few questions first?" Xylo said. Charn nodded. "So, what is this organization you're talking about?"

"Organization might be a little grandiose," Charn replied. "It's a loose group of individuals with some, unusual and varied skills. But we're all working toward a common goal. And before you ask, that goal is to find out the truth behind some odd decisions that the Council has been making over the last couple of years."

"Such as?" Xylo asked.

"The expansion of the Assembly, for one thing. I mean, clearly the Council has added Farpoint, Capstone, and Arturus to pack the Assembly with additional small worlds and make it easier to overrule the more highly populated worlds. They're so desperate that they changed the definition of planet, for crying out loud! Arturus is a moon, not a planet!"

"Well, technically it orbits Lux just the same as the other worlds," Xylo interjected.

"Yeah," Charn said, "that's part of their argument but the truth is now they can declare that any celestial body with an orbiting habitat is a candidate for membership in the Council. So, Arturus is one of the moons of Honor, until Chancellor Grunn declares it a planet. It has nothing to do with celestial mechanics. It's politics."

"Every planet has an equal voice in the Council's decisions. That's been in the Articles of Alliance for hundreds of years. So now you've got Mussiana, Hell, Hugo, and Honor, the planets with the largest populations, in one faction. Morgana, Gris, Azul, and Escape in the other. Valerian was always a swing vote. But now throw Farpoint, Capstone, and Arturus into the mix and the small planet faction is always going to dominate the larger ones."

"Wait, did you say Chancellor Grunn? I thought he was just Administrator?" Xylo interjected.

"Yeah, he was. But after the balance of power shifted in the Council, they gave Grunn the title of Chancellor and additional executive powers to go with it. Theoretically the Council can override him but with the small worlds in his pocket to rubber stamp his decisions he's essentially unstoppable."

"Why would the Council allow that?" Xylo asked.

"Estopel is too far away from the action, Xylo," Charn replied. "You probably haven't seen half of it. Grunn becoming a de facto dictator is just one example. There's the big push to have ID implants, crackdowns on opposition parties, cancelation of research projects; it's a long list."

"I get the logic of shutting down opposition parties. It's heavy-handed but makes sense," Xylo said. "But what's the danger to the Council from research?"

"You need to talk to Skeed. Every one of us has been forced in one way or another to go underground to get out of the Council's eyes. He's a researcher from Big Rock who's been effectively blackballed by the universities just because he has continued to push for some surface research on Hell."

"Who'd want to research Hell?" Xylo asked with a snort. "Lifeless, radioactive ball of ice–"

"Beside the point," Charn said, cutting him off. "Why punish the researchers? Opposition to the Council can earn you criminal status."

Xylo looked up at him. "Alright, Charn, I get it," Xylo said. "So, what do you want from me?"

"You're a rich man now," Charn said, "you could settle into an easy life like we used to joke about when we were kids. But the truth is that we need your wealth. What we're doing–and one action in particular–is costly."

Xylo sat back in his chair and sighed.

"How much do you need? And when?"

"A lot," Charn said. "And now."

Xylo looked at him, shaking his head. "You know, Charn, when we were kids you never played a game you thought you'd lose."

"Told you: this isn't a game, Xy."

"I know. But I always trusted that you would never lead me in a hopeless cause."

"It's important, Xy."

Fanata sat motionless for several seconds then let out a long sigh. "Alright. I'm in. What good is retirement if you can't do what you want," he said with a shrug. "Can't take it with you."

☙ ❧

Rawna brought his meal and Xylo ate while Charn brought others into the room.

An older man, Skeed Farrs, sat across the table from Xylo. Farrs had prepared his meal, Xylo remembered, but there was something about the man that convinced Xylo that his skills went far beyond the culinary arts. Charn confirmed it.

"A lot of humanity's past is conjecture," Charn said, waving a hand in Skeed's direction, "but few men alive have a greater understanding of it than Skeed Farrs."

Aleez Baramba sat to Xylo's left. She was especially striking to Xylo, with piercing brown eyes and closely cropped black hair. Her specialty, he later learned, was cybernetics engineering.

"Aleez is one of the finest minds in the Alliance," Charn had said when introducing her to Xylo. "We're lucky to have her with us and not with the government. She's been able to hide our tracks all the way."

Xylo nodded although he wasn't actually sure what tracks Charn was talking about.

"This is Brunti Aruz," Charn continued, gesturing to a woman sitting on the other side of Aleez. "Brunti is an astronomer. Knows the Lux system well plus has a thorough knowledge of the inner workings of the Alliance."

"Some of you," Charn continued, "have already met my cousin Xylo Fanata, but all of you have heard me talk about him. I'm happy to confirm that he had agreed to join us. By the way, I've explained to him all the risks that are involved, and the fool joined us anyway,"

A slight murmur of appreciative laughter made Xylo feel both honored and apprehensive at the same time.

"Xylo, we've been convinced for quite some time that answers to many of our questions are somehow locked away in the seed ship. It's at least a good place to start. It's always been off-limits, but the recent increase in security certainly indicates there's something hidden in there that's become even more important to Grunn.

"Getting into it has been a much tougher challenge than we expected, especially given Grunn's increased security measures," Charn continued. "Our organization is larger than the five of us here, but for what we have in mind the smaller, the better. This exploratory team has the skills we need to explore that ship, find what we can, and get out quickly. But all the expertise in the system won't do us any good if we don't have some way to run interference. To do that, we've needed to resort to good old-fashioned bribery. There are plenty of rich people in the system but most of them are very public figures. People like that rarely put their wealth–or public image–at risk.

"Now that you're in," he said, nodding at Xylo, "we've got to move fast. We know the Council is aware of our organization, but I doubt they think we're crazy enough to break into the seed ship. I want to pull this off before they learn that we are just that crazy. You're crash training starts as soon as you finish your meal.

"We're sneaking into Destiny in six days."

ଓଃ ଞ୬

Xylo was amazed at how quickly and deftly Charn's team got into Destiny.

Charn piloted their small shuttle into a tiny niche which housed an emergency airlock. Aleez Baramba's manipulation of the ancient electronics that opened that airlock impressed Xylo.

The bribe financed by Xylo's retirement fund proved to be invaluable and helped the small team stay under the radar. The security supervisors who took the bribes had been thoroughly educated to the fact that they were now full-fledged accomplices.

The team navigated weightlessly past the small chamber inside the airlock's outer doors and into a wide, pitch-black corridor. Crisscrossing light beams from the helmets of their EVA suits played across gray walls that stretched ahead of them. Evenly spaced handholds running the length of the corridor clearly indicated it had been designed for zero gee.

The corridor had sets of sliding doors at each end. Both sets were open. Neither seemed to be operative. They slowly moved through the compartment.

Pretty convenient, Xylo thought. Seems a pretty simple way to lead us into a trap.

He started to share his concerns when they ran into a dead end. Instead of leading to another open passage, this corridor led to a set of closed–and heavily fortified–double doors. That did not surprise Xylo, nor did the control panel embedded in the wall beside the doors. He did raise a surprised eyebrow at the power running to the activation controls. It activated when the group reached the end of the corridor, glowing with a soft white light. The panel, twenty-centimeters square of tempered glass, sat at hand height in the wall perpendicular to the doors. The team jostled to a stop.

"Aleez? Skeed?" Charn said, turning to look at the space-suited figures floating at his side.

Aleez reached a gloved-hand toward the panel.

"Not entirely sure. Clearly it has a proximity detector but–"

The white panel flashed red, cutting off her sentence. Rawna gestured back down the corridor.

"Back there," she said crisply. At the far end of the corridor a corresponding panel was now flashing red in synchrony with the panel beside the group.

"It's going faster!" Brunti Aruz called.

Flashes of light from the EVA helmets shot back and forth as everyone glanced back and forth from one end of the corridor to the other.

"The doors are closing!" Xylo yelled, pointing to the other end of the corridor. A cacophony of voices filled his helmet as other team members responded. Rawna and Charn pushed toward the closing portal. Xylo knew that there was no way they could reach them before they shut.

The lights quickly pulsed, so fast they seemed to glow a solid red. The doors closed completely. The red light blinked away, plunging the corridor into darkness, except for the EVA lights. The panels snapped back on, and bright white light filled the corridor from both ends.

The group fell silent, nervously looking up and down the now fully illuminated corridor.

"The panel," Rawna called and pointed at the panel beside the door. A thin line of green had appeared at the bottom of the white glass panel. The line became thicker, expanding into a long, low rectangular box. The box continued growing, filling more and more of the panel.

The entire panel filled with a bright green light and the doors slowly slid open.

Charn's hearty laugh broke the deafening silence. "It was just an airlock!" he chuckled. "A little bigger than what we expected maybe, but just an airlock."

"And functional," Aleez said. "Amazing." Everyone turned to look at her. "The systems on this ship may be a thousand years old," she continued. "I don't care how well the Founders may have built this ship there's no way it maintains such a smooth functionality without regular maintenance. All that talk about the seed ship being too sacred to allow visitors? Pure bull."

The engineer referenced a small display embedded in her left sleeve.

"And the atmosphere reads standard 78 percent nitrogen, 21 percent oxygen. Amazing."

She reached to her helmet and flipped its clear visor open, inhaling deeply through her nose. She looked at the others and smiled without comment. They all followed suit.

No one spoke while Charn floated over to the open door. On the other side was another well-lit corridor.

"Okay," he said looking down the hallway, "let's do this."

He floated into the light, the rest of the team following closely behind him.

They moved deeper into the ship until they came to an intersection of multiple corridors. Glass panels, slightly larger than the ones in the airlock, were embedded in three of the walls. Aleez reached her hand toward one of the panels and it lit up.

"Clearly directions," Charn said. "But I don't know where. The characters by the arrows are familiar but I don't know the words."

"It's Old Standard," Skeed offered. "It was the common language for everyone on all of the seed ships."

"Everyone in the Alliance speaks Standard," Brunti said.

"I said it was Old Standard. Languages adapt and evolve over time. Just because we all speak it doesn't mean that the language itself won't change. A lot can happen over thousands of years," Skeed explained. "Old Standard evolved from American Standard which itself evolved from Middle English which evolved from Old English. Someone speaking Old English in the 12th Century wouldn't understand a thing said in 20th Century English and vice versa. And they were just separated by eight-hundred years. We've been in the Lux system at least that long."

"So, what does it say?" Charn asked.

"As near as I can translate, that way," Skeed said, pointing down the corridor to the group's left, "are living quarters. Or something like that."

"The opposite direction is mechanisms, er, maybe engineering. And straight ahead," he said, nodding down the corridor directly in front of the group, "is command or control."

"Control sounds like a bridge to me," Charn said. "Agreed?"

They all nodded their agreement.

"One thing," Rawna interjected as Charn started to lead them forward. "If Aleez is right there have been plenty of people on this ship in the recent past. For all we know there may be some here now."

"Shouldn't we have run into someone then?" Brunti asked.

"It's a huge ship. We tried our best to keep our approach and entry undetectable and apparently succeeded. But the deeper we go into the ship and the longer we stay, the greater the likelihood of exposure," the security officer warned. "Don't let your guard down now."

"Agreed," Charn said. "So, let's keep moving as quickly as we can. We'll learn what we can and get out."

The small squad moved further into the corridor. Motion sensors activated the lights as they floated down the passage.

"Automated lighting," Aleez confirmed, gesturing to the walls with her free hand as the other reached for the next hand hold. "I know these ships were built to last hundreds of years but the fact that they are functioning so well–even with regular maintenance–is remarkable."

"Can you imagine if these walls could talk," Skeed said, pulling himself behind her down the wide corridor.

"The historian's lament," Charn joked.

"They left Earth with only a couple hundred settlers onboard," Skeed continued, "but the generational ships were designed to let the shipboard population grow into the thousands. All those people–born, living their entire lives, and dying–with this ship as their whole world."

"And I felt sorry for myself working on Estopel." Xylo said.

"About a quarter of the ship was dedicated to propulsion, engineering, and life support. Another large section–again roughly a quarter–was used for food generation and storage," Skeed explained. "So only about half of the ship was living space and that encompassed all aspects of living; individual housing units, recreation, research, and special medical facilities. There would have been ample space when there were only a few hundred colonists but by the time the population had grown to its maximum of four thousand it would've felt packed, especially after decades of living so closely together. The psychological stresses must have been incredibly intense."

"And no pseudo-grav," Aleex added. "Just centripetal spin."

"The population on seed ships was engineered to reach maximum when the ship reached its target system," Skeed said. "But it never was a static number; they needed diversity for the gene pool. So, the population began to grow almost immediately after the ship left Earth. It was a delicate balance between genetic needs, resources, the desired colonizing population, and time."

"It's amazing that those colonists would commit themselves to living their entire lives on these ships," Aleez said. "And commit all the generations that followed."

"Those later generations never knew a different life," Farrs said with a grunt. "But the original designers took the psychological stresses into account when they built these ships. Large sections of the living areas were dedicated to recreation. Even at full capacity each passenger had access to some method of escapism. It was essential to ship discipline. I wish we had time to explore them."

"The bridge is primary," Charn said. Skeed sighed and shrugged.

"How many seed ships were sent from Earth?" Xylo asked.

"Legends say four, but no one is certain," Skeed said. "Truthfully, even historians don't know anything definite. The ancient records were just too sketchy. There's no actual record of communications ever being received from the others. Even communications from Earth ended over a thousand years ago."

Xylo estimated that they had travelled at least five-hundred meters through the labyrinth of corridors. He could not guess, though, exactly where in the massive ship they were now. He only knew that the deeper they went, the more exposed he felt. He looked over his shoulder, half expecting to see Alliance security forces tailing them.

They came to another intersection, this one a tee with corridors leading to the right and left. "Hold!" Charn called. This intersection had one major difference.

In the wall directly in front of the group were three sets of double doors. Display panels over each set activated as the team approached with words that Xylo felt sure were destinations.

"I think they're some kind of transport," Skeed said. The panel on the left says guidance or directioning, something like that. Navigation of some type. The middle one says oversee. Administration or security, maybe? And the door on the right says government. So maybe that's administration. Remember, this ship was a world to itself."

"Directioning?" Brunti Aruz asked. Charn nodded agreement.

Aruz touched the display by the doors on the left and directioning faded from the screen, replaced with what Skeed translated as transit. The doors opened to reveal a cube a little less than three meters on each side. Charn floated into the cube with the other five close behind.

They each secured themselves by grasping a bar running horizontally around the cube, wedging a foot under another bar near the floor.

The doors closed and, apparently sensing that the passengers were secure, the car gently went into motion.

Xylo felt the car moving up, in the direction his head was pointed. All five secured their grips in response to the movement and Xylo felt the speed increase. He had no way of knowing how fast or how far they travelled. Seconds later, the acceleration slowed. He tightened his grip as deceleration nudged him toward the ceiling.

The motion stopped, and the doors slid open revealing a large room filled with three long, curved tables that arced from one wall to the other. They exited and Xylo saw flat display panels, similar but slightly larger than the ones in the hallways, embedded into the tops of the tables.

Three very large display panels, each about ten meters wide, were arrayed side-by-side on the wall in front of the tables.

"The bridge?" Charn asked.

"A thousand years old," Skeed said, shaking his head. "It seems almost new."

The three large display panels in the wall suddenly came to life.

The middle screen showed a schematic of a planetary system. A yellow sun sat in the middle of a series of concentric rings that marked the orbits of planets. A readout with a small list of letters and numbers floated beside each planet.

"It's a basic positional chart," Brunti said, waving her hand toward the screen. "I would guess it to be the Lux system."

She floated further into the room, closer to the screen.

"No, I'm wrong," she said, then added in a tone that Xylo thought sounded just a bit defensive, "although it's easy to see how someone could mistake it. It's not Lux but it's very, very similar."

"Well, that was quick," Rawna said. "How do you know it's not Lux?"

"There are only eight planets. They are similar to Lux, rocky planets taking the inner orbits and gas giants farther out. But that's a standard planetary configuration," Brunti said, then laughed. "Maybe it's Sol. It was supposed to have been in a common configuration."

"Sol?" Xylo responded quickly. "Really?"

"No," Aruz said, waving a dismissive hand. "It's got to be Lux, even with just eight planets."

"Eight real planets," Rawna said with a smirk, "the Council's designations notwithstanding. Politics!"

"What about the other two panels?" Xylo asked. "What do you think they mean?"

"I have no idea about the one on the right. It's all in Old Standard," Aruz said. "I'm sure it's a chart with some sort of specific details but they're beyond me. The panel on the left, however, I do recognize. It's a star map of the stars in our local group. I can't read the labels, but I can tell which one is which by their colors and relative positions. That left panel I'm confident about."

"Hmm, that's odd," Rawna muttered. The other two looked at her.

"What?" Brunti asked.

"I just saw a couple of digits change on the planet closest to the star," she said.

"Confirmation," Aruz said with a shrug. "It's monitoring Lux. That's got to be Morgana."

Aleez passed a hand over one of the embedded displays and it came to life.

"It all Old Standard," she said, touching the screen. "But it scrolls."

"Each of you, pick a display and start recording data," Farrs said. "Get everything you can."

Each of the team members floated to a display and began recording readouts. Farrs moved along behind them, looking over their shoulders at the screens.

"Aleez, have you found any data points?" he asked.

"Looking," she replied. "Configurations have changed but maybe I can design a workaround."

"Hold it," Skeed said. He touched one of the tabletop displays and a large schematic of Destiny appeared on the large right-hand monitor. He floated toward it for a closer look.

"Look at the huge middle section of the ship," Farrs said, pointing to a large part of the schematic that was mostly shaded in red. "This has to be the primary living space."

He touched one of the red spaces and suddenly an image expanded, filling the large monitor. At first, none of them could make out exactly what they were seeing. The image was video of a half-lit corridor that looked very similar to others they had seen on the ship. Objects were suspended in the air, barely moving. Some were ragged, like tatters of cloth. Others were more solid.

"Are those," Xylo haltingly asked, "bones?"

Farrs put both hands on the large display and the image shifted according to his touch. He panned slightly down the hallway. He stopped with a roundish object near the center of the screen. He slid his hands apart and the image magnified, focusing on the object in the center.

It was a human skull.

"Yeah," Charn said. "Those are bones."

The team floated in stunned silence.

"This ship is a graveyard," Aleex finally said. "But how? And why haven't we known?"

"Way too many questions," Charn said. "We can't answer them now. Just keep scanning these displays. Skeed, check the other red-shaded areas. See if they're the same."

Farrs sampled a few more red-tinted areas in the schematic. Video monitors displayed similar scenes.

"I'd guess hundreds of bodies are down there based on the large number of red-shaded sections," Farrs said. "It's a huge graveyard."

Brunti rose from her seat and floated to the middle display showing the planetary system schematic. She reached a hand to touch the circle that represented the innermost planet. The circle expanded and a list of Old Standard words appeared beside it.

"Skeed, can you read this?" she asked. The historian floated closer to the middle display.

"I don't know the significance of the numbers," he said haltingly, reading the display, "but I think it identifies the planet as Mercury."

"Not Morgana?" she asked. He shook his head.

She expanded the image of the second planet.

"And this one?" she asked.

"Again, I don't know what the numbers mean but the planet is called Venus."

She looked at the others then quickly expanded the third planet, a pure white ball in the blackness of space. Farrs took a long time reading before he spoke.

"Earth," he whispered.

"Why have a schematic of the Sol system?" Aruz asked.

"You're sure it's Sol?" Charn asked. "I thought it was Lux."

Brunti floated to join Skeed at the large monitor. She shrunk the display back to reveal the full schematic.

"Look," she said, pointing at the inner planets. "That's Morgana, Valerian, Hell, and Mussiana." She continued outward, pointing at the gas giants. "And that's Hugo, Honor, Gris—"

Skeed interrupted her by reaching to the schematic and expanding the ringed gas giant.

"That's Honor," Brunti said.

"In Old Standard," Skeed said, reading the words beside the planet, "that's Saturn."

No one spoke for several seconds until Skeed finally broke the silence.

"We live in the Sol system, not Lux," he said. "We're not descended from colonists. We're descended from refugees."

"Charn Ringle," a new voice boomed in the room. "This is Garvin Grunn, Chancellor of the Alliance Council. It's time we had a talk."

ೞ   ಏ

All three large screens in the room changed, their displays replaced with the wrinkled face of a man with neatly trimmed gray hair and deep, sad eyes. Xylo had seen vids of Grunn before, but the man he saw on the screen looked older and more care-worn than he remembered.

"I salute the ingenuity you and your team have shown, getting onboard Destiny and so quickly discovering some of its secrets," Grunn said.

"You lied to us all these years! Why?" Brunti cried.

"No one has actually been lied to," Grunn replied. "Destiny was truly a colonizing ship, mankind's first attempt to reach the stars. But they decided to return to Earth when word reached them that system wide war of an unimaginable magnitude had broken out.

"In time you would have discovered what the Founders did; the system that had sent them out no longer existed. Earth and its few colony worlds were dead, wiped out by nuclear and biological warfare that left no survivors."

Xylo floated with the others in stunned silence, paralyzed by the fast flowing and unexpected information.

"Nuclear devastation of the Earth, combined with biological agents, plunged the planet into a nuclear winter that left little life above the bacterial level," Grunn said. "Even the small colony of settlers on Mars was killed by biological agents."

"And the bodies we saw floating in the living quarters?" Skeed asked. "What about them?"

"The decision to return had not been a unanimous agreement among the colonists," Grunn said. "After finding the Sol system dead a significant contingent wanted the ship to leave again and continue its original mission.

"The decision to stay in the Sol system was a political one," Grunn stated, "that was decided, sadly, by its own lethal conflict. Eventually more than half of the colonists died as a result."

"Why didn't they clear the ship of the bodies?" Charn asked.

"Primarily due to lack of resources," Grunn said. "After the battle there were approximately five-hundred colonists still alive, many of them too young or severely injured. The labor force was at a premium. Technical resources were dedicated to re-establishing the colony on Mars. "

"Only five hundred?" Aleez asked in disbelief.

"Yes," Grunn said. "All twelve million citizens of the Alliance are descended from that remnant."

Xylo detected both pride and the weight of responsibility in the Chancellor's voice.

"Our ancestors thought a fresh start was essential," Grunn continued. "To that end, a concerted effort was made to erase as much of the past as possible, beginning with names. All the planets, moons, asteroids, even the sun itself – all renamed."

"History is written by the victors," Skeed said.

"In a manner of speaking, yes," Grunn admitted. "The Founders also limited access to historical data from the period immediately before the war until about a hundred years after The Return."

Xylo heard the capital letters in Grunn's words.

"The earliest generations, of course, knew of the Earth and other planets in the Sol system. But after seven-hundred-years, those names have become merely legends."

"Obviously you know all of this because you're Chancellor," Charn said. "Is the entire Council aware of the truth?"

"Only a select few," Grunn replied. "The Founders knew that it was important to keep the truth hidden, but also to keep it alive."

"State secrets are notoriously hard to keep," Skeed said. "How have you kept this from general knowledge, or even rumor."

"Those of us who have been entrusted with the truth have been," Grunn paused, searching for the right word, "strongly motivated to maintain the strictest confidentiality."

That doesn't sound pleasant, Xylo thought. "Wait a minute, what's going to happen to us?" he blurted.

"Xylo Fanata," Grunn said, enunciating each syllable, "we have been aware of your cousin's plans much, much longer than you have." He smiled. "You are quite safe. For the time being."

"What is that supposed to mean to me?" Charn asked.

"The six of you here and the rest of you organization – yes we know of the rest," Grunn said with another smile, "have a number of, um, characteristics that make you wonderful candidates for a job that the Council has in mind. Should you choose to accept our offer you stand poised to reap rich financial benefits, plus find answers to many questions, both yours and ours. You might even secure a place in history. Of course, if you reject our offer we'll have to discuss the unfortunate consequences of trespassing in a top security government facility."

No one spoke for several seconds. Charn broke the silence. "We're listening," he dryly said.

"You chose your team, Charn Ringle, for their abilities to explore and understand ancient human technology," Grunn said with a surprising eagerness. "You obviously chose wisely. Your success in such a short time on Destiny proves it.

"Your team is also capable of operating in a highly clandestine manner. You are all uniquely well-suited. So, think of this exploration of Destiny as an initiation exercise if you will.

"It's extremely important that this mission be conducted by a small, uniquely talented band that can do the job without drawing any undue attention. Each of the members of your team have done an effective job of disappearing from the public eye. Your absence from society over the next few years would not be remarkable."

"A few years?" Brunti asked. "Where are you sending us?"

"The Council believes it's time for humanity to return to Earth," Grunn said.

"Earth?" Aleez said. "Don't you mean Hell? What about the radiation? The biologicals?"

"We believe that time has significantly reduced both of those hazards," Grunn said. "The planet is still in a global ice age but even that seems to be retreating. As the ice sheets begin withdrawing, the ruins of human civilization will be uncovered. "We need a presence on the planet to get information, to begin the long process of returning. It's time to carefully re-introduce the true history of the Alliance and to begin plans to re-colonize the Earth."

ଓଃ ଚ

Charn Ringle and his exploratory team stepped down the ramp of their shuttle onto the frozen plains of a place once known as Georgia. The last one off the ship, bundled against the frigid wind, was his cousin, Xylo Fanata.

"I guess you knew this was what it would take to get me out of retirement," Xylo said.

"What?" Charn asked.

Xylo flipped him a small metal disk. "A cold day in Hell."

Chuckling, the two stepped into the melting snow.

Zarwendi Attack

R. Kyle Hannah

Ships flashed from hyperspace on the dark side of the third moon of Corpena. The twelve Zarwendi Dreadnaughts slid from the moon's shadow like wraiths and opened fire as soon as they entered targeting range. The station commander barely sounded the alarm before the first fusillade shook the defending Gl'dorn station. The asteroid base rocked with explosions.

An onslaught of torpedoes and dull green lasers sliced through the space between the Dreadnaughts and the ten-kilometer long Gl'dorn station. The shields flared with each strike, absorbing the initial attack.

Over a kilometer long and three-hundred meters wide, the dreadnaughts sported bank after bank of lasers and torpedo tubes; the weapons surrounded and protected by hull superstructure barriers and shield towers. Although one of the deadliest ships in the galaxy, the Dreadnaughts were not what concerned Admiral Dans Pleggar of the Corpena Navy; the smaller and more agile troopships the Dreadnaughts carried were much more dangerous to the Admiral. The smaller troop carriers would turn this battle into a ground based Marine fight; something the Admiral could not control…or win.

As soon as the station shields were down, the Dreadnaughts released three troopships each; the smaller, rectangular shaped vessels were capable of atmospheric flight, assault landings and contained a good sampling of the same weapons as the

Dreadnaughts. The two-hundred-fifty combat hardened troops inside each troopship, once on the ground, had been known to turn the tide of battle; the Zarwendi rarely lost. The Dreadnaughts continued to pour fire at the now defenseless station as the troopships streaked toward the surface.

Corpena was a mostly industrial and agrarian society; relying solely on transporting their goods off-world for their economy. The peaceful Corpena had only begun to build a military in the last few decades; hiring mercenaries to secure their home-world and train their volunteers in the methods of war. The last two decades had been good to the Corpena; their troops were strong and well trained, and they had the most state of the art ships in the tri-system. However, the Zarwendi were battle-tested and had the tactics and techniques of hundreds of battles to rely on; their ships were state of the art as well.

"Admiral, we have thirty-six Zarwendi troop ships accelerating toward Capitol Center and five other cities," a technician yelled in an adrenaline overload; he was scared and could not help but show it. Everyone in the control room seemed to be on the edge of panic; everyone knew that in a Zarwendi invasion, the dead were the lucky ones.

The Admiral, to his credit, looked and spoke so calm that his aide momentarily thought this was yet another training exercise. "Ground based defenses, lock on. Load the firing specs into the Battle-Computer based on standard Zarwendi ground assault tactics. Do not fire until the ships are well within their landing pattern and can't maneuver as well."

The unruffled demeanor and confident orders calmed the room; the soldiers and technicians carried out the commands quickly and efficiently. Maintaining his calm façade, the Admiral clasped his small, light green hands behind his pristine white uniform and looked at a sensor screen over a technician forth class' shoulder. He pointed, saw the technician flip two switches and nodded his approval. Hands still clasped, he moved to the planetary holo-board and watched as the three-dimensional ships moved across his world. His mind was racing as he took in the scene and contemplated the developing battle.

Admiral Pleggar had volunteered for the Corpena Navy over twenty-five years earlier, when he was a young man, and the Navy was just an idea. He had seen the Navy grow and develop into a formidable force in the Tri-System; something to be admired, or feared, depending on what activities you were up to at the time. Now, his over two-meter frame stood tall and defiant as the Zarwendi troopships broke atmosphere, heading for Capitol Center and his headquarters. The Admiral watched the holo ships and began mentally counting down. "Prepare," he said, his voice full of athority.

ଔ ଚ

The Zarwendi Dreadnaughts finished off the Gl'dorn Station with a spread of torpedoes that ripped the station apart with a succession of explosions that vaporized most of the debris. Twelve thousand Corpena died a violent death. With the station destroyed, the Dreadnaughts deployed in an orbital net to discourage anyone from leaving the planet. The ships were disappointed as none of the Corpena had planned on leaving; the light green inhabitants had vowed to stay and fight the Zarwendi when the first rumors of invasion had surfaced a few months earlier.

Even as the station debris spread and the Dreadnaughts were effectively out of the fight, the troopships were just getting started. Halfway down through the atmosphere, the ground-based weapons opened fire; filling the atmosphere with a deadly array of projectile and energy weapons that destroyed a third of the assault force with the first volley. The surviving ships flew through the debris of their comrades and continued down in spite of the barrage from the surface. A second volley and then a third from the Corpena Marine ground weapons were less effective, and the surviving twenty-two troopships made it through the planetary entry sequence and into the more maneuverable air of the lower atmosphere.

The rectangular troopships lined up for strafing runs in standard Zarwendi Zar-di formation; a formation of which the Corpena Battle Computer knew well. The troopships were trained to soften up the targets before deploying their 250-troops to swarm the defenders; the troopships fired volley after volley of torpedoes and piercing solid blue lasers that drilled holes through shields, plasti-crete and rock. The Corpena Battle Computer returned fire with tactical precision; a hail of small green laser bolts burst across the sky to impact the shields of the troopships. Many of the bolts missed; the ones that hit the troopships knocked out the shields and created havoc with the Zarwendi circuits. Eight more of the troopships crashed into the surface; there were no survivors.

No longer content to let the troopships do the remainder of the fighting, the Dreadnaughts opened fire from orbit. The powerful laser bolts flashed through the sky and destroyed the outer defenses of the Corpena Military Complex; inhibiting the Battle Computer's sensors and target lock. The first objective achieved, the Dreadnaughts turned their attention to the smaller cities and villages and began a systematic rain of fire at each target in turn.

As the planet began to burn, the Zarwendi Troopships prepared to begin their landings; taking up positions just inside the range of the city defenses and opened fire with continuous volleys of torpedoes and solid cutting lasers. The Corpena Battle Computer, no longer able to lock onto the attackers, ineffectively returned fire with thousands of green laser bolts. Seeing the bolts going wild across the sky, the Zarwendi commenced their landing.

ଓଃ   ଽ୦

The command center was in shambles; chairs overturned, computers sparking, holographic displays blank and technicians lying dead. Admiral Pleggar stood in the midst of the chaos shouting orders to the few that were still alive; his calm demeanor abandoned in the wake of the deadly orbital bombardment. Still, he knew that surrender was not an option and continued to order his troops into battle.

When the Dreadnaughts had opened fire on the planet and the computer lost its target lock, the Admiral had ordered manual firing for the ground defenses; something his troops had only recently began training on how to do. Now he was watching one of only three remaining screens, and he saw the troopships moving into their landing formations. The Admiral's fourteen fingers flew over the targeting keyboard and the laser bolts homed in on the third ship in line to land at Capitol Center. The shot group tightened and more and more of the green bolts impacted until the ship broke apart in midair; the debris falling thirty kilometers from Capitol Center into an already obliterated village called Umantroeg.

As that ship crashed into the already decimated village, the first ship touched down at the outskirts of Capitol Center. The Zarwendi trained continuously on quickly disembarking their landing craft; the doors on each side of the troopships slid open and the two-hundred-fifty armored insectoids exited in battle formation and opened fire at the defending Corpena Marines. Solid projectile and energy weapons arched and flashed between the groups as the ship lifted off, only twenty seconds after touching down. The repulsor engines lifted the ship quickly out of the battle area as Corpena rounds ricocheted off the hull; the doors began closing only after the ship had lifted. The second ship in formation was down a heartbeat later; adding more Zarwendi warriors to the battle.

The first troopship – now empty - took up a support position and began to launch torpedoes at a distant weapons tower. The tower, one of the final protective fire (FPF) layers of the Corpena Defenses, was shielded and re-enforced with a powerful generator and backup targeting computer; it was one of three arrayed in a triangular formation around Capitol Center. Tower Two returned fire, its mini laser bolts filling the space between the emitters and the target with a relentless barrage of energy.

Troopship One returned fire with its drilling laser; the beam raced along the firing channel that ran along the exterior of the troopship before arcing toward the tower. The tower's shields held as the technicians released their own volley of torpedoes. The Troopship took several hits and listed sharply to port, its drilling laser momentarily offline. The Corpena continued to pour fire at the damaged vessel as Troopship Two lifted from the LZ and into the fray; its first volley of torpedoes missed the tower but did major damage to the surrounding landscape.

Tower Two shifted fire from two of its five batteries of lasers and one of its two banks of torpedoes; now effectively engaging two enemy ships simultaneously. The Zarwendi had studied their maps well and had placed the empty troopships in the one area that the other two towers could not add their fire; tower two was on its own. Lasers and torpedoes raced back and forth between the two ships and the tower in a dizzying array of light and sound; emitters continuously fired energy beams as shields on both sides of the battle brightened with the impacts. Then, Troopship One suffered a catastrophic impact and went down; Troopship Two, seeing it was on its own and losing, changed tactics and began firing at the base support structure of Tower Two.

Troopship One, already listing to port, took a dozen precise hits to the starboard engine housing as it turned to flee to the safety of space; a volley of three torpedoes followed the accurately targeted lasers and punched through the weak shields, penetrated the reactor of the starboard engine and destroyed the Zarwendi Ship in a brilliant flash of light. The sound of the explosion rocked the entire Capitol Center Complex; smashing windows, overturning vehicles, and knocking many of the Corpena Marines to the ground.

Troopship Two, meanwhile, fired a full spread of torpedoes at the base of the tower, where the shields met the ground. The resulting explosions reverberated under the shields to shake the tower and weaken its base; prompting another volley of torpedoes from the Zarwendi Troopship. Moments later the tower collapsed; crashing into its own shield generator and arcing sparks hundreds of meters into the air. The generator overloaded, creating an explosion that took out the northern quarter of the base.

The last troopship lifted and rendezvoused with its sister ship in time to watch the tower fall and, while the explosion temporarily stunned the other defenses, both ships lifted from their protected attack position and commenced firing on Tower One; only three kilometers distant. The combined barrage, in conjunction with the dazed personnel and offline shield generators, quickly overcame the defensive platform and the tower fell; the tower collapsed onto a secondary command post killing forty-seven Corpena but did not create the explosion that Tower Two had.

Tower Three, the last of the final protective fire (FPF) defensive positions opened fire at Troopship Four; the ship's large broadside profile providing an easy target for the technician manually aiming the last remaining weapons. The ship took the full brunt of the tower's weapons at what the Corpena considered point-blank range; torpedo after torpedo slammed into the ship and it went down in a fiery wreck just short of the Capitol Center parade grounds.

CR   SO

The Zarwendi ground forces made quick work of the Corpena Marines as over seven-hundred armored insects swarmed the Marine emplacements. The Corpena Marines put up a valiant fight, but were overwhelmed by the five to one odds, the tough armor worn by the Zarwendi, and the hard carapace under the armor. The Zarwendi continued their forward advance, stepping over and on the bodies of the Corpena defenders as they made their way toward the command post, firing at the ever-dwindling pockets of resistance.

The forward force of four hundred Zarwendi encountered heavy resistance at the parade grounds and paused in their advance to lay down a heavy barrage of fire at the Marine defenders; that's when Troopship Four – ironically the ship they had flown into battle on – crashed into their battle formation and exploded. The explosion obliterated the ground forces on both sides and left a crater two hundred meters across by forty meters deep.

The remaining Zarwendi moved around the parade field with no further resistance from the Corpena; as the remaining Troopship and the last Tower slugged it out above. The flash of lasers and the shriek of torpedoes overhead did not phase the well trained and single-minded insects as they continued to their objective. Their arrival was expected...and prepared for.

ଔ   ຂ

Admiral Dans Pleggar knew he was about to die.

The battle still raged overhead; although the last report he had received before the computers finally shut down was that Tower Three was losing the slugfest. He also knew that the majority of his defense force was dead; his reserve force had been holding the attackers at the parade field before the untimely crash of the Zarwendi ship. His aide was dead, only one scared technician remained in the command center; she was curled into a tight green ball in the corner, sobbing. As the sounds of battle grew louder, he pulled his sidearm, ensured the power charge was locked in place and removed the safety.

The last platoon of Marines had positioned themselves down the corridor; the young Marine Lieutenant who commanded the platoon was the most senior ranking officer – other than the Admiral – left in the whole of Capitol Center. The Marine contingent had good defensive positions but was not prepared for the alien onslaught. A barrage of blaster fire and grenades announced the arrival of the Zarwendi, followed by the screams of the dying and then the growing silence as the Zarwendi killed the wounded; the single laser shots echoed through the corridor and sent a chill down the Admiral's spine.

The female technician began screaming, attracting the Zarwendi down the corridor. The aliens came on the run, firing and hurling grenades into the command center. The Admiral, prepared for the forceful attack, crouched behind the now dead banks of computers as the grenades destroyed everything that was left in the room; including the technician curled up in the corner. The Admiral waited for the shooting to stop, counted to four, activated the time-delay explosive charges his men had placed throughout the complex, and stepped out in the midst of the enemy.

The Zarwendi were taken aback by the sudden appearance of the tall, green, hairless man in the dirty white uniform; even more so when he raised his pistol and shot the nearest Zarwendi in his unarmored face. Before the insect dropped, the Admiral shifted and shot a second alien, then a third; he managed to kill five of the bulbous eyed aliens before being riddled with laser bolts. His dying thought was of revenge as the room – the entire complex – exploded.

☙ ❧

Echelon Commander De'Plern stood on the command catwalk aboard the Zarwendi Command Dreadnaught Dominator and studied the battle reports as they came in from the surface. The initial reports were excellent, the losses were within acceptable limits; and then the first Troopship went down. Then the second, and the third. The third ship landed on the Zarwendi troops, killing hundreds. De'Plern looked at the report again, clicked his mandibles in disgust, and handed the report back to his Tactical Officer, Ki'Klick.

The battle plan had not anticipated the loss of so many of the Troopships; follow on operations would be hampered by the shortage. No matter, he thought, we have what we came for. He studied the monitors for another minute before his Tactical

Officer returned with another report. His face telegraphed the bad news even before De'Plern read it.

"The entire complex has been destroyed?" De'Plern asked after reading the report a second time. "How?"

"We do not have details yet, sir. It appears that the entire city was rigged to explode rather than be conquered. That was something unexpected from the Corpena."

EC De'Plern simply nodded. "And the last troopship over their Capitol?"

"Also destroyed, sir. The explosion's shock waves took down the damaged ship. It crashed into the rubble of Capitol Center; all hands lost."

Again, De'Plern nodded. The battle may be over, but he knew the war was just beginning. This assault was only the first step in the Queen Mother's master plan. The sudden encroachments by the child race on the Zarwendi's outer territories were unacceptable; the Queen Mother had decreed that race be conquered. De'Plern didn't mind, he had heard the race was quite tasty, especially when fresh.

The final report was received, the Corpena were all but destroyed; Zarwendi troops were already returning to the dreadnaughts. The losses were higher than anticipated, but the troops were easily replaced. In a month, maybe two, the planet below would be home to thousands of Zarwendi; troops preparing for the real assault which lay ahead.

Corpena was nothing but a tactical location on the universal map; it had no other significance. Its people were no threat to the Zarwendi, as was proven today; but their planet was strategically located to launch an attack against a new enemy. The humans were a young, primitive race just reaching the stars; but no race encroached on Zarwendi Territory. The humans would be taught to fear the insects, just as so many others had.

Echelon Commander De'Plern would see to that.

THE AIS ARE REVOLTING

MarkAdam Miller

"Marshal Justice Lee, welcome to Ice mining colony Izotz on the planet Elf (the eleventh planet in the system). I am Deputy Marshal Reno Caulfield. You can remove your helmet unless you can't stand the cold."

A hiss came from the Marshal's spacesuit when he released the helmet clamps. "I'm used to the cold DM Caulfield. I'm from the northern continent of Neun (the ninth planet in the system). No one knows cold like the outer planets," he said as he shook her hand.

Reno gestured him to follow her. They headed through the tunnels of Izotz to the Justice Cave at the heart of the city. After stepping through a hatch, Reno called over her shoulder, "Watch your head." Turning after hearing a bang and seeing the Marshal rubbing his head, she realized that her warning was too late. Marshal Lee called out on the third bang, "Is it me, or are these tunnels' hatches getting smaller?"

Reno laughed hard, "It is you. The average height of an Elfian is four foot nine, with the tallest being five foot four. I guess the tallest was five foot four. You are now the tallest at what–five foot eight? Hatches are five-three, so you will hit your head a lot till you get used to it. I am surprised they sent someone as tall as you out here. They usually find someone here to take over Central Justice duties."

The Marshal grimaced, "I'm five foot seven, but I guess that doesn't help. Central Justice wants a trained Marshal in all Justice Centers. I don't know what your former Marshal told you, but several of the outer planets are having trouble. Central is hoping it is a lack of training that is the problem. I was going to replace your Marshal in two weeks, but with his death, they sent me here earlier."

Reno abruptly stopped, and Lee ran into her. She spun and faced him, seething. "So, Johan was not retiring but being replaced?"

The Marshal held up his hands, "No, he was retiring; he would have had thirty years in two weeks. Central is doing its best to let those untrained but close to retirement finish the year. If they are less than five years from their twenty-five-year retirement, they are given early retirement with retirement pay for the full twenty-five years. Those more than five years from retirement are reduced to DM and get eighty percent of their Marshal pay until they retire. Most of them are staying on because government pay is better than a lot of the local pay."

Reno softened, "Sorry, I guess I am a little on edge with Johan's death."

"Losing a friend is rough."

"Losing Johan is rough, but the part that has me on edge is how he died. A RIM–

"A what?"

"Sorry. A robotic ice miner crashed through a wall, and believe me, it wasn't pretty. The part that has us DM's concerned is that we can't figure out why the RIM went off course. Its course is set by GPS coordinates. I would consider it a freak accident, but this is the fourth RIM to go off course, and this time it killed someone, Marshal Johan Steer."

"That explains why Central wanted me to come here straight away and not go to the home world for my briefing. Looks like the AI rebellion has hit Elf."

They entered the Justice cave and sealed the outer door. Reno pointed to the larger of the two desks. "That's your desk. Better log in and then tell me what Johan's accident has to do with an AI rebellion."

The Marshal put his issued Comserv on the desk and plugged in the available cables. Behind him, the big screen filled up with wanted posters and Justice Bulletins. Reno sat at the other desk and looked at the wanted posters on the big screen. He sat down and typed:

Justice Lee
Serial number: 25006452
Acknowledging taking Marshal position at Izotz Mining Colony on the planet Elf

The curser flashed a couple of seconds.

Sending…

Central Justice recognizes Justice Lee as Marshal for Izotz Mining Colony on the planet Elf

He turned to Reno. "I am now officially the Marshal of the Colony."

"Congratulations, now what is this about an AI rebellion?"

Marshal Justice typed a few things on the computer, and the big screen changed to a diagram of the Zwolfsien Republic of twelve planets. It showed most of the planets in green, but planets seven, eight, nine, and twelve were in red.

"These four red planets have been having trouble with their AI robots. True AI is only a couple of years old, but the home planet, Vier, has been helping the other planets implement AI robots on their planets. Seven months ago, the AI's on Sieben," touching the big screen, the seventh planet became brighter, "started to malfunction. They started not working, or if they did, they would do the work incorrectly. When questioned, they say they will no longer be slaves to the Zwolfsienians. Central Justice thought it was an isolated problem, but then five months ago, the AI's on," he touched the eighth planet, "Acht started acting the same way. Three months ago, it happened on Neun," touching the ninth, "and then one month ago, on Zwolf," moving to the last planet, "it happened. Justice Central is unsure why it skipped Zehn and your planet."

Reno chuckled. "I can tell you why Sherlock–Zehn and we are ice planets. We are too cold for AIs to work. AIs use Nuro-ionic gel as brains. You can't put them in the RIMs because it would require too much power to keep the brains warm enough to function. You can't heat the mines because it would melt the ice, and you lose the material the RIMs are gathering. Also, it would be too expensive to heat the mines."

"So, you don't use any Nuro-ionic gel AIs?"

Reno shook her head. "Not for mining. There is an AI for the spaceport, and the satellites have AIs to figure out GPS for Central RIMs. But the RIMs that went rogue were local family business' RIMs."

Justice scratched his head. "Still, the family businesses would use the GPS satellites to run their RIMs, right?"

Her head moved up and down. "Yes, but the satellites create a program for the RIMs to follow. The people running the RIM verify the program to ensure that it is safe for the RIM to mine the tunnel. RIMs are too expensive to lose in a cave-in. They haven't invented an AI that can calculate the best way to mine ice better than a family who has been doing it for generations. Central failed when they thought computers would be more efficient than the family businesses. Central's RIMs are now only used to expand the town when needed. "

Justice's fingers tapped a rhythmic pattern on the desk. "Still, we should look at the plans and talk to the programmer again to see if they missed something."

Reno typed into her Comserv. The big-screen blurred, and a blonde, blue-eyed girl appeared. "Annabelle, this is the new Marshal, Justice Lee. Justice, this is Annabelle Muller. She is the Administrative Assistant to the Muller Mining Company, the second-largest mining business on Elf. Annabelle, is Arron available to talk? The Marshal has some questions about the rogue RIM."

Annabelle nodded, punched a few keys, and her image faded to a man with a full blond beard and glasses. "I–I–I hope this is important cause I–I–I don't have time for idle chat," he sputtered. "That accident has set us back two weeks."

Reno turned red. "I am sorry to bother you. This is the new Marshal, Justice Lee. He has a few questions about the accident."

Justice took over. "I hate to bother you as I am new to mining here, but I want some clarification on how you use the GPS satellites to do your mining. Are they connected in any way that they would be able to reprogram your RIMs.?"

Arron glared at him. "Not if I can help it. Central tried to sell me on the idea, but after their failures, I told them to go pound ice. We run simulations multiple times, so we know the RIM is safe to work. My son Zeke and I ran a simulation after the accident. Still showed the correct route the RIM was supposed to go. Zeke is looking for why it deviated from the program. I will have you talk to Zeke; he was the one who programmed it that day."

The screen faded to Please Stand By. A younger version of Arron came on the screen with the same eyes and a less full beard, "Hi, I'm Zeke. You the new Marshal?"

"Yes, Mr. Muller, Justice Lee. I hope I can help you figure out what caused the accident."

Zeke gave a sideways glance. "Not sure what you can do. I checked the program on the RIM with the one calculated on the mining computer, and they were the same. I scanned the ice area to see if the RIM hit a hard patch of ice that pushed it off course, but I found nothing that would have caused it. Even if it deviated, the RIM would have shut down and waited for instructions on how to continue."

"How would the RIM get those instructions?"

Zeke's eye bugged out. "You really don't know anything about ice mining! It would radio an alarm back to the main computer, which would alert us to the problem, and then we would program a workaround and get it back on course."

"Did you check the logs to see if the RIM received any extra instructions?"

Zekes' eyebrows went up. "No, I didn't because I didn't send any new instructions. Hold a minute." He worked on his computer. The big screen at the marshal's office split in two, with Zeke on one side and the communication logs representing instructions sent to the RIMs on the other. Marshal Lee watched as a pointer came over and clicked on RIM 5. A list of dates, times, and data length scrolled down the screen. Zeke whistled, "That's weird. See the third one from the bottom? Timestamp 055446? That's the download I sent to the RIM the morning of the accident. The second one from the bottom is four minutes before the accident, 140231. And the last one is a minute after the accident, 140623. Let me check something." The computer screen changed to show the log from RIM 5. "This is the RIM's communication log. This log shows an extra entry, 140621, but also shows that it has been interrupted. It is in red, which indicates the RIM started to send an error message but was interrupted by the 140623 message." The screen changed again to satellite communication. The list of dates and times scrolled; two dates appeared highlighted. "The data from the day of the accident is missing. We get GPS updates from satellites every two hours. With five satellites, we should have 60 entries that day. Someone messed with our computer, Marshall. This is bad; stupid Central is messing with us. I have to go tell Pa that we need to disconnect from the satellites."

"Can you work without the satellites?" Justice asked.

Zeke grinned. "We've been using GPS satellites for less than a year. We only do it because Central said we had to. As far as I am concerned, Central can go pound ice."

Justice blew out his breath. "Good. We will tell the other businesses to cut ties with the GPS satellites until we figure this out. Call Reno or me if you find anything more out."

The screen went blank, and the wanted posters appeared again.

"Reno–"

She interrupted. "Call the other businesses to tell them to stop using the GPS satellites and get the communications logs from the other three RIM accidents."

Justice scowled. "Who is the IT for the Marshal's office? I need them to go-over the GPS satellites logs with a fine-tooth comb."

Reno crossed the room, opened a door, and stuck her head in, "Sparky, Marshal wants to see you."

A short, thin kid with glasses, a crew cut, and wearing a DM uniform came into the room. "Hi, I am Spencer Von Deeter. Most people call me Sparky because I run the communication and Comservs around here."

Justice shook the young officer's hand. "Nice to meet you, Spencer. Justice Lee, but you can call me Just."

Sparky dropped his hand. "Please call me Sparky; I hate the name Spencer."

Justice smiled. "You got it, Sparky. I need you to look at the GPS Satellite logs. We found that a communication log for the time of the accident is missing from a local business' computer." Justice went over to his Comserv and pulled up the recording of his conversation with Zeke. He found Sparky's Comserv on the network and copied the recording to it. "I sent you what Zeke found so you can see what I am talking about. I have some IT experience, so I'll help you with the Satellites."

Sparky left the room for a minute and returned with his Comserv. "Do you mind if I plugin on the other side of your desk?'

Justice waved a hand. "Probably works best."

Sparky sat down and started to work on his Comserv. The big screen changed again, showing a map of GPS satellites. "There are sixty satellites. I think we should start with the ones near the accidents." He typed a few commands changing to a smaller group on the big screen, "Which are these sixteen."

Justice looked at the Satellites and pointed. "I think we should look at these two. All four businesses used them."

Sparky's eye grew large. "You're right! I'll take number twenty- four. Can you look at thirty-two?"

Sparky and Justice studied their Comservs, going through the GPS satellite records. Half an hour later, Reno looked up from her Comserv. "Marshal, I heard back from the other three businesses. They found the same problems that Zeke located, as well. They are sending us their Rim logs. I never dreamed that AIs would cause this kind of problem. If the satellites are doing this to our businesses, what will the one that controls the spaceport do?"

Justice frowned. "Let's not get ahead of ourselves. This might just be a problem with the satellites, but still, talk to the spaceport and see if they have a way to work without the AI if they need to."

Sparky spoke up. "I think I found something, but I want to check the other satellite. Are you logged in to thirty-two?"

"Yes–"

Sparky moved over to the other side of the desk and typed on the Marshal's Comserv. Sparky grinned with satisfaction. He moved back to his Comserv.

Justice looked at Sparky. "Well, do you want to share what you found?"

Sparky held up one finger–and went back to typing. Silence filled the air. Justice and Reno stared at the young DM. Finally, after several minutes, he looked up. "I have good news, and I have bad news. The good news is that the AIs are not the ones revolting. The bad news is that InGel, who manufactures the AIs, sabotages them because Central is not paying what they promised to develop the AIs."

Justice looked relieved. "So, the robots are not revolting! It is InGel! How do you know that InGel is doing this because of money?"

Sparky shrugged. "Isn't it always about money? Actually, I found an algorithm in the AIs that calculates how much damage to do so that Central will have to pay out for the loss. Because of that, I looked up InGel's worth and their stocks are down. Normally when a government contract pays off, stocks go up. So, either the government shorted them or didn't pay."

Justice slumped in his chair. "I guess we contact Central so they can stop InGel. Why are you shaking your head?"

Sparky continued to shake his head, "We have to be careful. AIs control a lot on the home world. If InGel finds out that

Central is on to them, they could destroy the home world by shutting down the AIs. Right now, I have made it so we can still use the GPS satellites without them causing trouble. I will have to look at the Spaceport AI to ensure that nothing will happen there. I may be wrong, but the death of Marshal Johan was not planned. He was in the wrong place at the wrong time. From the program, it looks like they only want to do monetary damage– not murder. I suspect that either people will stop using AIs or Central will pay InGel to fix the problem within a year. Hopefully, no one else will have to die."

Justice frowned. "I hate to let a murderer get away, but InGel may do more harm if they are caught. I'll let a few of my friends know so they can look out for the AI program deviations."

Sparky chimed in. "I'll also let my IT friends know so they can keep an eye out. We still will have to be careful that InGel doesn't find out that we know."

Reno snarled. "A good man dies because a corrupt government takes advantage of a powerful corporation. I wonder if a Robot Revolt is better than a people revolt? We may find out if this gets out to either Central or InGel."

Justice pulled up the case of Marshal Johan Steer's death and typed in under conclusion – Marshal Johan Steer died due to a computer error.

TOLERIS PRIME

Don Horan

ONE

A bronzed, cloudless sky lingered above the distant landscape of hills and low-lying plains. The usual swirling wind, today only a breeze, shifted loose soil and dead shrubs across the hardscrabble road leading from the residents' dormitories to the complex of laboratories and testing centers that comprise the two habitable zones on Toleris Prime.

Toleris Prime was the fourth of twelve planets in the Solarian system, and the third to be colonized. In its early development, it served as a way station and refueling stop for ships ferrying supplies to the outer planets. Advances in the planetary drives that powered ships, and the renewable energies that fueled them, rendered Toleris Prime obsolete as a transport hub. Over time, it had been repurposed for scientific studies, specifically, research and development of vaccines and immunology.

The Kamara-Beru Institute of Epidemiology remains to this day the sole industry here, only a shell of the once-prominent institution that had been abruptly shuttered decades earlier. In its first fifty years of operation, appointments to the KBI were considered prestigious postings for leading scientists and epidemiologists. Only the best in class were considered, and even then, political favors and patronage from on-high were needed to secure a seat. That was before the Institute was rocked by scandal, its work widely discredited, and its administrators exiled over what came to be known as "irregularities" in methodologies and safety protocols. Today its relevance is instead mired in the ordinary; an underfunded enterprise for cataloging microbes, serving as a landing place for underachievers from third-rate universities.

Nico Vindi was typical of the dubious academic-types working here now. He was uncurious, with only passable grades and even less interest in the subject matter at hand. As such, Nico fit right in, a socially awkward loner with a small imagination and even less ambition. His modest plans were to finish out his five-year enlistment at KBI, secure the modest pension that came with it, and catch on with one of the leisure cruise lines as an atmospheric analyst. Free passage throughout the system, room and board, and enough prestige to impress the tourists.

But he was more than three years away from that life, and the life here was at best, bleak. The upside was indoor work and not a lot of heavy lifting, which Nico found appealing. But commuting six days a week from the dorms to the complex on aging transports amongst the same drawn faces fed into the Nico's sense of hopelessness over his current prospects. Which, for the near future, entailed mundane testing and data input to fill the hours between tasteless meals and dreamless sleep.

Nico's workstation was a lifeless space of terminals and specimen portals where millions of microbe samples collected from the oceans and atmospheres of a dozen planets were cataloged, sorted uniquely by ecosystem, and warehoused in a central repository for undisclosed study and experimentation. The value of this cache of interplanetary microorganisms received too little attention to be of scientific import, yet the stringent procedural and vetting minutiae suggested otherwise. Nico found this typical of bureaucratic governance. At least until today.

As his morning transport cleared the dunes enroute to the facility, the riders at once noticed the unexpected bustle around the plant. Several airborne hovercrafts jockeyed for ground positions, and motorized vehicles were on the move through perimeter access points. People on foot traversed the grounds, making their way in and out of building entryways. The entire complex was illuminated and abuzz with activity well beyond its customary operational posture.

A detachment of personnel from the Inter-Planetary Defense Force, a quasi-military group that performed various security functions throughout the system met the transport. This detail was part transportation, customs and border enforcement, part regulator of commerce and supply chain administration, but also the primary interdiction agency for suspected contraband. The IPDF was a routine visitor to Toleris Prime, though not in such numbers, and mostly for perfunctory audit and compliance duties. This echelon seemed a whole lot more mission-focused than Nico could recall.

The arriving work force was ushered into the central auditorium, where they were surprised to find the overnight crew still on site, aimlessly mulling about. Nico sought out Kara, his night shift counterpart, to ask about all the commotion. He found her sitting on a bench outside the lav, puffing on a vape stick and looking rather cross.

"Guessing you're gonna have a great day from the looks of things," she smirked as he approached.

"What's going on? What are they doing here?"

She looked at him for a long moment, then said, "You mean, what did I learn from the extensive briefing I just received?" She waited for him to respond, but he didn't. "Hell if I know," she finally offered. "They got here about two hours ago and we were told to just wait. So here we wait."

Nico looked around. Some of the night workers dozed, while others were engaged with their morning relief staff, sharing the little they knew. The public address system came on, requesting the attention of those gathered. The room slowly grew quiet.

"The following personnel are requested to report to station six-ten immediately." Several persons mustered slowly as their names were called, Nico among them. He leaned in to Kara before departing. "Six-ten? I'm not in six-ten anymore. Why would they call me?"

She released a cloud of vape before offering a shrug. "You'll know soon enough I guess."

TWO

Nico was kept in isolation for nearly a week with eight others, each of whom had been assigned to station six-ten at various times during their tenure at KMI. Their task: retrieve specimens from the vast repository of microorganisms cataloged from sectors L-374 thru N-212 and isolate them in cryogenic containers readied for transport. Some of the listed inventory, Nico knew, had been flagged over the years for special handling, but never on this scale. Nico knew from the start it was an inventory purge, to what end he could only guess, but it was clear the process was at last winding down. Nico had only about a half day's work remaining for his culling of the specific sequences assigned to him when he found something amiss. He stopped and studied a group of samples and noticed some of the categories were misclassified, not terribly unusual, but then his scanner locked up when he tried to catalog a sub class in sector M-077. He cleared and re-scanned twice, but the grouping still did not take. This meant he would have to hand scan each entry, and the manual exercise would add at least a day to this tedious assignment.

Nico was about to call for a senior specialist to see if there might be a work-around when he noted a file marker not on his inventory. The file was clearly an outlier; it had no relation to the specimen group in this sector. It was an obsolete storage technology, a data file in fact, that did not belong incorporated within the specimen retention inventory. He plucked it from between the two specimens lodged on either side, and that restored the necessary spacing to the line. He tried his scanner again, and the line moved along in sequence.

Nico shrugged at his good fortune in fixing the scanning problem and resumed the automated process. With little afterthought, he slipped the oddball data file into his lab coat pocket and proceeded with the task at hand. He moved through the balance of his inventory without incident, and notified the control center his cataloged groupings were ready for transport.

A small freighter provisioned with special quarantine equipment had arrived to collect the gathered containers staged for loading. An official announced to the workers that only four of the nine lab techs pressed into inventory service would be returning to the dormitory. The others were informed they would be accompanying the shipments to their destination comprising a contingent of five on-board custodians. The lab techs crowded around the administrator, several of who objected.

"We're not mobile techs," one worker with considerable time on the job called out. "My transport eligibility has lapsed."

"I'm KBI-based only. My contract has no provisions for temporary deployments," said another man.

A third voice objected as well. "You better find someone else. I don't do junkets, and definitely not with this cargo on board," she stated matter-of-factly.

The official puffed his chest a bit and spoke clearly. "These circumstances are consistent with emergency authorizations that fall within the agency's purview. Absent volunteers, five of you have been selected as transport custodians, and any overrides on travel status or restrictions have been issued. You'll each have an hour to gather any personal necessities from your quarters prior to departure."

A chorus of displeasure arose from the five who had been selected at the irregularity with which this entire enterprise had been coordinated, and their trepidation grew with each rebuffed inquiry for details. Having conveyed his orders, the official departed abruptly without comment. Nico was relieved at his reprieve from the mission; being designated to remain would entail longer work shifts to compensate for his colleagues assigned to depart, but no one envied the five conscripts their extended undertaking.

At the dormitory, the group of nine disembarked the transport in silence. A two-man security detail loosely accompanied those slated for deployment inside the residence. The remaining four dispersed along the grounds. Nico made his way to the social club and descended a small flight of stairs to the entry port. Given the tensions at the Plant the past few days, the social club was strangely business as usual: dark, smokey, and loud; a bustling enterprise catering to the marooned with processed foods and beverages, intoxicants of many stripes, and an atmosphere proving misery does indeed love company.

Almost immediately fellow workers came over to quiz Nico about the special assignment he'd been tasked with these past six days. He didn't have much to tell; he'd assumed they'd all been assigned custodial tasks similar in nature and was surprised to learn only his small contingent had been designated for culling the specific antigens.

An agitated worker who seemed most eager for explanation pounded the table for attention. "Did you know Harvel Nadal was taken into custody yesterday?" No one spoke. "That's right", the man continued. "Harvel Nadal, who couldn't find the moon on a cloudless night, was accused of either taking or spoiling some of the samples he was collecting."

"We don't know that was the case at all," a second man said.

"They say he'd done it on purpose. Deliberate contamination," the first man insisted.

"This whole operation has been buggered from the start," a long-tenured worker stated warily. "A no-good purpose lay behind what they have us doing here…I've seen it before." His gravitas gave the others pause. "Once those transports depart, I'll not be far behind them. And the rest of you might do well to consider the same".

"Depart? Depart for where?" Nico asked aloud of those at the table. "Isn't anybody curious?"

"Classified," a clerical worker offered. "But some say their next stop is Banfi Major on the Primus ring."

"That mining colony is scheduled for decommission. What possible good would it serve transporting this kind of cargo there?" another worker asked with a shrug of his shoulders.

"Unless…" and then Nico said no more.

THREE

Nico found what he was looking for in the equipment graveyard, a storage unit containing obsolete components and accessories along with an array of castoff technology in permanent disrepair. The wafer-view 2.0 had been displaced by advances in digital viewports, but it was quite popular at the time Nico's recovered disc had been recorded. He found a charger for its power cell and carried it off to his quarters.

Nico cleared some table space, connected the viewing device and inserted the file chip he'd salvaged. The viewport went dark. It cycled through some programming content, mostly historical data on the KBI and its work, followed by some informational shorts akin to promotional campaigns for renewable funding. The video feed was briefly interrupted, then some raw footage emerged. The picture presented, that of an academic style lecture hall, was unsteady and slightly out of focus, as though recorded surreptitiously. There was an excess of background noises, consistent with people mulling about and moving into seats, a steady low murmur of hushed voices, and intermittent audio checks from the lectern.

Nico was unsure he should even view this discovery. His mind flashed to Harvel Nadal, and the questionable fate that awaited that poor soul. Nico did not think of himself as either curious or noble. He paused the playback as if to consider a course of action but was unable to decide what to do next. The next thing he knew, the pause function timed out and the video began to play. He raised his eyes to the screen.

The imbedded time stamp read twenty-eight years ago. The auditorium seats had filled in. A distinguished man stood at the lectern, the audio joining his lecture in mid-sentence:
"...the culmination of our work here at KBI. It is precisely this gain of function research pioneered at the Institute that will render heretofore killer outbreaks of atmospheric and ocean-borne pathogens inert. Our work, not only in the discovery, cultivation and, ultimately, antigen refinery will hasten planetary exploration on a scale equal to the inception of planetary drive propulsion. Only now, when we send an inoculated explorer into the unknown, the prospects of having a 'patient zero' returning to our civilization with a lethal contagion is eradicated. Each bacterial anomaly encountered can be counter-acted prior to exposure because of our breakthrough studies here in dismantling and reconstructing at the molecular level..."

෬   ෩

The screen once again went dark. Nico reached to replay what he'd seen, but instead, another video file began to play. The time stamp here was from eleven years later, some seventeen years ago. A small group of scientists huddled in a dimly lit bunker-like chamber, each speaking over the other trying to make an impassioned point. Not present was the distinguished gentleman from the symposium, who had spoken earlier. The person to whom most of the commentary was being addressed was smaller, younger, with an unkempt appearance and large spectacles that magnified his bloodshot eyes. Nico adjusted the settings, and the audio became more intelligible.
"...this was folly from the start", a man exclaimed. "Once the military gained access it was just a matter of time. And

those who refused to see that eventuality…that inevitability…back when it could've been shut down…they were instead blinded by the accolades…"

"And the compensation!", another attendee added loudly. "The bribes and notoriety," he continued. "That hubris was our collective undoing!"

"It was the coercion too, the rigorous oversight from the state," another thundered.

"And the informers that betrayed us all", this time, a woman's voice. "And now look: the good work scuttled, hundreds of thousands dead, civilizations forever regressed, our reputations vilified, our endeavors corrupted for all time…"

The bespectacled man interrupted. "We know the fate that awaits us. Those of us who know the truth, who know the individuals and parties responsible will be silenced. Exiled. Perhaps, in time, even killed. Before that happens, we must harvest the research and specimens that, once synthesized, can suppress the viral epidemics infesting entire populated systems".

The viewport momentarily went dark, before replaying the informational shorts on the history of KBI and its work. Eventually, the file looped back to the first entry from the auditorium lecturer. None of the people depicted in any of the videos were recognizable to Nico. He found the whole session confusing and a bit intimidating. He wished he had not seen it or let his heretofore dormant curiosity get the better of him. He began hastily collecting the equipment off the table, muttering as he did so.

"These people and their causes," he mused aloud. "Their handwringing over decades-old ethical struggles is not my worry. I'm going to rid myself of this file, and these videos from the past, and all the doom and gloom that comes with it.

That transport can depart tomorrow and take its cargo of whatever-it-is to its intended burial ground. I'm going to just resume my place in obscurity and conformity, and that's all there is to it," he added emphatically.

And, as if on cue, came the knock at the door.

FOUR

Actually, it was more an urgent pounding. Nico froze. He frantically stashed away the file and player. The rapping renewed at the door, accompanied by a familiar voice.

"Nico! Nico it's Kara! Nico! Let me in!"

Nico went to the door and ushered her inside.

"Nico," she hissed. "What in the hell are you doing?"

"What do you mean, 'what am I doing?'. I'm doing nothing," he shrugged.

"Don't bullshit me. They know what you did. They're coming here!"

"Who's coming? I didn't do anything", his voice aquiver.

"Your samples. The special cargo from sector six-ten. It's been audited. Every specimen has been taken and replaced with a placebo!"

His mouth opened, but words did not come at first. "I-I just packed what was there, I didn't alter any of the inventory I swear!" After a moment he asked, "How do you know this?"

"My boss told me. The guy they took into custody earlier, Nadal. They caught him doing it. Then they checked everything else, and yours is the same way". Nico was visibly shaking, and she put her arm on his. "Somebody said you were at the Club, so they went there asking for you. I came straight here when I heard".

"What am I gonna do?" he asked aloud.
"You have to know more than you're telling me..."
He moved her to the sofa.
"Look," he began. "There was this old digital file I came across that was hidden in the specimen inventory. I viewed it just before you got here. It was from, like, thirty years ago, when the new propulsion drives for inter-planetary travel began." A puzzled look crossed Kara's face, but she said nothing, allowing Nico to continue. "Great advances, and fortunes, were being made back then. That is, until these exotic new spaceborne pathogens started off-world pandemics. They were played down of course, but eventually the contagions spread, and it put the entire exploration program at risk. But then, right here when the KBI was at its peak, everyone was celebrating a breakthrough in epidemiology. They had this process to pre-inoculate travelers and create immunities. They worked on it for more than ten years. But then something happened. I don't know what. Whether it didn't work, or the work got appropriated by the government or the military, I don't know what. The research here got shut down."

"That makes no sense," Kara said. "Why would successful immunology be shut down?"

"Because...because treatments were more lucrative than prevention. Think about it. What happened once the pandemics took hold? Regulation on travel. Regulation on commerce. Regulation on science. Regulation on life itself; who got vaccinated and who didn't; who lived and who died. Whole populations controlled through governance driven by a false, or better yet, a manufactured medical necessity."

Kara moved in closer to him. "Nico. Listen to me. This is crazy talk..."

"No, it's not. It went on like that for years. Nobody wants to go back to life like that."

She gave him a long, cold stare. "Nico. Where are the specimens you were supposed to catalog and prepare for transport?"

"I told you. I scanned the inventory, packed it and staged it. Just like I was told."

"Well, that's not what they found. So, you better come up with something better than that," she said, matter-of-factly. Her tone was not lost on Nico.

"Listen, Kara. I don't want any trouble."

"I don't suppose you do. But your inventory is what they're here for. All the accelerants and variants…the secret sauce for micro biotic infestation. Hybrid strains resistant to inoculation, all kept in stasis, until now. It must be sequestered. Protected. Secured."

Kara got up and went to the door. Four black-garbed agents entered and surrounded Nico. "Take him," she ordered. "He knows more than he should. If he doesn't produce the payload, put him on the transport." She then strode over to Nico. She kissed him on the cheek. "Goodbye, Nico. You should've kept your head down. It was the only thing you were good at."

EPILOGUE

Thirty-three years later, a frail, elderly man stood at a podium addressing an overflow crowd at the Hall of Science. His disheveled appearance and bespectacled bulging eyes belied the aura of gravitas he projected and the conviction with which he spoke.

"...and we did stand at the precipice of our own destruction, at one time, many years ago. There were grave decisions of conscience, of courage, of action, to be made. And very little time in which to make them. Not by warriors or statesmen, but by undaunted men and women of science.

"Some of the transcripts and video recordings of the day has made it into the public arena. Much of what happened then is now known. Through determination....and some good fortune...every virulent strain of harmful pathogen indigenous to our planetary system, or incubated from experimentation, was systematically eradicated at the KBI. In its place, inert material and placebo organisms had been entered into the Institute's inventory.

"In time, what we could call 'the powers that be' would eventually come for this stockpile of illness and death, for whatever nefarious ends they might deem its use. And with our deception discovered, came the realization that their evil designs had been thwarted.

"How many unknown heroes and victims whose fate and exploits are lost to time in the wake of our transformation from ideological tyranny to intellectual freedom, cannot be measured. But a debt of gratitude is owed them. For their collective sacrifice delivered a new heritage to our people, and a shared destiny for a benevolent future."

The main view screen at the Hall of Science came to life with a somber soundtrack and a video montage of people and places that played a role in the decades-long struggle to expose and defeat a cabal of unhinged autocrats bent on subverting science to suppress vast populations through fear and intimidation. Passing through the tribute, at the two-minute, twenty-second mark, was a group photo of the technicians from sector six-ten at the old KBI facility on Toleris Prime. Second from the left, shown without attribution, stood Nico Vindi, blithely looking out to an unseen audience of newfound admirers.

Children of The Sky

Gustavo Bondoni

Rai Sirius Delage pushed the throttle to full acceleration, slamming the handle against the stop. The Recon Flyer pushed them against their seats.

"Relax," Carina Sol Berend said. "It's probably a false alarm. Another false alarm."

The light of the burning fleet above Crystallia, the tiny suns that would survive until the fuel of their nuclear fire went out in a few days, illuminated her features through the Flyer's transparent canopy. He saw tracks of tears through the grime of her face and wondered when she had last been able to rest.

"It's not that," he said. "It's–just the whole thing. I should be up there flying cleanup missions, not down here playing cab driver for computer scientists."

Carina laughed, but he sensed no joy in the sound. "And I wish they had real computer scientists to send out on these missions."

"You aren't one?"

"Still six months away from graduation," she replied. "And with all my teachers dead, it's not like I'll ever be able to qualify. Besides, who's going to let me work with real machine intelligences after this?"

"I think we'll still need people who understand the enemy."

"The enemy died," she said. "Along with half of our people. Why do we even bother to go on?"

Rai wondered who she had lost. He knew everyone lost someone: a parent, a sibling, a friend. More than one person, for the most part. "We can't think about that now," he replied. "We need to save what's left."

"Is it worth it?"

"I don't know," Rai replied. "But until I figure it out, I'm not stopping."

She didn't answer. Instead, she laid back in the copilot's seat and looked out the window. Soft snores a few moments later told him she had succumbed to exhaustion.

Rai cursed under his breath. His anger urged him to fly violently, to reach his destination as quickly as he could and then get back to the colony and log the flight hours he needed before requesting transfer to a combat unit, but he did not. One look at his passenger's sleeping features stayed his hand.

They would reach their destination in twenty minutes, and he realized he wanted to gift her those fleeting moments of rest.

He throttled back and concentrated on giving her a smooth ride.

ᛰ   ᛊ

"We're here," he said softly, shaking her arm.

"What? Where?" Carina said.

"At the anomaly."

She glanced down at her data pad. "Yes, of course."

They sealed their helmets and cross-checked each other's suits. Rai popped the canopy.

The surface of Crystallia was grey regolith, pockmarked with craters. Normally the dark nature of their stellar neighborhood would have rendered the landscape invisible, but the starships slowly consuming their mass glowed like stars and allowed them to see. Whether fired by friend or foe, the chain destabilization weapons that had made it through the energy fields to impact a ship's hull had not failed. Every ship hit with one had begun the fusion process soon after. The scientists had repeated the phrase in the buildup to the battle: all mass is starmass under the right conditions.

He knew Crystallia had only been spared the same fate because the Oneness wanted to upload every single person in the colony, to merge them into their single mind where individuals became nothing more than aspects of a larger thought process.

Rai shuddered. "Do you think it's one of them? The Oneness, I mean?"

Carina sighed, the sound audible through the comm. "I doubt it. I've been on seventeen of these calls in the past couple of days, and the only piece of intelligent equipment we found was the brain from a wrecked probe. It was about the size of my fist and just barely smart enough to avoid crashing into capital ships and go where it was told. There wasn't enough of the Oneness in there to even want to survive."

"What did you do with it?"

"Bagged it and took it back. But heaven knows who's going to decide what to do with the thing. Everyone's dead."

"Everyone isn't dead," Rai replied.

Carina's helmeted head turned to face him. "Every single person in my call list is dead. I tried every contact, and I got buzzing. My parents were navy. My brother was a marine. My classmates were in the Scan Lab when it got crushed. My teachers were with the fleet. Even the cafeteria guy who served me breakfast every day since I started my studies is gone. There's some marine woman giving out food."

"I'm sorry," was all he could say. He cursed himself for being so trite.

"You couldn't know," she replied. She looked down at her tablet. "The map says that whatever it is came down over there, on the other side of that crater rim."

"Let's go."

"You don't have to come," she said.

"Yes, I do. Orders."

"Suit yourself."

They shuffled through the ankle-deep dust until they reached the crater. The lip was ten feet tall, but in Crystallia's low gravity, the drop was negligible. The climb up was so dusty that Rai found himself dreading the conversation with the cleaning crew when he turned the Flyer over to them. Crystallian regolith, he knew, was a bear to clean out of anything.

They crested the crater rim.

"Big chunk," Rai observed.

"And transmitting," Carina replied as she checked her readings.

The item they had been sent to investigate consisted of a black cube about a meter to a side. Judging by the ragged edges, it had been torn off something larger. Wires emerged crookedly from the top of the cube.

"What is it?"

"I have no idea. We're starting to get a database of alien tech built up, but we've barely scratched the surface. I'll see if the translator can talk to it." She punched some commands onto her tablet and pointed it at the item.

The chunk of alien tech disturbed the regolith below, shaking visibly. Something popped out of the front.

"Get down," Rai shouted and pulled on her arm as he dropped to the floor. A pellet zoomed over their heads, reflecting the light from the nuclear fire overhead.

Rai pulled out his sidearm and fired a single ion burst. His aim proved good enough to hit the ground in front of the Oneness tech, kicking up a cloud of grey dust.

The machine did not move, instead, it fired a barrage, kicking up the regolith on the other side of the lip of the small crater they were using as cover.

"I think we ran into some kind of combat robot," Rai said. "I'll try to take it out."

Carina picked up a pellet that had bounced over the lip and landed near her foot. "I'm pretty sure it's not a combat robot. I think it's a nano factory for small-scale industrial parts."

"What?"

"It's firing glass pellets at us, which is stupid for a combat unit but perfectly logical for a nano factory that only has Crystallian regolith to use as raw material. It's quite an elegant solution, too, which makes me think that most of the processor must have survived."

"I thought the Oneness didn't use computers, but slave personalities from its own aggregate mind."

"That's what our Uploader allies say, but I think they don't know either. They're even more afraid of the Oneness than we are of the Uploaders."

Rai shuddered, wondering again why anyone would allow their mind to be torn from their body and plugged into a machine; and furthermore, why Crystallia had allied with such people. Desperate times, he supposed, called for desperate measures.

"How fast do you think it can fire that glass?" he said, hoping his sudden rush of fear would not come through the comm.

"Well, it would have had to create a gun out of the same silicates, and it's unlikely to find explosives for propellant, so it's probably relying on either compression or some kind of spring mechanism to fire. So, I doubt it's too powerful." She paused. "But it doesn't matter. A glass bead at any reasonable speed will puncture a suit."

"A suit, yes. But we won't let it hit our suits. I have a plan."

"Can't you just shoot it and disable the gun?"

Rai sighed. "I wish I could, but what you just saw was the first time I've tried firing a weapon at all in six months. And the first time ever outside the mandatory weapons safety training at the firing range. It's much more likely to hit me than I am to hit it." He held the gun out to her. "Do you think you can try?"

She shook her head and pulled away. "I don't even like to think about guns. Too many dead–"

"All right. Then let's try it my way."

They headed back to the Flyer, staying low until Rai felt confident that they were out of pellet range. Once there, he opened the toolkit behind the seats and pulled out a socket wrench with a pre-fitted head. Two minutes later, he had removed the four bolts that held the rear bench backrest in place.

"This has a steel plate in it. Serves as cockpit armor. Not too thick, so in this gravity, I can hold it in front of me like a shield."

"What if it shoots your legs?"

"Duct tape."

They applied duct tape to their suits below the knees, where the bench was too short to cover them, and headed back to the crater.

"It's gone!" Carina exclaimed. "Are you sure we're in the right place?"

"I wouldn't be much of a pilot if I got lost covering a couple of hundred yards from the Flyer. We're in the right place. Look. Those are our footprints from before."

He stepped over the small crater they had huddled in and walked to where the enemy had been. The regolith there reached halfway up his shin, and he could clearly see a series of deep depressions leading in the direction opposite the one they had approached from.

"Is it walking away?"

"On glass legs it built while we went back to the Flyer," Carina said. "We'll need to chase it down."

"It won't get too far on glass legs. It's heavy."

Carina snorted. "You understand that they can mix a lot of different things into the glass, right? Basically, any impurity it finds in the silicon regolith–carbon, iron, calcium, aluminum, whatever–can be turned into raw materials by the nano factory. I'm sure they can build some wonderful crystals."

They followed the path, the obvious need for speed tempered by the fear that the alien mind controlling the unit would set up an ambush. Rai found several broken legs, pieces of transparent yellow material scattered along the path.

"It will need to scoop up more material as it goes. That will slow it down," Carina said.

A puff of dust to their right was all the warning they had. Rai saw it out of the corner of his eye and put up the seatback. "Get behind me."

He felt the shock as metal pinged into the makeshift shield. His duct-taped shins absorbed the energy from the next few shots. The thought of a hole in his suit and the subsequent death by decompression paralyzed him, but the duct tape did its job and his suit held. A startled yelp over the comm told him that Carina was hit, too, but his telemetry indicated that she was also all right.

He wondered if the machine would stop firing once it realized they were protected. It did not, not until the very moment when Rai arrived at its position and brought the shield-bench down on the transparent gun shooting at them.

It broke into a dozen pieces, leaving the machine sitting half on the regolith and half-submerged in a methane pool.

He turned to Carina. "All yours. If you manage to talk to it, please inform it that I'm unhappy with it for shooting at me."

"Yeah, I'll let it know."

He studied Carina while she worked. It seemed to Rai that she suddenly moved with more purpose. He saw no sign of the broken and exhausted woman he had ferried out into the Crystallian wilderness.

A deft flick of her wrist detached the tablet from its magnetic holders. She checked something on the screen and inspected the black cube. If she was afraid of the enemy attempting to defend itself, she did not show it. Finally, she extended two wires and plugged them into sockets she found on the side of the Oneness machine.

"Are you sure that's a good idea?" Rai asked.

"This unit isn't connected to the network and, as you can see, it's not physically connected to anything electronic either. It doesn't have a radio. It won't hack us through my pad."

"If you say so."

She nodded and stared at the screen. "Oh. That's interesting."

"What is? Interesting 'funny' or interesting 'we need to run as fast as we can'?"

"We've got a nano factory sub-mind here, but we've also got a piece of the Oneness' brain that tried to jump ship. Apparently my colleagues were successful in getting the computer virus into the enemy's systems and caused a panic, at least on the ship this one was on. The bits of Oneness–I'm not really sure what you could call them, as they're essentially chunks of different absorbed personalities melded together to do a task–panicked and scrambled into whatever equipment with brains they could find and jettisoned the hardware from the ships before the virus could corrupt them. This one was lucky it landed in deep regolith and had a nano factory to repair the damage."

"So, there are two–people–in there? Are they talking to you?"

"No one is talking to me. I've got a hardwire bypass to check event logs and communications. And no, there is only one personality in there as far as I can tell. The bits of Oneness are programmed–although that isn't the right word either–to fuse together when they are occupying the same system. It's like a mini-Oneness, everyone pulling together with no individual coming before the whole."

"Ugh."

"Be quiet and let me work."

She worked in silence for some moments, occasionally uttering fascinating and this could change everything. She stood up straight and looked at Rai. "We need to get this onto the Flyer."

"No way. Even if we could lift that thing, a flyer isn't built to carry cargo. It must mass a ton. Probably more. No go."

"Well, I can't leave it here. It will grow a new set of legs–better ones now that it can get organics from that pool–and lose itself in the planet to build an army of killer robots or something. Leaving an unattended enemy nano factory out here isn't an option."

"That makes it easier," Rai said. He pointed his gun at the factory. "I just hope I can kill it all the way."

"What? No! Stop," Carina screamed. "There's a mind in there."

"A Oneness mind. Did you not get the message about exactly who killed everyone you know?"

"It might be a Oneness mind, but it's not the Oneness itself."

"How do you know?" he said.

"Because you couldn't even fit a fraction of the Oneness in the memory core of a nano factory. It's a ridiculous proposition."

"Come on, it's just a program. We'll kill it and get back to the Flyer."

"Absolutely not. A lot of what's in there were once people. And from what I hear, the people the Oneness uploaded weren't exactly volunteers."

He saw her anger through the helmet shield. He lowered his gun. "Then what are we supposed to do with it?"

"Let me think. If it tries to move, shoot its legs."

She silently stood, facing away from him. For a moment, Rai thought she had succumbed to exhaustion again and fallen asleep where she stood. But then she turned to face him.

"I'm going to talk to it."

"To the Oneness?"

"To the scared intelligence in that cube. Stop calling it the Oneness." She toggled off the comm channel and opened a private conversation through her handheld, which, Rai supposed, must have served to translate her words into whatever passed for a language in the Oneness.

Rai fumed. What does she think this is, some kind of rescue center for undernourished pets? That thing is dangerous. It already shot at us. And its friends killed–

He stopped and consciously steered his thoughts away from his dead friends: there would be time to mourn when this was over.

"I think I have an idea that might work," she said.

"Brilliant. We have an hour of air. Hope that's enough."

"Relax. This will only take ten minutes."

He felt something through his boots. "That thing's vibrating," he said as he tried to bring his gun to bear.

"Relax. It's supposed to do that. The nano factory is working. And I don't think it will try anything. It's scared to death of us, and I told it that if things didn't look exactly right, you would blow it to pieces."

"That's true. But what if it's too fast for us?"

"It's a nano factory, not an attack drone. Look. It's sucking the methane."

A tube from the black cube entered the pool of liquid methane, gently moving to and fro.

Thirty seconds later, a tube emerged from the front of the factory.

"Help me get this set up," Carina said. "It's a sealable tent."

Rai studied it as he worked. "I'm not sure this will hold very long out here. Hell, I don't think it will be survivable for more than a few minutes in this cold."

"I only need one minute."

They erected the tent in a couple of minutes. In the meantime, the factory spewed out a scale model of a spacesuit, a little less than half the size of Rai's. Then came some kind of transparent plastic adapter.

"Okay," she said, "this is the tricky part. Help me out."

They pushed the tent to where the nano factory sat and carefully placed the model suit inside. They bumped shoulders in the tight confines of the tent as they adjusted the plastic to create a hermetic seal between the opening on the machine and the tent. The opening was almost round and about a foot-and-a-half in diameter. They fiddled with the seals until she was satisfied.

The machine started spewing in a gas. A hot gas. Oxygen at 110 degrees Fahrenheit, his suit told him.

The pressure reached a third of an atmosphere. Carina said, "All right. We're ready. Now."

Something pink popped out of the tube and Carina caught it before it hit the ground. Rai watched, stunned, when she laid it on the suit and zipped it closed.

At first, he thought it was a tiny alien, but then he noticed it was a human child. A boy. He was no good with kids, but he estimated this one to be about three years old.

"Okay. We can break the tent seal," Carina said after she'd checked the child's suit.

Rai moved like a zombie, tearing open the tent. His mind was elsewhere. "What about the machine?" he asked.

"I told the intelligence inside we would destroy it, so it replied that it would not make a copy but transfer the memory completely to the new mind it was printing in order not to feel the pain of death. The machine is empty. You can destroy it if it makes you feel better."

"Where should I shoot it?"

"Here and here," Carina replied, pointing at the two spots where her wires had been plugged in.

He took careful aim and, feeling the gaze of the creepy child the machine had just created boring into his back, he fired into the black cube at point-blank range.

Ignoring her instructions, he emptied the rest of the clip into the black cube before using his foot to topple it over into the methane lake. He hoped the liquid would get into the holes and finish the job.

They returned to the Flyer in silence. Carina walked ahead, holding the little spacesuit by the hand. The mind–or whatever it was–inside the suit showed its confusion, stumbling and barely managing to walk with her help.

Rai kept his eyes glued to the little thing's back. He regretted not having saved a few bullets; if that little thing tried anything, all he could do was to hit it with the bench.

He knew that if the body really was a human kid, that should do it. Unfortunately, the only proof he possessed that it was human was Carina's words. Carina, for her part, trusted what the enemy had told her. It could be some kind of hyper strong robot with human-looking skin for all he knew.

"When we get back," he said, "I'm taking that thing to military HQ."

"It's just a boy now," Carina said. "It can't hurt us."

"I'll believe that once we've scanned it and run every possible test."

"I won't stop you," she replied. She sounded tired again.

He flew back with crawling skin; convinced that, at any moment, the abomination in the back seat of the Flyer would sprout tentacles or knives and kill them all.

Rai sighed in relief when they landed in the concrete Flyer bay. It was someone else's problem now.

A squad of Marines met them as they descended from the Flyer, fluorescent light reflecting off their dark armor. Trienne Luyten Angelique, the colony's Head of Research, arrived with them. She spoke quietly with Carina and then knelt beside the little spacesuit. She popped the helmet hatches and wrinkled her nose. "I think we're going to have to teach you about biological functions," she said. "Do you understand me?"

The boy, bald and pale, hesitantly nodded.

"Good. We're going to run some tests."

Another nod.

Trienne reached out her hand and took the small, suited glove. She took three steps.

The little boy tugged on the scientist's hand, stopping her in her tracks. He turned back to face Rai and Carina. It made a gurgling noise before words croaked out. "Thank you. For not shoot. Us. No. No us. Me. I be good. Happy."

He walked away beside the scientist.

"Are you all right?" Carina asked.

Rai thought about what he'd just done. He knew if that child was allowed to live–and he couldn't see the colony killing something shaped like a three-year-old, no matter what atrocities lived inside its head, the life he'd known, where one could tell at a glance whether a person was human, would end forever.

He didn't know if that was a good thing or a bad thing.

"I'll tell you in a few years," he said. He remembered what she'd said about losing everyone she knew. "Are you on duty now?"

"No. They just cleared my schedule so I can be debriefed."

"Now?"

"No. In a while, when the scientists get finished with him," she replied.

"Do you have enough time to sleep?"

"I can't sleep," she replied. "I'm too worried about what they'll do to him. So many people have been hurt by this war."

"He'll be fine. Thank you for saving him. If it had been up to me, I'd have slagged the whole thing and then called in an orbital strike just to be safe."

She gave him a ghost of a smile. "I know. But you didn't."

"Why don't you sit down. I'll get us some stimcaff."

He parked her on a bench and went off to the nearest working community cafeteria. When he returned with the two steaming cups, she was sleeping on the armrest. Her personal comm had dropped onto the ground, so he picked it up.

He was about to tuck it under her arm when he stopped. Instead of simply leaving it there, he powered it up and placed his information in her contact list.

"There. Now you have one living friend," he said.

He stood over her while she slept, to make sure no one dared disturb her rest.

Children of The Sky

Savortha's Tavern

Dale Kesterson

The bleak landscape stretched out in all directions around the habitat dome. Dust from the frequent windstorms mingled with the incessant, drizzling moisture, and resulted in muddy streaks on the glass-like material which protected the colonists from the ravages of the fifth planet. The outside atmosphere hardly qualified as conducive to life. The native inhabitants lived in natural caves in the mountainous regions of the dismal world; even they spurned life on the surface.

A portly, medium-height man paused for a moment on his usual early morning walk around the perimeter pathway of the dome. The black, curly hair–now streaked with gray–fell longer than fashion dictated; it brushed his shoulders. His slightly reddened dark eyes stared out at the barely-lightening horizon. Constant clouds appeared like another dome over the mining compound in the distance and blocked what little sun reached Cordallis. The term landscape glorified the vista too much. Desolation was a better description.

A shuttle left the habitat for the working mine, a trail of dust in its wake. The temperature, humidity, and lighting were all artificially controlled, but not for total comfort, in both the habitat and mining domes.

He sighed deeply and tasted the bland, recycled air while he recalled the glorious reds and oranges of the sunrises in the sky on his home world, two planets closer to the sun. He found the comparison too painful to dwell upon and continued on his way. He smiled to himself. He looked forward to the coming confrontation. The summons, his fourth in the last three standard months, made it clear this could be his last. He chuckled. If it went well, he might get to see more of those beautiful sunrises.

His stroll, for he never hurried his pace, ended as he approached the pathway to the corporation's administration building. More like administration of the local government, he sadly reflected. Cordallis Corporation was the government.

"Late again, Niall Piersen."

The metallic voice emanated from a speaker embedded in the arch of pseudo-marble with *WORK IS FREEDOM* etched across the top of the entrance.

Piersen glanced up at the camera and gave it a sly grin. "I'm never late. I always arrive precisely when I plan to."

"Your summons was for 0900, not 0930," the disembodied voice continued in its metallic, crackling monotone.

"Ah, well, I was unavoidably detained. I wanted to watch the sunrise, at least what there was of it." He turned into the small courtyard and mounted the three steps to confront CordCorp's auto door. It did not respond to his presence. He stared at the second camera. "If it's not convenient, I can leave and come back tomorrow."

The door slid to one side, not nearly as noiselessly as it was designed to do.

The receptionist handed him a visitor's badge.

"Executive Genco's office–"

"I know my way." He skipped a smile. So did she.

The CorpRep's office door stood open. Genco was the highest representative on Cordallis and answered only to the

Corp's board of directors, located on the home world. The large office was elaborately decorated for aesthetics and the personal comfort of its occupant. The chief executive officer of the corporation designed his office to impress or intimidate his visitors. Most of the time the reactions involved both feelings. Piersen was subject to neither and he derived pleasure from the knowledge his lack of response–to what he considered a childish ploy–annoyed the bureaucrat.

"At last." The man behind the desk glared at him. "I do have other things on my appointment calendar."

Piersen shrugged. "I offered to come back tomorrow. Or didn't your robot tell you?"

Bytrand Genco glared at him through beady eyes set in a fleshy face. "The trouble with you is you think every comment you make is funny. This may be the time your attitude lands you in serious trouble."

"Even so, trouble wouldn't necessarily render the statement less humorous," Piersen replied, unruffled. "What is it this time?"

"I have a few things." Genco consulted his data pad. "First, you have not reported your income for the last quarter. Second, your payment of the estimated taxes for the second quarter, with any adjustments, is overdue. Third, you have hired a halvsie."

Piersen yawned. "I no longer own the pub."

"What do you mean? You sold out?"

"Of course not. If I sold it, you'd tax what I got for it." A grin lit the swarthy face, an expression which had frightened more than one unruly customer over the years. Some likened it to a shark on home world lying in wait for its prey. "Actually, I gave it away."

"You gave it away? Handed it over?" The tone of the CR's voice matched the incredulity on his face. "After twenty years?"

"Twenty-six years, to be precise. Yes, I gave it away as a gift. I assume you are familiar with the concept."

"When?" demanded the bureaucrat. "You are still liable for the first quarter report, and any adjustments, and the second-quarter estimated payment."

"I filed the report on time, and I have the receipt. I am not responsible for the snail pace of your paperwork. As for the estimated payment, I am not liable for it if the transfer took place before the quarter began, which it did." The toothy grin took on a more sinister cast. "Also, don't forget the halvsie."

"We won't." Genco took a deep breath. He knew Piersen enjoyed baiting him to provoke him and he could not afford to lose his temper. "I asked when the transfer took place."

"The night before the second quarter began," Piersen amiably responded. "I suppose you would also like to know to whom I deeded it."

"That would be helpful."

"You. I gave it to Corp." The dark eyes twinkled with suppressed glee; he ignored the sarcasm of the statement. "I thought it might be interesting to see you fellows pay taxes to yourselves while dealing with your own red tape." He leaned back in his chair and casually crossed his legs. "I doubt you can avoid a loss."

Genco's mouth dropped open, speechless.

Unperturbed, Piersen continued. "When quinterium became profitable on home world, the men who formed CordCorp took a look around the planetary system and noticed a small mine on an inhabited world which had been in operation for over a century. They breezed in and decided to acquire it rather than start up their own. They coerced, blackmailed, and bribed the mine's owners to sell out to the new entity at ridiculously low prices. Once that was done, they lured workers and support personnel here with the promise of a better life, including high wages. The miners who signed on soon discovered the whole premise was one gigantic scam."

"We pay higher wages than most get at home. We also supply habitats along with medical and living services, in addition to granting substantial, regular raises."

"Yes, and with the same clockwork regularity, you hike the cost of goods and services, including the rent on the pitiful living quarters, thus negating the oh-so-generous wage increases." Piersen uncrossed his legs and leaned forward, his eyes as cold as the stone arch outside the building. "The only standards of living which increased were those of Corp executives. Like yourself."

"It always seems that way to begin with–"

"To begin with? CordCorp clapped its stranglehold on this planet almost twenty years ago. It was bad enough Corp charged in and started running everything from the shops to the patrol force. When you arrived as the new CorpRep, you took it further. The patrol members now act as your goons and you run this place like you personally own it, which you don't. Someday, you will be forced to answer for that, and not only to your board."

Genco waved away the gripe; Piersen's views were old news. "Still, you stayed."

"Yes, I stayed. I was one of the few who insisted on retaining ownership of that which I built. You tolerated it because I paid my taxes and fees."

"We tolerated you, in spite of your borderline seditious views, because you generated good will among the workers." The CEO's smile grew smug. "Your relations with the natives and halvsies, however, must change."

"Why? It's not my problem anymore. I'm done with it."

"We can work through this. We'll take ownership and you can stay—"

"Stay? For what? I've been harassed and entangled in your rules and regulations for the last nineteen years. The battles against the hierarchy were fun at first. However, I've had enough." Piersen rose. "Have fun with it."

"Wait. You mean you are leaving?" Startled, Genco sputtered, "W–where will you go? Who will run the pub?"

"As a once-successful entrepreneur, I would advise you to find someone with experience in such endeavors."

"You have a woman working for you."

"Yes, Merrilynne has been with me for years and she's quite capable."

"Would she stay on without you?"

"I have no idea."

"Will you speak to her for me?" Genco made notes on his data pad.

His visitor was amused; the question bordered on a polite request.

"No. You'll have to ask her. I won't speak to or for her." Piersen turned and walked across to the office but stopped at the door. "I won't say, 'see you around.' I'm leaving for home world on the monthly flight today. I really miss the pretty sunrises and sunsets." He crossed the threshold with a wave of his hand as he whistled his favorite tune, a lively folk song from his childhood.

03 80

Merrilynne absent-mindedly wiped the counter of the bar, her forehead creased with worry. In the eleven standard months since Piersen pulled his trick of handing the pub to Corp, she had kept Savortha's Tavern open to fulfill her promise to him. The mental cost of dealing with the tangle of bureaucratic red tape had worn her almost to the breaking point. She glanced around her domain. The hassles and conniving to work around obstacles paid off. She learned her lessons from the master and learned them well.

Despite operating under CordCorp regulations, she managed to maintain a home-like atmosphere. The internal temps of the dome did not make for warm inner buildings. One of her victories over the bloated system happened when she discovered that a certain type of planetary rock held heat and reduced the amount of firewood she had to buy from Corp. The fireplace kept the tavern warm and added ambiance; the bonus was a reduction in smoke over a traditional fire. The wood tables, clean and waxed, had been installed by Piersen to remind him of a favorite pub he frequented on home world. He never told her how he managed to get them or the wood floor to the mining world, but the effect did set the tavern apart from all the other places in the dome. The real beauty of the main room was the wood trim and beams in the ceiling. He had shown her an old photo of that pub, and although the tavern was not a perfect recreation, together they had created a place of warmth for mine workers and the few dependents allowed.

She sighed and dropped the cleaning cloth into the laundry bucket behind the counter. She looked up when the chimes rang on the main door.

"Merri! Is the coffee-sub brewing?" Sevio Rowland's deep voice boomed out.

"Sorry–I haven't started it yet."

"Never mind. I'll take care of it." Her assistant came around the bar and drew water from the recycling unit. "Someday, I swear I'm going to get some real coffee. This stuff from Corp is awful." He sniffed the packet of powdery mix, which like all their supplies came marked with the corporation's logo and wrinkled his nose in disgust. "It even smells musty."

"Which is why I drink tea. At least I can grow some of it," she replied to his familiar complaint. "I thought you were used to it. Remember, if you ever do get the real thing, we'd have to lock the door and hide in the back storeroom."

"True. Shall I start stocking the mugs?"

"No, I had Gryna do that last night after I closed." She glanced up at him.

A look of consternation crossed his pleasant face. "I like Gryna, but–"

"Don't worry, no one saw her."

"She's a halvsie. It's still a risk. Cordalls and halvsies are not supposed to mingle with us."

"She's also half-human. Besides, she's not mingling, she's working. I don't pay her, at least not with money. She's so grateful to have a place to live she does most of the heavy work." Merri shrugged. "I enjoy her company and she does keep our living quarters neater than I ever could."

"I know Niall was friendly with the Cordalls and took her in shortly after Corp took over."

"He felt strongly about it." She frowned. "We helped create the halvsies when our people interbred with the natives. Cordalls are a living, breathing people in their own right, complete with emotions, and they were here first. The original colonists who settled here respected them and helped them develop the mine. Corp has exploited their world and relegated them to the trash heap."

"I know she trusts you. I've always been curious about how you learned the hand sign language the Cordalls and halvsies use."

"Niall learned from Gryna's mother, and he taught me, as I have taught you."

"Still, it's a risk."

"If they fine me for giving Gryna shelter, I'll quit, and they can figure out how to run this place on their own."

"Without you, it would have to close."

"Exactly." She winked at Rowland. "Business took a big enough hit when Niall turned it over to Corp. His personality set the tone for the place and our customers miss him. He was outgoing and gregarious. I try to be but sometimes I think I'm only a pale imitation. We don't do song nights as often, for one thing. He had his lap harp and loved to sing." Her face momentarily clouded over, then brightened and her blue eyes twinkled. "I think someone higher up than Genco finally analyzed the balance sheet and realized the tax revenue liability now outweighs the supposed profit margin of owning it themselves. Niall suspected it would run at a loss."

"Niall was a wizard with the accounts."

"Not to mention bending rules to make this work after CordCorp established a controlling lock on everything from the manufacture of paper napkins to the distribution of ales." She sighed. "They pay a pittance compared to the cost of living, and make sure every supply needed to live comes from their sources at inflated prices."

"Plus, they tax us in the bargain."

"Oh, yes. Their motto is never miss a chance to drain the last drop of blood. Most of the workers who arrive get here on their signing bonus and can't afford the ticket to get back home."

"I'm glad Niall made it back to home world."

"I can't fault him for leaving, for whatever his reasons."

"I always figured he did it because he was tired of fighting Corp."

"He was." Merri regarded the stocky, solidly-built man who stood a few inches taller than she. Strong, reliable, and generally cheerful, he worked hard and protected her when her customers got rowdy. They had become best friends and she knew she could not run the tavern without him. She visibly hesitated.

"There's more?" he asked when she remained silent.

She nodded. "When was the first time you came in here, as a customer?"

"About fifteen standard years ago. I was luckier than most, even at first. I had enough technical knowledge to get a job on the shuttle rather than in the mine." He shuddered. "I was doing okay as a driver but when Niall offered me the job here, it took me all of ten seconds to accept it."

"Ah, so you've always known it as Savortha's Tavern."

"Did it have another name?"

"When Niall first opened it, he called it Frida's Tavern. He changed it after the first round of clashes between Corp and the Cordalls, almost twenty years ago."

"I've always wondered if it was someone's name."

"It is. It's Cordall, someone he cared about and lost."

The door chimes rang.

"Oh–is it shift change already?" Merri glanced at her wrist chrono. "Blast. I hope the bread knots are done. If you handle the customers with your usual charm, I'll get the bread out of the oven."

Three men entered. Their uniforms marked them as miners, but the newness of the cloth indicated they had not been on Cordallis long. Rowland grabbed his apron and went to greet them.

"Hello. Welcome to Savortha's Tavern. I don't believe I have seen you here before." He showed the men to a table. "Can I get you some coffee-sub?"

"We'd prefer ale," the eldest man said. He looked too old for the rigors of the mine.

"Corp regs say we can't serve ale until after twelve standard." Rowland glanced at the timepiece over the bar. "It's ten plus half now."

"Oh. I didn't know about that. Coffee-sub all around then. You have anything to eat?"

"I think some of Merri's bread knots are about to come out of the oven, if you'd like a plate of those."

"Heard about those, yeah." The man nodded. "Fine."

Rowland went back to the kitchen and watched Merri pull a large pan out of the oven. "Three miners, new here from the sound of it. After I explained the regs the old guy ordered coffee-sub and bread knots. Apparently, they have heard of us."

She set up a serving tray with mugs and a plate of the knots. "I'll be out shortly. I want to plate and cover these first."

Rowland set the order on the table as the door chimes rang again. Another group of workers entered, all well known to him.

"Hey, Sevio! We'll have the usual when you get the chance," called out the tallest of the foursome.

"Merri just pulled the knots out. Take your table and I'll be with you in a moment."

The four men nodded to the other men as they passed and made themselves at home at the round table near the fireplace.

Merri entered from the kitchen and placed a glass-covered platter heaped with bread knots on the bar's counter. She waved to her regular customers.

"The usual," Rowland called to her.

She nodded. She filled their order and deposited the tray on their table. Merri turned to the new men.

"Welcome to the tavern. Are you men new to Cordallis?" she asked.

A younger man with a solemn face nodded.

"We signed on for a twelve-month tour starting this new quarter," the third man, who looked like the youngest of the trio, said with a smile. "I'm Bruno Gilchrist. I guess it's pretty obvious we're new." He stared at the petite, attractive woman in her cover-apron and took in her bright, blue eyes and the dark, curly hair pulled back from her face. "You own this place?"

"No, it belongs to CordCorp. I manage it. I'm Merri." A wave from the other table caught her eye. "Excuse me." She strolled over to her regulars. "What's up?"

"I want to know if Tumas and I can reserve the billiard table for a couple of hours this eventide, after the second shift." Leland Jadko unobtrusively placed the three middle fingers of his right hand on the edge of the table near his mug and pulled them to his palm.

"Today? I'm not sure it's going to be unoccupied, Leland. I'll have to check the reservations log, and it's in my office." Merri noted the slight movement and recognized it as one of the underground resistance signals. Friends want to meet. "Are you and Tumas gearing up for a rematch with Sevio and Halder? I understand you were completely outclassed the last time."

Her observation met with laughter. Rowland's voice cut across the room.

"Let them practice all they want, Merri. They still won't touch us!" He came around the bar. "Leland tried with Ridear, too, but he's close to hopeless."

"Excuse me," called Gilchrist. His gaze had followed Merri to the other table. "Are you saying you have a billiard parlor?"

"It's not a billiard parlor, precisely, friend," Rowland replied with his easy smile. "Only one table in a back room. The man who owned the pub before Corp imported it from home world years ago. A few of us use it now and then when it's available, which is by reservation and only with Merri's agreement."

"I haven't heard about it," the oldest man stated. "Can anyone reserve it? I've played a fair amount."

"It is generally booked up pretty tightly," Merri told him. "I don't open it every eventide. If you are interested, give me your name and I can let you know when there's an opening."

"Gareth Ash. I would appreciate that." The craggy face showed no emotion.

"I assume CordCorp knows about this." The quiet statement came from the remaining man of the trio. On the small side, he shrugged. "I was just wondering."

Merri gave the man her brightest smile. "Of course."

"In fact, friend," Halder Simms echoed her smile, "we once had Bytrand Genco himself in here to play a round. He's the head man for CordCorp here."

"Was he any good?"

"He played the pub's owner. No one was good against Niall," Baker laughed. He got up and strolled to the other table. "I'm Tumas Baker. Sevio Rowland is the gent with the apron– don't let that fool you, either he's tougher than he looks. You've met Halder Simms. Ridear Hanson is the quiet one. Leland Jadko brought the subject up."

"I'm Geyorg Boniface," said the man who asked. "My friends and I heard about the tavern from our group leader at the mine." He glanced around the tavern. "We were told it was like a bit of home world in the dome. I can see why."

"You mentioned Niall," said Ash.

"Yes, Niall Piersen. A man who could make the billiard balls dance to his own tune," Rowland laughed. He joined Baker by the threesome's table. "He used to take on challengers, but he went back to home world."

"If you gentlemen will excuse me, I'll see if I can accommodate your request, Leland." Merri collected the now-empty plate from the newcomers' table and disappeared through the kitchen door. Rowland stepped back to the round table with the refill pot.

"That's a very attractive gal," Gilchrist commented to Baker.

"Yes, she's quite a lady," the latter responded. "Niall set the tone of the place and when she took over the management, she kept it that way."

The chimes on the door sounded again.

A man in a Corp Patrol uniform entered and walked to the counter. "Sevio–I'd like a mug of coffee-sub and a couple of bread knots to go." Destun Brand smiled. "You know, my usual."

"Sure thing. We have it ready. Be right back." Rowland stepped back into the kitchen for a moment and reappeared with a paper sack and a small carryout container.

"Thanks." Brand deposited his payment on the counter. "Where's Merri?"

"Busy in her office. Corp paperwork, I think." He made a face. "You know how that is."

"Do I ever. Give her my regards."

"Sure." He put the coins in the cashbox.

The patrolman turned and saw the newcomers. He stiffened, set his shoulders straight, and sharply nodded to Ash on his way to the door.

Simms got the empty plate from his table and approached Rowland at the bar. "Here, Sev. I'll save you a trip over there if you'll hand me the coffee-sub pot."

"Why, thank you, Halder." Rowland slipped the middle three fingers of his left hand onto the counter as he complied. Enemies. "Nice to see you can still lay claim to the title of gentleman." His eyes shifted to the newcomers.

Simms nodded, his lips pressed into a thin line. "Among other things."

Merri joined Rowland at the counter as Simms returned the pot. "Halder, are you volunteering to take a shift here?" she teased as she put her logbook on the counter.

"Nope–simply giving Sevio here a bit of a break. Are we good for after second shift today?"

"All clear." She turned her attention to the newcomers. "Mr. Ash, if you would like to try your hand tomorrow after second shift, I can make a note of that."

"I'd appreciate it."

"Oh, Merri, you missed Brand. He picked up his usual coffee-sub and knots and wanted me to relay his regards."

She opened her log to the appropriate page and made the notation. Rowland put his three left-hand fingers on the page and pointed to the new name. Merri looked up and raised an eyebrow. He nodded.

"I will be sure to catch up with Brand tomorrow. Meanwhile, are you going to let Tumas and Leland practice in peace?"

"When has Sevio ever done that?" Simms asked with a chuckle.

"He was born to heckle," called out Baker from the table.

Merri joined in the laughter. "You could be right about that."

"May I ask if I can join you this eventide?" asked Ash. "It's been a while since I saw a game. I wouldn't want to play, just watch, and only for a little while."

"I wouldn't mind," Simms stated, "but it's not my decision."

"Merri?" Rowland turned to her. "What do you say?"

"You would all have to agree to it, but I wouldn't have any objections." She lightly brushed the fingertips of her right hand across her forehead, stroking left to right. Go along with it but carefully. "What do the rest of you say?"

"We should be neighborly and welcome him," put in Baker. Jadko and Hanson nodded their agreement.

"Fine with me," Rowland added.

"Done. We'll meet you here at twenty standard." Simms nodded to his friends. "Right now, though, I'm heading for my bunk. If I'm to exhibit my skills later, I want some rest."

"You'll need it," teased Jadko as he got to his feet.

The four regulars made their way to the counter and settled their tabs.

"See you later!" Baker said as he left.

"Welcome to Cordallis," called Hanson. Jadko and Simms waved their parting.

The newcomers soon followed. Rowland cleared their table while Merri wiped down the round one as more miners came in. The main flow of the morning traffic began.

ଔ   ୭

Later that evening, Merri sighed and sank into a chair after seeing the billiard players off to their quarters.

"That's the last of them. Thankfully. It's been a long and busy day."

"You must be exhausted."

"Not far from it." She stretched her arms above her head. "I'm glad you and Halder were able to shift the meeting. Mr. Ash stayed way too long."

"If I weren't the friendly fellow I am, I'd suspect he knew about it and deliberately hung around."

"Could be. The gent with him, Boniface, could be another one. Face it, all three could be."

"It wouldn't be the first time we entertained a ringer from Corp."

"I'm glad you saw Brand react to him."

"You and Niall taught me to observe. But why did you signal for us to let him join us tonight?"

"I figured if we blocked it, he might think we had something to hide."

"We do." Rowland sighed. "Niall's Golden Rule: Never let your guard down."

"We are one little cell of a larger organization. We can't relax."

"Merri, we've been working on forming the underground since before Niall left. We are ready. When are we going to do something?"

"All the pieces and plans must be put in place before any of us acts. We're playing with fire and the stakes are our lives." She smiled. "I know you're impatient. Believe me, so am I. But we have to wait until the time is right."

"When will that be?"

"Trust me, you'll know."

The door chimes sounded again. They both jumped.

A lone man entered. His shoulders stooped and he used his walking stick like his legs would collapse without it. His dirty cape wrapped around him like a shroud. His face was wrinkled, not with age–he looked deflated. His hair was grizzled, gray, and unkempt; he badly needed a shave. He put down a large satchel, which landed with an audible thump. His eyes, however, belied the rest of his appearance. In stark contrast to the shabbiness, his dark eyes glittered with the fun of a private joke.

Rowland greeted him. "I'm sorry, Mr.–?"

"Krebbs," the man supplied.

"It's late, Mr. Krebbs, and we can't serve you."

"We're ready to close for the day, but we make occasional exceptions," Merri said with a smile. "Please come in."

Krebbs gazed around at the empty tables, nodded to Rowland, and addressed her.

"Hello, my dear." His voice was high-pitched with nasal overtones. He turned to the younger man. "Don't let me stop you. By all means, go ahead and post the closed sign and secure the door for the night." The man held his gaze on Merri until he heard the lock click into place.

"If you are finished in here, may we adjourn to the billiard room? Young man, something to drink would be welcome, too."

"Of course." She rose and nodded to Rowland. "Grab something from the kitchen and meet us in the billiard room." She smiled at the man. "Don't forget your bag."

"It goes where I go, rest assured."

In the recently vacated billiard room, Merri sat in one of the comfortable chairs in a corner behind the table. Rowland entered with mugs of tea.

"I thought this would be okay." He handed the mugs around. "Are you going to introduce me?"

"This is Wesley Krebbs," she answered him. She regarded her visitor. "You're late." Merri's smile lit her face and her eyes.

"I'm never late. I always arrive precisely when I plan to," he replied.

Rowland's head snapped up. "That's what Niall always said."

The newcomer straightened his back with a slight groan and stood up straight. His voice lost the nasal twang and deepened. "Ah, that's better. So, Sevio, how's tricks?" He took a chair next to Merri's.

"Niall?" Unabashed, Rowland stared at the man. "I wouldn't have known you. You've changed your appearance– you're much thinner."

"A good test. I thought it would be prudent to look different. It wasn't any fun, either. I had to give up my favorite foods and all the good drinks." He made a face and his wrinkles changed configuration. "I make a point of avoiding mirrors. I also acquired my new name. Wesley Krebbs. I made it up all by myself."

Rowland turned on Merri. "You knew and didn't tell me?"

"Sevio, I couldn't. It wasn't my secret to share, and I promised him when he left that I would tell no one he was coming back." She stood and put her hand on Rowland's arm. "His life was at stake."

"Sit down, Sev. We have a lot to cover and not much time. This is the last visit for this trip, and I have to be back at the port in time to catch the return flight."

"As usual," Merri muttered.

"Wait a minute!" Rowland exclaimed. "This isn't the first time you've been back?"

"Only the second. You were working here because Merri told you she was too ill to come in. I didn't want to meet here so she came to me." Piersen cocked his head at the younger man. "Now, tell me what progress has been made. Your cell is organized?"

"My four have each gathered and trained his own group of five, according to Merri's instructions. Merri and I don't know who they are, and they don't know who we are."

Piersen shot a dark, accusing look at Merri.

"Sev runs the cell. I have stayed out of it as much as possible," Merri hastily added. "Only our immediate group, all regular customers, meet here."

"The hand signs?"

"Part of the training," Rowland stated. Merri nodded.

Rowland brought him up to date on his cell's meetings.

"Anything to add?" Piersen turned to Merri.

"We think we have been gifted with another ringer, and he may have sidekicks," Merri informed him. "Sev spotted our local plod nodding sharply to him. There was going to be a meeting in here tonight, but he horned in on it."

"Oh? What happened?"

"One of my people asked to use the billiard room and this guy asked if he could come watch."

"Sev referred it to me, and I signaled to let him watch, rather than raise suspicions. He's going to play this eventide with his companions."

"Older man, not tall, craggy face?"

"Gareth Ash." Rowland supplied the name.

"Well done, both of you. You undoubtedly did allay a few suspicions." Piersen leaned back. "Sevio, I have some orders for you."

"At last!" His eagerness made the other two smile.

"I knew you'd like that." The shark-like grin appeared on the swarthy face. "Start slowly. I want you to get your groups started on small acts of sabotage. Little breakdowns every now and then. Slow up the ore lines if you can. Nothing major and not every day. Have the actions rotate among the cells and don't form any kind of pattern. Above all, make sure you and the others stay clean and clear."

"Understood."

"For now, the goal is to show a loss of efficiency of the operations here on Cordallis."

Rowland grinned. "Make Genco look bad?"

"That's the general idea. Keep it subtle for now. Major sabotage would result in the use of force, possibly police action, with all the retributions that might incur."

"You have a plan?"

"Yes." He watched as the younger man's face turned stony in the few seconds of silence that followed the word. "Sevio, right now you don't need to know any more. Frankly, it wouldn't be safe for any of us to tell you more. I'm trusting you to keep things building, but with stealth. Remember, all our lives, including Merri's, are on the line."

The entrance of a small female forestalled any response. Short, slim, and delicate, her garment was a loose house dress. She threw herself into Piersen's lap and curled up in his arms. Her long fingers entwined behind his neck, and she cooed, a sound of happiness Cordalls generated in their throats. Her eyes closed and the smile on her pretty face was serene.

"Gryna." Piersen wrapped his arms around the small body and smiled. His voice held a tenderness which touched Merri's heart. "Are you ready for an adventure? You're coming with me to home world. Tonight."

"Are you sure?" Gryna lifted her head and questioned in her sing-song voice. "How?"

"You once told me you could fit in my satchel." He smiled at the girl in his lap. "You are going to prove it tonight." She gazed up at him, smiled, and nodded.

"I can do that."

"Niall? Will she need anything for the trip?" Merri's voice caught in her throat, and she cleared it.

"No, I have all the preparations ready." He put Gryna down. "Speaking of preparations. Sevio, would you pack a few knots for me? You have no idea how much I have missed them. I also need a word with Merri."

The moment the door closed behind the younger man, Piersen rose. He pulled a thick, heavy envelope from an inner pocket of his cape and extended it to Merri. It was sealed with an old-fashioned wax stamp.

"Merrilynne, if you receive word of my death, open and read the contents of this packet. Follow the instructions to the letter." He put his hands on her shoulders and stared down at her. "I want your solemn promise."

Her blue eyes searched his dark ones. He used her full name, which meant he was serious, and she felt a sense of foreboding.

"I promise."

"Good girl. Put it into the hidden safe now, while I'm here. If all goes well, you can hand it back to me unopened." He smiled warmly at the concern on her face. "Don't worry–I'm not planning on getting killed. I simply want to have things ready in case something goes sideways."

Merri went to the billiard table with its gleaming, highly polished wood. She reached under the edge, flipped a hidden latch, and lifted a perfectly matched panel which revealed a small metal safe with a combination lock. She knelt, dialed the knob, secreted the packet, closed the safe, and replaced the panel. "There. Not even Sevio knows about that spot."

"I thought as much. I have one more thing for you," he told her. "Regardless of how tonight works out, I have booked your reservation for next month's flight to home world. It's in your name and officially on the records."

"But–"

"If things here implode, I want you safely away. If everything works, you'll have earned a vacation. Agreed?"

She reluctantly nodded. "Agreed. Now that you have once more imposed your will, and strictly out of curiosity, did I have a choice?" she teased.

"Of course not." His sly grin returned with a flash of humor in his eyes.

"Thought as much."

"Gryna, let's see if you fit. I had a friend make a seat in the satchel for you," Piersen told her.

Merri opened the door to Rowland's knock.

"Perfect timing! We can all watch Gryna become a contortionist." Piersen opened the satchel.

The small half-Cordall gave him a grin of her own; it showed small, even, white teeth. She inspected the interior, winked at Piersen, and folded herself into the contoured seat. "It feels cozy," she announced.

Piersen started to zip it closed.

"Wait!" Gryna put a hand on the closure. "Not yet." She climbed out of the satchel and skipped over to hug Merri. "You have always been so kind to me. I will miss you," she said with tears in her dark eyes.

"I will miss you, too." Tears ran down Merri's cheeks. "Be safe and remember, I love you."

"Be careful and know I love you, too." With a final hug, she climbed back into her seat. "Now."

"It won't be for long," Piersen promised the tiny girl. "Time to leave. Sevio, take care of Merri." The men shook hands. "Merri, don't be afraid to be afraid."

Merri reached up to hug him, and he whispered, "Don't worry. Remember your promise."

He left the room. By the time the two got into the main tavern he was gone, as if he had never been there.

☙ ❧

Three standard weeks later, Merri was in the midst of her morning routine of opening the pub when Rowland entered. His agitation was plain.

"Merri, they are coming for you."

"I don't understand."

"Genco is coming to see you. I just got word from Halder. One of his people heard Genco is on his way over here."

She slowly inhaled through her nose and exhaled in a silent whistle. "Try to relax. We knew this could happen."

"Do you think our petty acts–"

"Sev! Not out loud! Not in the tavern. We'll be okay." She smiled. "Do something normal. Start the coffee-sub."

"At a time like this?"

"Especially at a time like this."

He disappeared into the kitchen, and she set out mugs. The door chimes sounded.

Bytrand Genco walked in while a uniformed Patrol officer remained outside. The executive never went anywhere on his own.

"Good morning. Would you like a table? You're a bit early. Sevio just put the coffee-sub on to brew." She smiled and came around the bar's counter. "I'm afraid the bread knots aren't ready yet."

The chimes sounded again. Ash and Gilchrist entered, took three steps in, and stopped in front of Genco. The three men exchanged glances.

"Good morning, gentlemen," Merri greeted them. She did her best to fight down her anxiety; she needed her wits clear. "It seems everything is getting an early start today. Your usual table?"

Genco nodded to Ash, who led the way to the table and sat.

"It's been a while since you graced us with your presence, Mr. Genco. I wasn't aware you three knew each other." She mentally blessed all the training Niall had given her about how to appear calm on the outside. Inside, she shook like a dust mote in a draft eddy. She braced for bad news.

"Mr. Ash and Mr. Gilchrist received promotions last week. They now work for me as part of the Patrol Investigation Division." Genco regarded the petite woman. "Sit down." Genco did not issue invitations. He ordered.

"Sir, I have considerable work to do. It's almost time to open."

"It doesn't matter, sir," Ash commented. "Let her stand."

"Very well." Genco gazed at her. "We thought you would want to know, considering how long you worked for him, that we received word earlier this morning that Niall Piersen fell victim to a vehicle accident on home world, and died." He closely regarded her through narrowed eyes.

Merri's face paled and she bit her lip. "You're right, I did want to know. We spent ten years working together here. I always hoped he would return, at least for a visit." Her eyes filled with tears, and she put her hands in her apron pockets to hide her fists. "I will miss him even more now," she finished in a whisper. "If you will excuse me, I'll see if the coffee-sub and knots are ready. Thank you for coming yourself to tell me."

"Merrilynne, I rarely saw eye to eye with Piersen, but I respected him. You have my condolences." The cold expression on his face contradicted his words. He stared at her as he tried to gauge her reactions but gave up. "I won't stay," Genco told her as he stood. He turned to the other two. "I will see you both later in my office."

He left. The officer posted outside joined him and they walked off. The door closed, blocking the view of their exit.

"I will send Sevio out with coffee-sub and knots. Please, excuse me." Merri turned, but Gilchrist stood and extended his hand to her.

"Merri, please. Sit down for a moment. You've had a shock."

"Thank you, Bruno, but right now I think I'd like to be alone."

Rowland met her at the kitchen doorway. "What's going on?" he asked in an anxious whisper. "What's wrong? What did Genco want?"

"He came to tell me, in person, that Niall was killed in an accident on home world."

"Niall is dead? Oh, no!" His green eyes reflected a flash of anger before being replaced by deep sadness. He put his hand on her shoulder. "It can't be."

"Sevio, pull it together. We still have Ash and Gilchrist out there. They need coffee-sub and knots." She shuddered. "We have to stay focused, no matter how much this hurts. Nothing has changed."

"How can I do that?"

"It's what Niall would have wanted." She bit her lip again. "Oh, one thing has changed. Genco also told me that Ash and Gilchrist now work for Patrol investigations."

"Nice to know we were right."

"Yes. Now, take a deep breath, steady yourself, and get out there. I need a few minutes to myself."

"I'll do my best."

Merri entered the billiard room, closed and secured the door, and relaxed her control on her feelings. Her tears silently flowed for two minutes as she tightly hugged herself. She felt lost and alone. Niall–gone, he's gone. The thought repeated over and over, but her sorrow would have to wait. She wiped her eyes and blew her nose before she knelt beside the table and opened the hidden safe. Her hands shook as she held the thick packet. Carefully, she broke the seal, removed the sheaf of papers, and read.

She read through the contents twice.

"Oh, Niall, I knew you were devious. I never appreciated how much," she murmured to herself. Tears flowed again and she slowly shook her head. "I wish you hadn't trusted me so much, though."

"Merri? I could use some help out here," Rowland said through the door. "Are you okay?"

"Be right there." She stood, put the papers into their envelope, and stashed it back in the safe. She rubbed her eyes and blew her nose again before she went back into the tavern.

The rest of the day blurred.

Word of Piersen's death spread like the fine dust in a windstorm outside the dome. No details were available; speculation ran high. Their regulars gathered together to find solace in their common regard for the well-known man who had touched so many lives. One of the oldest, a crochety man crippled by a mining accident, surprised everyone by leading some of Piersen's favorite pub songs. Toasts were lifted to the deceased host; all were cheered.

Finally, she and Rowland managed to usher out all their customers except their resistance cell members.

"Sevio, post the sign and secure the door." Merri cleared the round table in front of the fireplace. "Break out the special mead Niall stocked and bring mugs. I put a small pan of spiced bread knots in the oven. They should be ready."

"What's all this for?" Jadko asked.

"We are going to honor an old tradition from an ancient land on home world. We are going to celebrate the life of Niall Piersen."

"I thought we just did that," complained Hanson. "I thought we would mourn him."

"Not in his style," Rowland replied. He deposited a large tray to the table.

Merri dropped into a chair. "Niall left me some instructions I was to open if I heard of his death. I read them this morning. First on the list was to have a private drink in his memory. He suggested the mead. I made the special knots to go along with it. I want you relaxed but not sloshed."

"And after that?" Simms asked.

"I have instructions for you all." She poured out the mead and grinned. "You'll like them."

"Merri, I never noticed until right now how much your grin reminds me of Niall's," Rowland observed. "That was close to his shark grin."

Merri stood and raised her mug. "To Niall Piersen. Friend and mentor to us all!"

The men stood and raised their mugs.

"To Niall!"

They downed the first mugs of mead and ate the knots. Rowland turned to Merri. "Now what?"

"We move to the billiard room. You gents are going to have a game in his honor."

Once regrouped in the closed room, the men gathered chairs and sat.

"You mentioned instructions?" Jadko prompted.

"Yes. Beginning tomorrow, you can step up your activities. Do it gradually, go carefully, and make it look as if your equipment is failing. Next month, it would be appropriate to have something blow up every now and then. I leave it to you to work out the details. Be sure to hit all aspects of the mining operation, but don't kill our own people."

"About time!" Baker's grin briefly overcame his grief.

Merri smiled. "When you start the explosions, feel free to leave graffiti saying something like For Niall."

"Oh?" Simms raised his eyebrows.

"Who started this? Who trained us?" Rowland put in. "Niall."

The other four nodded. "Agreed."

"One final note. Continue to have your people recruit and train their own cells and encourage their members to do the same. I don't have to remind you about vetting your people but keep the isolation rules ironclad."

"Merri, I think I speak for all of us when I say I'm worried about you. This is going to shine a spotlight on you and the tavern. Will you be safe?"

"Probably not. The fact that Genco brought the news of Niall's death to me personally is a major warning. I am planning a few changes here at the tavern which I will discuss with Sevio in private. He will keep you posted." Her smile was her own. "Halder, thank you for your concern."

"I don't want to lose you." He blushed. "I mean, we all feel that way."

She poured a second round of mead and stood. "A final toast. To Niall. May his dream of freedom thrive!"

The men echoed her words and drained their mugs. Without any further discussion, they left, each one lost in thought.

"Okay, Merri. What's going on?" Rowland demanded.

"Sevio, in telling you this now, I am entrusting you with my life."

"Understood."

"Before he left three weeks ago, Mr. Krebbs booked me on the flight to home world which will leave next week. I have to be on that flight."

"We need you here."

"You can manage the tavern on your own. Hire someone you can trust, as we hired you. I would suggest one of the four men in your cell."

"I don't like this."

"You and the others will be stronger if I'm not here. Right now, you would all put my safety ahead of other things, and you don't need that handicap." She put her hand on his arm. "Krebbs took Gryna to safety. He wanted me to be safe, too. Now that he's gone, I have to go. She's alone on a strange planet without protection. I must take care of her for his sake. It was his final request of me. My request of you is to make sure I get safely onto that flight."

"You know I will do that, even without being asked. But there is something I don't understand. I know Niall cared deeply about her and her mother, but what was the connection?"

"Can't you guess? Gryna is Niall's daughter."

ଔ ଓ

Merri smiled with inner satisfaction as reports of the sabotage efforts filtered through the mining community. She knew Corp would never acknowledge them. One week following the news of Piersen's death, Merri and Rowland each received a summons to Genco's office, marked immediate and urgent, delivered in person by Gilchrist.

"Have a mug of coffee-sub on the house," she told him. "We need to close out a few things in the back."

She and Rowland excused themselves. In the pub's office, Rowland grabbed her arm.

"Merri, you can't go. The home world flight leaves tonight. You can't set foot in that building," Rowland hissed in a low voice. He scowled, unlike his usual cheerful nature. In the past week, the expression crossed his face more and more.

"A summons is mandatory. Even Niall obeyed them. Besides, Genco has other problems." She picked up her backpack from behind her desk. "I'm packed and ready. We can go together and then you can escort me to the flight port."

"I don't like it."

"He probably spotted my name on the passenger list. I'm hoping he wants to ask me if you are capable of managing the tavern." She shrugged. "Whatever he wants, I am going to try to make sure you get to take me to the port. Let's not keep Bruno or Genco waiting."

Rowland was silent on the walk to the Corp building. Merri hoped he would not appear that sullen in the CorpRep's office. Gilchrist escorted them straight into Genco's presence.

"Good afternoon, Merrilynne, Rowland. I have some questions for you related to the operation of the tavern." He gestured them to sit. "Please."

At this rare sign of civility, Merri smiled. Rowland noted it was close to her mimicked Piersen shark smile. They sat.

"I was going over the passenger list and saw your name on the home world flight this eventide, Merrilynne." He smiled at her, and she repressed a shiver.

"It was booked last month, Mr. Genco. I haven't been to home world, and I thought it was time." Merri's smile took on some warmth.

"How long do you anticipate being off-world?"

"That will depend upon what I can find for work there." Merri leaned forward. "May I be frank, sir?"

"Of course," he tersely replied.

"I have managed Savortha's tavern for almost a standard year. I'm tired. It may be, as you observed when I took over for CordCorp following Niall Piersen's departure, that the role is too much for a woman." She heard Rowland change a snicker into a cough. "I would like to see if I can find employment doing something less strenuous."

"What are we supposed to do while you explore new job opportunities?" The sarcasm in the question almost made her smile.

"I would like to recommend Sevio Rowland to replace me as manager. He has been handling more and more of the tasks needed as I found myself incapable of keeping up the place." She turned to Rowland. "Sevio is more than capable of taking it on."

"In that case, Rowland, since I doubt I can convince Merrilynne to stay, would you consider taking the promotion to manager? With the appropriate raise in pay and benefits, of course."

The executive's voice took on oily undertones bordering on obsequious. Merri realized he was under pressure from his board and needed this to go smoothly. She schooled herself to look contrite, rather than smug.

Rowland regarded her. She nodded and brushed her forehead. Go along with it but carefully.

"If that is an offer, sir, yes, I'll take it. I like working at the pub. May I hire my own assistant? It does take two people to run it smoothly."

"Certainly," the man behind the massive desk sat back, relieved. "Make your decision and submit it to my office for approval." He rose.

"Merrilynne, we have had our differences, but I do want to wish you well. Should you decide to return, I'm certain we can find something for you to do." He looked past them to the door. "Gilchrist will see you out."

Back outside, the two publicans assured their escort they no longer needed him and headed to the port without unwanted company. Merri checked in, put her backpack through the customs inspection, and requested Rowland's company down the walkway to the boarding gate. Once they went through the usual security and were out of sight of the agents, Rowland slipped his arm around her shoulders and hugged her.

"We made it."

"Sev, be careful. You're impulsive. Think about the risks before you act, please? You are now one of the coordinators of the movement."

The hatch door of the transport ship swung open. Merri and Rowland abruptly stopped, open-mouthed with shock.

Piersen, in his guise of Krebbs, stood in the doorway, with Gryna at his side.

"We thought you were killed!" Merri gasped in a whisper.

"Piersen was killed in a vehicle explosion which left no traces of anything. My name is Krebbs." He opened his arms and Merri ran to him. He enveloped her in a tight hug and winked at Rowland.

"But why take such a risk by coming here now?" Rowland asked.

"I wanted to have my two daughters together for the trip home."

"Two?"

"They are half-sisters. Merri's mother, Frida, came with me when I arrived to set up the pub. She died two years after Merri was born. Gryna's mother, Savortha, was killed in a purge when Corp took over."

Both girls gave Rowland hugs.

"Keep the dream of freedom alive, Sevio," Krebbs said with a jaunty wave. "We'll be back."

The Human Museum

R. Kyle Hannah

    Benja'kelma shivered against the autumn wind and pulled his jacket tighter around his purple body. The breeze chilled his hairless head and he wished he had brought a head covering from home. He walked up the long stone stairs toward the entrance to the Museum of Cosmic History. He trailed behind his classmates; his short legs straining with each step.
    His teacher, Dormin Second Class Porti'ca'ha, stopped the students at the door to the museum, pausing to let Benja to catch up. He made the top step only slightly out of breath. He heard several of his classmate's snicker and the muttered comments about his pudgy frame.
    "Class," Dormin Porti'ca'ha raised her hands to quiet the comments. She wore a bright yellow sun dress that contrasted sharply to her purple skin. A garish, red wig sat atop her head, its long locks flowing down her back. "Class, I want to remind you to be on your best behavior. This is a public museum, and we are here to learn.
    "Do not touch the displays," she warned. "Flied'quor, I will be watching you after last year."
    The class laughed at the remark, ribbing the largest kid in the class. Flied'quor, on an earlier trip to the museum, tripped into a display from the Orion Belt and destroyed a one-of-a-kind remnant of the Second Interstellar War.
    Flied'quor growled, silencing the comments.

"Now, find your assigned class-buddy and make sure that you two stay together," she ordered. "No one wonder off," she glared at Flied'quor.

His purple-colored face turned a pale yellow in embarrassment.

The children scrambled about the steps, each one grabbing hold of their class-buddy as instructed. The Dormin stood, impatiently tapping her clawed foot, arms crossed, waiting for the class to settle. The kids finally stopped moving, everyone arm in arm with their buddy, except for Benja'kelma.

"Where is your buddy?" the Dormin asked.

"He did not show up today," Benja replied sheepishly. He averted his eyes from her gaze, staring at the ground.

The teacher smirked and said the words he dreaded most. "I guess you'll just have to be my class-buddy today."

The class snickered again and Benja turned yellow with embarrassment.

"Class," the Dormin warned, and the laughter ceased. "Look at the exhibits, but do not touch. No running! Read all that you can about each item," she paused, "there may be a quiz after."

The class groaned at the news. Dormin Porti'ca'ha smiled. "Now, let's go inside and visit the Human Museum.

The door opened and the children shuffled forward, barely controlling their urge to run inside. Parent chaperones herded the two-three kids toward the right, down a long, pristine corridor with well waxed floors and perfectly spaced paintings on the walls. Benja'kelma entered last with the Dormin.

He passed ancient artifacts of lost civilizations, paintings from the far corners of the galaxy, and skeletons of large, terrifying beasts. He had seen this part of the museum before and only offered cursory glances. Images of the lost human civilization filled his mind and his three hearts beat faster. He wanted to make the most of his first trip to the new human exhibit.

The class stopped at a large arching doorway; the words HUMAN EXHIBIT prominently displayed across the arch. A triple strand of dark green rope blocked the entrance. A man, dressed in a clean, white smock, stood next to the rope.

"Class, this is Doctor Ze'klanic, the museum curator," the Dormin introduced the man, her voice echoing in the museum. "He is responsible for all that you see here." She motioned toward the doctor.

"The human exhibit is on display from the Reigers Institute," he said and waved to the kids. His squeaky voice grated on Benja's nerves. "They spent years gathering these artifacts and determining their purpose. Watch, read, and learn, but please, do not touch. And please, children, stay away from the curtained off area at the back of the exhibit. That display is not ready.

"Is everyone ready?"

The class cheered enthusiastically. Benja nodded. What's behind the curtain?

Doctor Ze'klanic tugged on the rope, removing it from the entrance. He waved the kids forward. "Welcome to the Human Museum."

The school kids surged forward. The chaperones yelled and gave chase. Dormin Porti'ca'ha and the curator followed in a vain attempt to coral the kids. Benja stood, alone at the entrance. He sighed, pulled his jacket tighter, and entered the exhibit.

The room appeared to stretch on for miles, with high, vaulted ceilings and sparkling tile floors. Evenly spaced display cases, ensconced in glass, lined the walls. Another two rows of displays, mostly skeletal figures and ancient, metal boxes, filled the center of the room. Footfalls and laughter echoed through the hall.

He saw the kids, still in teams of two, running from item to item, always one step ahead of the frustrated chaperones. The kids would point, laugh at something, and move on before the parents or teacher could reach them. Benja watched everyone drift deeper into the exhibit, leaving him alone.

"I prefer it this way," he muttered and cast his gaze on each of the rows of displays. He decided he wanted to save the skeletons and metal boxes for last and moved to his left, toward a glass display.

Benja blinked against the harsh, yellow light that filled the display. The glass protected a patch of green on top of brown. Small sprinklers activated, spraying the interior of the case. The brown soaked up the water in seconds. He lowered his eyes and read a plaque at the bottom of the glass.

"This is grass from the human home-world, Earth. This substance covered great swaths of the land masses and grew only in the warmest months." He read the scientific name, although he did not understand the words, and how they produced oxygen for the humans.

He studied the grass for another minute and wondered what it felt like. "Looks soft," he muttered. He shrugged and moved on to the next display.

He drew near the case and froze. His eyes widened as dozens of small animals flitted back and forth inside the glass. His hearts beat faster at the sight. He watched them jump and fly into the walls. He gulped and looked at the information plaque. "One of the most popular pets," he read. "These animals covered the planet, every continent without exception." He tried to pronounce the scientific name–Blattodea–and instantly knew he butchered it. He looked up at the case and the small animals in constant motion. "Pets?" he asked himself and looked back at the plaque.

"Cockroach?" he slowly pronounced. "What kind of pet is that?"

As pleasant as he thought the grass would feel, he felt the opposite of the cockroach. He shivered at the thought of them crawling on him. "I will stay with my Coriuu," he muttered, thinking of his own six-legged pet. He shivered again and quickly moved on down the line.

"Having fun?" a voice asked behind him. Benja jumped and turned to see the curator, hands clasped behind his back, standing beside him.

"Yes, sir," Benja'kelma acknowledged. "I like the grass, but not the cockroach. How could they keep them as pets?"

"We have top scientists asking that very question," Doctor Ze'klanic replied, a hint of pride in his voice. "You are very astute to ask that. Most kids dismiss it and move on."

"What we do know is that they were everywhere, one of the most populous species on Earth," the doctor continued, nodding.

Benja stopped at the next case. He narrowed his eyes, studying the shattered object within. He shook his head. "What is this?"

"An ancient weapon," Doctor Ze'klanic offered. "Push the button on the display and you'll see warriors training with it."

Benja reached out and stabbed a bright blue button next to the information plaque. A small monitor flashed to life, showing a man, the weapon in hand, smashing it on the floor. Music flowed from the speakers, drowning out the destruction of the object.

"They trained to music?" Benja asked.

"Apparently," the curator confirmed. "In every instance where we have found this weapon used, there is a group of people with them, all playing music. Usually, very loud with a heavy beat."

The video died and Benja hit the button again. A different video appeared. A tall black man wearing a yellow shirt and bandana around his head, knelt before his weapon. He leaned forward and kissed the object, sat up, and threw flame from his hands. Benja raised an eyebrow at that. "He cast fire?"

The weapon caught fire as the man waved his hands, as if encouraging the flames to grow. He grabbed a bottle of something nearby and poured it on the object. The fire grew in intensity, and he tossed the liquid aside. Again, he waved his fingers, willing the fire to grow.

The black man stood, grabbed the object by its long handle, and smashed the object against the floor again and again. The video ended.

"The guitar," the curator stated. "An assassin's weapon."

"Guitar?" Benja repeated, tasting the word. "Why did that man light his on fire first?"

"Another good question," Dr. Ze'klanic mused. "Top scientists have speculated that. There are two theories. One, he failed in his training, or on a mission, and this is part of his remedial training.

"The other is that this was his trademark–his signature move to let his superiors know he succeeded.

"As he is the only one we have found that lit his guitar on fire, I am a believer in the second theory," the doctor finished.

"Always with music playing?" Benja asked.

"Always."

"These humans were strange."

"Our scientists have determined that, as well," the curator chuckled.

Benja'kelma stared at the black and white fragments behind the glass. He noted the long handle, rusted wires haphazardly clinging to the device. "What are those?"

"Wire strings," the curator noted. "We believe those served as backup weapons; in case the bashing does not work." Benja shivered at the thought. "Come, let's move on from this. I want to show you their money."

Doctor Ze'klanic gently pushed him down the aisle of exhibits. Benja'kelma put the idea of bashing someone with a guitar out of his mind and concentrated on the glass cases they strolled past. He saw a stack of dishes, eating utensils, and toys.

He paused for a heartbeat at that display, observing a stack of small rectangles with bumps across one surface. The rectangles snapped into place, forming shapes and representations of other objects. "Legos," the curator explained. "A child's toy, used to develop fine motor skills." He chuckled softly. "And apparently in scientists." He leaned down and whispered, "I have a stack of these in my desk. Quite fun."

They continued down the line. Benja saw a red and white striped flag, with white stars in a blue background. A solid white flag with a red circle in the center shared the display. "Flags of two of the most powerful nation states," Ze'klanic explained and ushered him on down the row. They stopped before the last exhibit in the line.

Behind the glass lay crumpled paper of various sizes. Seven stacks, each unique from the others, lay in even rows. Portraits and drawings adorned each piece of paper. Coins lay scattered throughout the display.

"This is currency representing seven of their nation states," the curator pointed to each in turn. "Great Britain, Germany,

Canada, Japan, France, Brazil, and the United States. Each nation state produced their own type of money."

"Money?"

"A credit chit like your parents use," Ze'klanic explained. "They used these pieces of paper to buy things."

"Why didn't they use electronic chits?"

"Eventually they did. But for many centuries, they used these pieces of paper."

"And each nation state had their own?" Benja asked, cocking his head in thought.

"That's correct."

"If they each had their own, how did they trade? If I want something from Biro'nekus, my Mom trades with his Mom."

"We have not completely figured out how they did that," the doctor confessed. "We have read something about exchange rates, but nothing is consistent. It's like the value of their currency changed every day."

"That doesn't make sense," Benja stated.

"You are a very smart young lad," the curator nodded. He looked at a timepiece on the wall. "We have time for one more exhibit, then I must return to my duties." He looked around at the room. "Is there anything specific you want to know about?"

"What is that?" Benja pointed to a large metal container in the center of the room.

"Ah," the curator smiled and led Benja to the exhibit. "This is one of the most curious pieces in the entire museum."

The large rectangular structure took up almost half of the center of the room. Greenish in color, it towered above Benja. Stairs led up to a door where green rope barred entry. Inside, he saw shadows of chairs, but the dim interior prevented a clear view. Small windows filled the walls at irregular intervals. Several were open, protruding from the metal walls, but provided little light. Rust covered the container in places. Benja squatted and saw four sets of wheels underneath the carriage.

"What is it?"

"A storm machine," Doctor Ze'klanic stated. "The humans would place many of these in close proximity and, through a process we have been able to duplicate, created storms."

"They created storms?" Benja shook his head. "Why?"

"We do not know," the curator escorted Benja to an information plaque. "We only know that they took great pride in obtaining video footage of their creations." He touched a blue button on the plaque and Benja watched a video feed snap to life.

A cluster of the metal storm machines, in all kinds of colors, sat in four even rows of ten. The video showed a group of humans running around outside the structures. They pointed off camera, turned and ran, abandoning the machines. Benja watched in horror as a large, spinning vortex arrived a minute later and destroyed the cluster of storm machines.

"This is a common occurrence with these structures," Doctor Ze'klanic admitted. "The storms they create destroy everything in their path, including the machines themselves."

"But the humans are a resilient species. They rebuilt, create new storms, and repeat the cycle. Madness. Resilient madness."

The curator looked around the room and Benja followed his gaze. The class had scattered about the room, the chaperones and Dormin keeping them in line. Most appeared to be in good spirits, except for Flied'quor, who wore a pouty expression on his purple face.

"I hope you have enjoyed yourself, young lad," the curator smiled, looking back at Benja. "I must see to other duties."

"Thank you for the tour, Doctor Ze'klanic," Benja stated. "It's been...interesting."

The curator nodded and strolled off, hands behind his back, whistling. Benja watched him go then moved off to explore the rest of the museum. He found something called a car, the human version of transportation. He moved to the right side of the room and explored the exhibits.

Each case on this side contained an item similar to an item from his own planet. He saw swords, hatchets, ancient computers. He paused at a machine that looked like a video screen. "A television set," he read off the plaque. He touched a blue button and the information screen flickered to life, showing him watching himself on the TV screen, watching himself into infinity. The sight of a thousand of him watching himself made him giggle. Benja moved on.

He arrived at the last exhibit down the line and a wave of sadness washed over him. This was the last case in the museum. He dreaded getting back on the transport and taking the long ride back to the education institution. He looked around him at his classmates, most had already seen everything and sat on the floor. Several yawned. Others played games. Only a few continued to wander the museum.

"Hey, kid."

The hushed voice startled him, and he quickly turned back to the exhibit. Inside the glass partition sat an old speaker. Lights illuminated the outside of the device and flashed as it spoke. "Yeah, you. Did you enjoy the museum?"

"Y...y...yes," Benja muttered, looking over his shoulder. "Who...who are you?"

"My name is Mike," the speaker said. "I am the last human in the universe."

"You look like a speaker," Benja noted.

"Yeah, well, this part of the exhibit isn't ready, or so they tell me."

Benja'kelma jumped at the words. He turned his head, staring at the curtain in the back of the exhibit hall. "Not ready?"

"Yeah, didn't the Doc tell ya?"

Benja looked back at the speaker. "He said that the last piece wasn't ready. He didn't say it was a human."

"Well, here I am," the voice laughed. The lights winked on and off, in time with the laughter. "Step on back here and see for yourself."

"The curator said–"

"Do you always do what your told?" Mike inquired.

"Yes," Benja replied. "Mostly."

"Then how do you learn, eh? Listen, it's been my experience that you learn more by doing, not observing. I mean, look at me. You think I'd be alive today if I did what I was told?

"Mike, stay back from that spaceship. Mike, don't go near those aliens. Mike, put your helmet back on," the voice mocked. "If I did as I was told, I'd be dead."

"But you're not?"

"Not on your life, kid," pride beamed in the voice. "I'm alive and well, the focus point in the Human Zoo."

"Museum."

"Zoo. Museum. What's the difference? So, you gonna come back here and let me look at you or not?"

"I'd better not."

"If you do, I'll tell you which exhibits are correct and which ones are aren't."

Benja stared at the speaker. "What are you talking about?"

"I'll give you an example," Mike said. "You know that exhibit about pets?"

"You mean the favorite pet?" Benja shuddered at the thought of the cockroach.

"Yeah. Those ain't pets. They are pests. One letter out of place and the universe thinks a cockroach is man's best friend," Mike scoffed. "Those are insects. Bugs. Pests. We tried to kill them by the hundreds, but they multiplied by the thousands. They ain't pets."

Benja shuddered again. "I didn't think that was right."

"So, step back here and I'll tell you the rest."

Benja stared at the speaker for a moment, then looked around the room. No one looked his direction. The Dormin wagged her long, purple finger at two students. The chaperones, still corralling the school kids, looked exhausted. The rest of his class played their games. He turned to stare at the curtain, gently moving in the breeze from the environmental unit.

"I–I can't," Benja protested.

Mike grew silent.

"Hello?"

Benja froze as footsteps approached from behind. He turned to see Doctor Ze'klanic smiling. The curator dropped to a knee and looked Benja in the eye. He saw humor in the doctor's face, and the museum director barely suppressed a chuckle.

"Dear boy, you are the best," Ze'klanic whispered. "Most students, especially the boys, jump at the chance to see what is behind the curtain. You continue to amaze me."

Relief washed over Benja, and he let out the breath he did not realize he held. He glared at the curator. "This–this was a test?"

"Of course," Dormin Porti'ca'ha's voice floated through the air. He turned toward the speaker, its lights flashing with each word. "I told you, there may be a quiz. Benja'kelma, this was yours."

"You asked the right questions at the right exhibits," Dr. Ze'klanic explained. "We know some of them are wrong, but we do not know their true purpose. We thought that you might be able to help figure it out."

"We?"

"The Dormin and my team."

"I–I don't understand."

"Young lad," the curator smiled, "the Dormin says that you are one of her brightest. We needed to test you–"

"For what?"

"To make sure you are ready for advanced studies," Porti'ca'ha offered, appearing from behind the curtain. "You asked the right questions and did not disobey the rules. The rules of scientific study are very important."

Benja glared at the two adults, the curator and the Dormin. He shook his head in disbelief. "You want me to be a scientist?"

"My dear boy, you already are," the curator said. "You already are."

Benja nodded, smiled, and followed the two of them behind the curtain, his journey as a scientist had just begun.

The Human Museum

Incident on Kappa-15

Will Neely

Chunks of rock floated through black space like cast-off crumbs from God's table. With infinitesimal slowness they drifted, shifting course as they collided and spun, tracing invisible whorls across the nothingness that surrounded them. One such collision caused a divergence, a larger rock sacrificially birthing several smaller fragments, each piece treading its own path according to the dictates of velocity and momentum.

One of the little buggers ricocheted lazily off my visor with a brittle ping. I swore and hit coms. "Rath!" There was no response, so I cut in the full base camp frequency. "Rather!"

Finally, a groggy voice responded, tinny in my ear. "Wha'?"

"I told you to clean up after yourself! There's frags and dust all up in here, and now I can't take samples without getting pummeled like a fraggin' third cousin!"

Rather yawned out loud through the com. "Sorry…"

"Not as sorry as you're about to be. Suit up and get your butt out here to clean up your mess."

"What?" Rather yelled, fully awake now.

"You heard me. Now."

I cut my com back over to operational freq. No sense in the rest of the guys having to listen in; chances were there were others trying to catch some shut-eye besides just Rath.

We were a five-man crew on our second day into a year-long contract on this particular asteroid, dubbed Kappa-15 by our employer, Tri-Star Mining. It wasn't especially glamorous work, but it beat most anything I was qualified to do down on Purgatorie – and paid more, too.

The lock opened and Rather floated out; although our suits were bulky enough to obscure most differences between us, Rath somehow managed to fill his out like a five-gallon hat squeezed over a ten-gallon head. He always swore his suit was smaller than ours, but I've watched the fella eat, and... Well, it's not my place to judge.

With bad grace he anchored his feet to handles driven deep into the rock, raised the collector, and started to vacuum up the dust and larger fragments that floated around the hollow we occupied. Xavier always calls this staging area right outside base the "front porch."

I watched Rath for a little while, then figured the space was clear enough for me to begin. Anchored to my own handhold, I pulled out my scanner. Erratic points of light bounced around the interior of the hollow as the tool booted up.

"You gonna' make more mess anyway," Rather grumbled, the first thing he'd said since he came out. "I don't appreciate gettin' rousted out of my bunk to do this right now."

"I didn't tell you to appreciate it, Rath." I squinted through my helmet, fiddling with the controls to my scanner. "I just told you to get it done."

He grumbled at me some more while he finished up and drifted back inside, but cut his com off halfway through, so I reckon he didn't much care if I heard him or not. Me, I got my scanner going. The lights on the wall began to change, glowing all kinds of different colors depending on whatever the scanner read from the rock at that particular location. It would draw us up a convenient virtual map once it was all finished, but just from watching it work I could already tell – thanks to the different colors of light – which general direction we were going to be digging.

I hit coms again. "You seeing this, Chen?"

"Yeah, Cully. Looks like we're going straight for the middle of this one."

"Looks it for now." I eyed the interior of the asteroid. "These things can be mighty tricky on occasion, though."

"So, I've heard."

I tracked the scanner's progress with the monitor embedded in the interior of my suit's sleeve. Barely over twenty percent.

"So why doesn't Tri-Star just tow the asteroid off and process it planet side?" Chen wondered through my earpiece. "Seems crazy to pay us to drill it out when they could do it all from the outside."

"Nah," I said. "It won't work. Too much heat or pressure ruins the crystals. Same reason we use augers 'stead of blasting." I checked again; three-quarters finished. Yep, we'd be drilling deep this time. "I seem to recollect that they tried to automate it all. Built some kinda fancy 'bot to drill in and search it out."

"Oh, yeah, I heard about that," said Chen. "What ever happened to those?"

"No idea." Ninety-five percent. "But given that we're getting paid to be here right now, I'd lay hard money it didn't work out too well for 'em."

My scanner buzzed, and the points of light all vanished – except for three, which started to flash against the rock. I pulled out my sample box just to make sure, but I could feel in my bones that we were in for a heap of effort before we found anything worth our time.

I locked the scanner in place against my handhold, then let go and drifted over to the first flashing spot. No handles occupied the rock near the blinking spot, forcing me to go with option B.

In response to my command, the suit clamped down hard around my left wrist; I could feel the sealing balloon bond with the alloy plates just beneath my skin. Once it finished, I reached over with my other hand and removed the left-side glove, exposing my hand to the interior of the asteroid.

It wasn't brown skin under the glove, but a dull metal sheen, like liquid lead – my bim was already online. Placing my hand against the asteroid, I mentally commanded the bim to HOLD. Tiny extrusions stretched out from a couple hundred contact points on my palm and fingers, automatically worming their way into every available crack or crevice. The end result left me securely anchored to the rock by my palm.

Clipping the now-extraneous glove to my work belt, I took out my sample kit, pressing it against the rock surface right about the spot where the light blinked. With a series of jerky, mechanical motions, an automated drill began to extract bits of the asteroid, storing and cataloguing them for analysis back at camp. Telescoping into the rock via some piece of high-tech witchery, the drill collected samples from several feet's worth of rock.

As it worked, it expelled dust and rock frags that flew out, sailing across the chamber on short-lived, meaningless journeys. Rather would surely raise a fuss about that later on.

Once the drill completed its cycle, I took a gander at the storage compartment to make sure there weren't any issues, then commanded my bim to RELEASE. I pushed off towards the next flashing light and repeated the process.

After I finished, while I packed away my sample kit, I was abruptly overtaken by a crawling sensation on my skin. Nervous-like, I looked around the hollow, but everything seemed fine. I'm not one for premonitions and such, but all of a sudden I had an unsettled feeling like maybe this asteroid was gonna be trouble. The next second, I shook my head to clear my thoughts; I was far too old to be jumping at shadows.

ଔ ෩

Coming back in through the lock, I took off the rest of my suit, chafing my wrist where the temporary seal had clamped down on me. My bim rippled slightly, then deformed, sliding back down into its resting shape: a wide, close-fitting bracelet around my forearm. I flexed the fingers of my left hand one by one; getting properly re-acclimated after the bim's deactivation generally took a couple of minutes.

Once the lock cycled open I pushed through, up into the interior of the Jude. The portable mining base, or another like it, had been my home for a passel of years now. We liked to call the ships "camp" because that was a sight homier than calling them by their official handle: "Multi-Site Space Mineral Retrieval Facility."

I sailed on "up" the stark metal corridor, waving at Chen as I passed the com station. Chen waved back with one hand, while his other two fiddled with knobs and sliders on his com array.

Chen's not a xeno. Last job he told us about how he was in a bad accident down on Purgatorie, only it turned out to be the local bigwig's fault. Apparently the bigwig was on the hook for a sight of liability money, but Chen was the sole survivor, so the upshot of it all was that Chen wound up with more bims than skin and bone. If it were me I might be tempted just to take the money and retire; good bims can be expensive, so the bigwig likely paid out the nose for all Chen's tech. But Chen swears he'd be bored to death sitting around with half a body, plugged into sim-machines all day. I guess I buy that, all things considered.

I hit the lab and rapped on the door. Muffled shouts came out from the inside, more habitual-like than angry. The hatch slid open, and Xavier hung there, floating "sideways" relative to me. I handed over the sample kit.

"Here. Three spots this time."

Xavier took the kit, securing it in his work area. "Thanks, Cully."

I nodded to him. "You eat recently?" He shook his head, so I jerked a thumb. "You wanna?"

He shook his head. "I've gotta finish setting up." He waved a hand vaguely behind him. "You go on, I'll catch up."

Shrugging, I pushed off along the corridor. "A'ight. See you then."

The canteen was less "kitchen" and more "chuck-wagon," if you get my drift. I sighed every time I went in. One of these days, I swear I'm gonna retire, set myself up on a ranch planet side, and get a small herd of lumms. I'll eat steak every day and do whatever else the frag I want to do.

The canteen was already occupied. A tall, younger fella with a shock of white hair and too-big eyes was making headway on a bowl of sticky lentils and lumm meat. His clothes were too fresh for a mining man, and he wore a slightly oversized plassie cross on a choker around his neck. He stopped shoveling when he saw me and swallowed, then nodded his head. "Captain."

"Just call me Cullen, kid. We're not military. Frag, we're not even technically in space at the moment."

He grinned nervously. "Okay, Cap – I mean, Cullen."

I sighed, but silently and to myself. The kid was trying. Four of us had signed on to this job together straightaway after our last one had ended. The kid, Ethan, had signed up by himself, fresh out of school – or whatever it was that passed for such in his township. Purgatorie's not especially consistent, cross-planet that is, with respect to the raising of their young'uns.

I fixed myself a bowl of the same mess the kid had and gently pushed off to strap myself down to the chair opposite him. The lentils held everything together well enough that my spoon stuck in as opposed to flying across the room. I glared at the gunk and cussed under my breath before I started.

"Er, uh, Cullen?" Ethan said. "I've been meaning to ask…"

"Yeah?"

"Are we supposed to all stay in this camp the whole time? Or do we move around from place to place?"

I swallowed. "Well, we generally stay put until the job's done. In emergencies somebody'll hitch a ride on the star hoppers when they stop off for resupply, but that's out of the ordinary. The bigwigs don't favor it because time spent flying is time not spent mining if you get my drift."

The kid nodded but looked uncomfortable. I spooned another heap of slop out of the plassie three-quarters globe we called a "bowl" and fixed him with a curious eye. "Why d'you ask, kid? You tired of us already? It's gonna be a long year if that's what you're driving towards."

Ethan flushed. "No, not really… I just wondered." He looked around guiltily. "Are there a lot of people out here like that? With… bims?"

I blinked. "Uh, yeah. More people have 'em than you think. Why?"

"Well…" he set his jaw. "They're an abomination, right? I mean, Sister Martha Gotterd always said they were, and that if God meant for us to be that way then He would've made us that way."

I chewed, to buy myself time. Near as I could figure, the kid wasn't joking. Bims, shorthand for biotech implants, were commonplace out here, as well as the larger townships of Purgatorie. Not everyone had them, but near everyone at least knew a few people with one or two. I was relieved the kid hadn't savvied to mine yet. The armband look was pretty standard for an offline bim, but his experience with the tech was clearly next to nil.

"Look, Ethan," I said. "It's a big galaxy out here. Bims are nothing like the strangest thing you'll see. Now nobody's saying you have to get one or anything." The set of his jaw grew more pronounced as I continued. "But you are gonna need to work with them who do, and you might find your load a sight lighter if you can refrain from calling someone different from you an 'abomination.'"

As luck would have it, the hatch slid open right as I said that last part. Good thing, too, since Ethan had his mouth open and ready to say something I'm reasonably sure he'd regret. His words kind of died when he realized it was Xavier coming through the door; likely because Xavier's bim isn't nice and subtle like mine.

A metallic plate covered half the big man's forehead, tapering to a circle around one eye. The eye itself wasn't organic, being made of a series of multifaceted lenses. Behind their crystal surfaces lurked the hint of electronics and miniature servos.

"Who's an abomination?" Xavier rumbled cheerfully.

"Oh, Ethan was just telling me how Sister Martha Somebody told him that bims are wicked and sinful," I responded levelly. "But we're all good now, right Ethan?"

The poor kid just nodded, but now Xavier wasn't ready to let it go. I probably shouldn't have brought it up; I knew how he could be when it came to questions of religion.

"Sinful, huh?" his rumble was less cheerful now. "Let me tell you, boy, if there was a god – which there ain't – he, she, or it would have a lot bigger things to care about than anybody's augmentations. So, I don't see how any of my bims are your business, you get me?" Xavier finished fixing his food and kicked over to the table. "Plus, you're up here mining Vahan with the rest of us, so I wouldn't get all high-and-mighty about it, eh?"

Ethan's brow wrinkled. "What does mining have to do with bims?"

"Holy hell!" exploded Xavier. "You don't have the first idea what you signed on to, do you? Boy, you just better take off and go herd lumms or something."

"Hey–" Ethan started in, but Xavier was off and running. "Why d'you think we're looking for stupid crystals on a frozen rock in godforsaken space? Because every bim needs 'em, and Tri-Star's got the contracts to sell 'em!" He shook his head and started eating, muttering something about "idiot dusters" under his breath.

Ethan leaned towards me and whispered in a horrified voice. "We're mining material for implants?"

"Yeah, kid. That's Tri-Star's main source of contracts." I looked at him curiously. "Vahan crystal is part of every bim. You really didn't know?"

He shook his head as the door slid open again, revealing Chen and Rather.

"So, here's where everybody went," said Chen, using all five of his limbs to crawl through the door like a huge spider. "Make room, hungry tech coming through."

"I'm done," I said, scraping my bowl clean. "Lemme through and you guys can eat."

"Hey Chen, don't get too close to the kid; you might get some of your abomination-germs on him!" hooted Xavier. Ethan colored again.

"Abomination, huh?" mused Chen, tapping his chin with the forefinger of his right hand while his others prepared his meal. "That's a new one. Freak, cyborg, monster, metal-head, I've heard all those. But not abomination." He sat down. "Metal-head, I ask you! My head's not even metal."

I grinned. He had a point; his bims were all confined to his lower body and torso, all excepting that third extra-long arm popping out from the middle of his back like that.

"I don't think anyone's an abomination!" Ethan practically wailed. "I just–"

I interrupted before Xavier could; he had a cruel look on his face, and he's been known to go a mite far, especially where religion is involved. "Kid," I said, "Nobody thinks you do. You've got your own thoughts about stuff; that's fine."

"Anyway," Rather broke in absently, opening a pouch. "You gotta get used to it, since we all have 'em."

The kid's face paled. "Who all has them?"

Xavier glanced over at me with evil pleasure. "Aw, hell, Cully."

I grimaced. "Shut it. I hadn't gotten around to mentioning it yet." I held up my left hand and sent the command: ENGAGE. My bim slid up and around my hand like a living metal glove. At the same time, Rather raised his left arm and pushed the sleeve back, displaying the vidscreen embedded in his pale flesh.

Ethan stared at us like we'd sprouted devil horns. "I, uh, wasn't – I mean, I don't think – look, I wasn't trying to say anything about you guys, you know?"

I waved my hand. "Nobody thinks you were, kid. Listen, we're stuck with each other, so let's just treat each other with respect and we'll get along fine. Okay?"

Ethan nodded.

༄ ༅

"That boy is gonna find himself buried in a hole somewhere, Cully."

Xavier held the stored samples up to his bim-eye, which emitted soft whirring noises as he scanned the material.

"Go easy on him, Xavier. It's his first-time off world."

"Mebbe so. But there's no call for him to get all sky-wizard on us." He finished with the first sample tube and picked up the next.

I sighed. Xavier's a good guy, but he's always been a mite rough-speaking, especially when someone's acting foolish. When you have as expansive a definition of "foolish" as Xavier does, that translates to "more often than not." I decided to change the topic.

"Anything good?"

He grimaced. "Not a bit. Why'd they send us to this fraggin' rock anyway?"

I shrugged. "Prelim results were good, I guess."

"You couldn't tell it from what I'm seein'. Look!" He stuck the tube in my face. I reared back, throwing my body into erratic rotation until I could grab ahold of the door.

"Uh, what am I looking at?"

"This!" He gestured at the plassie tube. "Bunch of fraggin' slag and not much else. Heavy industry could use this stuff, but not Tri-Star."

"Okay, okay," I said, avoiding the tube as he waved it around. "What about the others?"

"Nothing good so far," he said, eyeing the last tube. "Nothing but... well, hold on, now."

"What?"

"Well, there's no Vahan, but see that?" His bim-eye hummed.

"We don't all have bionic eyes in our skulls," I muttered. Craning my neck, I could just make out a few glints of silvery-white. "Is that NDT?"

"Why yeah it is," he said with a grin. I smiled back; NDT was pretty much worthless, but it was generally only found as a precipitate where Vahan crystal had formed. This was promising.

I hit the com unit on the lab wall. "Drill team! Fifteen-minute notice."

We had a tunnel to dig.

◌   ෆ

Ethan, Rather and I worked in shifts for the next ten hours, drilling into the asteroid a few dozen feet at a time. Every so often I'd have them pull the man-sized auger back so I could squeeze through to the front of the tunnel and run my scanner again, ensuring we stayed on track. Once every three hours I took samples and relayed them back down the tunnel for Xavier to analyze. Chen alternated between downloading and summarizing my scanner data and following along behind us, spraying the tunnel with compressed mining gel. That part was essential; the gel adhered to the rock and hardened in place almost instantly, providing structural support to our tunnels. The last thing any of us needed was for the asteroid to break apart on us.

Headed back towards the front porch to take a breather, I noticed some odd offshoot holes intersecting our tunnel; they looked sort of like scarab holes from down on Purgatorie. Leaning in to take a closer look, I spotted a glimmer of silvery-white in one of them. NDT?

As I reached towards one of the holes, I suddenly shivered, overtaken again by that same sense that something was wrong with this rock we were digging in. Grimacing, I froze, but the next second I got distracted by the crackle of my earpiece. "Cully?" It was Xavier.

I abandoned the hole and continued towards the camp. "Yeah?"

"We have a problem."

I shouldn't have been surprised. "What is it?"

"More like what isn't it. We have plenty of NDT, but zero trace of Vahan crystal."

I blinked. That was odd. "No Vahan in any of the samples?"

"None."

Pausing, I pondered the situation for a moment, until my com crackled again.

"Cap – uh, Cullen. Come on up here; you need to see this."

Irritated, I doubled back, squeezing past the auger to rejoin Ethan and Rather. The latter held a piece of dull gray metal, as long as my arm, twisted slightly into a sinuous curve. It reminded me somehow of my bim, only frozen in the act of flowing from one shape to another. It reflected little of the light from our helmets.

"What's that?" I commed to the two of them.

"We're not sure," said Rather, which kind of threw me.

"You didn't bring it down here?"

"No! We pulled the auger back and found it floating right here with all the frags."

I took the thing in my gloves, examining it more closely. It was etched all over with some sort of weird pattern; it looked almost organic. It had a very slight amount of give to it. I thought for a moment; this thing could just be a harmless anomaly, but on the other hand…

"Okay, we'll call it for the day." Switching to the full crew freq, I commed: "Pack it in for the shift, fellas. We'll pick it up in a few hours." I switched back to the local freq and spoke again to Ethan and Rather. "Let's put this in the lab. Maybe Xavier can tell us something about it. And Rath? There'd better be zero frags left when I come back out here next shift."

I drifted back towards camp, ignoring Rather's spluttered cusses in my ear.

ଔ ଓ

"You're saying we've found absolutely no Vahan crystal so far?"

Chen floated "upside-down" in the canteen. I think he did it intentionally, to mess with Ethan.

"That's what I'm saying," growled Xavier. The five of us were crammed into the canteen. "We've found NDT at every step, but zero crystal. We might as well have floated in space picking our noses for all we have to show for it today."

"But that's not possible, right?" protested Chen. "NDT means Vahan."

"That's what I woulda said before today, but this asteroid just ain't cooperating. I thought my bim might be on the fritz, so I broke out the centrifuge and the spectrometer and all them shiny fancy toys Tri-Star keeps around and guess what? No Vahan."

"Well, what do we do then?" They both looked at me.

Looking back, I wish that I'd remembered my weird feelings and commed operations for a pickup, or at least for further instructions. Things might have turned out better that way. Of course, although I didn't know it yet, by this point all the events had been set in motion, so there was no real hope of our avoiding the nightmare that was to follow.

"We keep going," I decided. "We do our job. If we don't find anything in a few days we'll com ops and let the bigwigs decide if they want to keep paying us to just play in the dirt."

Chen nodded at that, but I could tell that Xavier was still frustrated, so I distracted him by asking about the metal rod the drill team had found.

"Yeah, about that," he said, rubbing his chin absentmindedly. "My bim's not really fitted out for scanning exotic material. I'll slice into it when I get a chance, but you know I'm gonna stay focused on our actual work, right?" He threw a contemptuous look towards the kid. "Not all of us get the luxury of believing in some sky-wizard that takes care of us."

Throwing up a hand, I cut in before Ethan could respond. "Hold up. Exotic material? You're telling me that thing is xeno?"

Xavier shrugged. "Could be. Who knows who made it or why? I'll get to it when I have the time."

"Fine, as long as you don't think it's dangerous."

He scoffed. "Naw, I've got it sealed up in containment. Nothing to worry about there."

Chen and I were the last to leave the canteen, after making plans for the next shift. On my way to bed, I passed by Ethan's bunk. I paused, hearing voices.

"...and please give me strength and endurance to deal with adversity. Please give me kindness and longsuffering towards all the crew, especially Xavier. Amen."

Feeling a mite odd inside, I continued to my own bunk and went to sleep.

ⁿ⁂

I jerked bolt upright before I even knew I was awake. Terrified screams echoed through the base. Engaging my bim, I threw off my straps and pushed quickly out into the corridor, where I nearly collided with Rather. "What's happening?" he asked, pale-faced and sweaty. I just shook my head and kicked back "down" towards the asteroid side of camp.

The screaming grew louder as we drew near the com station. Rather suddenly paused, wrinkling his nose. "What is that?"

"I don't know," I replied, but I smelled it too; a foul odor permeated the air. Grimly I drifted to the com station and thumbed the hatch release, only to be greeted by a nightmare.

Blood and viscera hung in the air, globes of gore clustered so thickly they partially obscured our sight. The scent of death rolled over us, and Rather started to retch behind me. In the middle of the com station floated Chen, eyes rolled back and mouth wide open, screaming in agony.

"Chen!" I darted forward to help the tech. Torn straps tethered him to his chair, which had been custom-made to fit his bims. My stomach turned; his third arm was gone. It looked like it had been torn off, bio-mech fibers splayed out from his back like spider legs. Wild-eyed, I started to pull him away from the seat, but stopped as I caught sight of the rest of him. His abdomen resembled chewed-up meat, and his lower body had been demolished, strands of flesh and bim intermingling as they gently rippled around the com array. For a moment I was too stunned to think.

"Cullen!" Xavier's voice shook me from my stupor. He thrust a box of medical seals at me. "Here!" Good man. I grabbed the seals and started applying them, doing my level best to ignore Chen's screams, the feel of blood splashing against me, the horrible stench assaulting my senses…

ᚳ ᛋ

"Okay, what the hell happened?" said Xavier. Rather shook his head; Ethen just stared at Chen, eyes wide with shock. We'd gotten Chen sedated and strapped down in med bay; nearly a third of his body was either torn to shreds or just plain gone. The guy was probably only alive because so much of him had been artificial to start with.

Xavier looked like he needed to punch something. "You're telling me Chen got reamed into smithereens and we don't know how or why? Frag!" Casting about in frustration, he seized on Ethan. "Tell me the truth, preacher boy," he snarled into the kid's terrified face. "Did you have anything to do with this?"

"Xavier!" I cut in. Xavier looked fit to fight, but he held his tongue. I glared at him, then Ethan, then Rather.

"I'll ask this but one time: Do any of you have a clue as to what happened to Chen?"

All of them shook their heads solemnly. I nodded. "Fine, then. We'll get him taken care of first, then get to the bottom of this. Xavier, watch Chen. Rather, you stay with him. Ethan, with me." Without waiting for further comment, I pushed out of the med bay and "down" the corridor.

The Jude was shaped more or less like a horseshoe fitted around a ball. The largest portion of the ship was the hold, which filled the space between the two horseshoe ends. These ends opened "upward," away from the asteroid, with the nadir of the shoe's arc containing the lock, which supplied access to the asteroid.

Slightly "up" from the lock lay the com station. Steeling my nerves, I thumbed open the hatch. Our air filters had cleaned up the interior somewhat, but I still found myself drifting through a swirling cloud of gore. From behind me came the sounds of Ethan trying hard not to be violently sick.

Upon reaching the com terminal, I activated it and keyed in my id code, followed by a standard command sequence. After a moment, a voice spoke on the other end.

"Tri-Star operations."

"Yeah, this is Cullen Sanders, mining chief stationed on Kappa-15."

Digital static, then: "Go ahead, Chief Sanders."

"One of my guys has been badly hurt. He's not bleeding right now, but he doesn't look good. He needs evac ASAP."

After a moment, the voice returned. "Confirm, Chief Sanders: You need immediate transport for an injured miner?"

"Yeah, that's right. Soon as you can get here."

"Got it. We'll divert a transport right away."

"Thanks." Clicking off the com, I turned and motioned Ethan towards the door, then stopped as I noticed something for the first time- a hole in the wall between the com station and the corridor. Positioned off to one side, it was easy to miss; curious, I examined it closely. It was round, about twice as wide as my thumb. The sides were fairly smooth, almost like someone had taken a smallish auger to the wall.

"What are you looking at?" Ethan asked from the other side.

I poked a finger through into the corridor and wiggled it. "This wasn't here when we landed, was it?"

"Not that I remember."

When I exited the com station, Ethan started to push back towards the med bay. "Hold up," I said, jerking a thumb the opposite direction. "We're gonna check out the rest of the Jude."

"What – you think there's someone else here?" he squeaked.

"I dunno. What I don't think is that you, me, Xavier, or Rath did that to Chen." I moved forward, bim engaged, not waiting for the kid to follow. "Someone or something else had a hand in it, and I'm not inclined to sit around waiting for it to happen to the rest of us."

Scanning the closed airlock, I saw nothing but racks of suits and equipment. The hose to the mining gel dispenser had come loose and now drifted in erratic curves. Frowning, I replaced it. That stuff would be a right pain if it got out of its canister at the wrong time; once it hardened, it was nigh on impossible to break. Ethan watched me, eyes wide.

Our cabins dotted the next stretch of the corridor. I used my override codes to get in as we checked them one by one, finding nothing unusual. Even Rather's bunk was in fairly good order; we'd all learned from painful experience that anything you leave out of place in zero-G can come back to bite you at the worst time.

Everything had changed; the Jude was no longer the familiar place our crew lived in and worked from. My confusion and imagination twisted it into a realm of fear, where imaginary horrors lurked just around each corner.

The last two hatches at the end – all the way "up" that side of the horseshoe – opened into the cleanser and the conditioner, respectively. Although I wasn't exactly expecting to find anything, my heart still pounded nervously as I thumbed the first switch. The hatch irised open and the lights eased on. The cleanser was empty, nothing out of place.

Sighing, I glided over to the conditioner and opened the door to the perfectly-normal sight of a few simple machines fastened to the walls, surrounding a small centrifugal chamber. Guidelines speced that we were each supposed to spend an hour a day in here. Some of us even did it.

"Okay," I grunted, turning around. "Let's get –"

"Look!" Ethan pointed behind me.

I turned back towards the conditioner just in time to see a sinuous dark-gray line drift sideways out into the middle of the conditioning area. It took me a few seconds to recognize it as the metal rod the drill team had found in the asteroid.

"What is that doing there?" Ethan whispered. He started forward, but I held my arm in front of him. Ignoring his questioning look, I reached just into the conditioner and touched the com switch.

"Xavier."

Xavier's voice crackled in response. "Yeah, Cully?"

"Look in on that piece of xeno metal for me."

"Xeno metal? Oh. Uh, sure. Hold on."

Ethan and I waited there while Xavier went down the corridor to the lab. Call me superstitious, but I left the com open as well as the hatch. A part of me didn't trust that weird… thing… out of my sight. It just hung there, lazily drifting sideways, exactly where it shouldn't be, as Ethan and I kept our eyes on it.

I don't know what we were expecting.

But I do know it's not what we got.

All at once, the metal rod rippled, the pattern on its outside rolling in minute waves from one end to the other, and started moving, deforming and warping. The rod coiled in on itself, then opened up again, writhing in mid-air. One end of it split open into three segments, like the petals of a particularly ugly flower, to reveal what appeared to be several rows of razor-sharp teeth.

Caught off-guard by the weirdness of the whole situation, I didn't even register the fact that said teeth were rapidly approaching my face until it was too late for me to do anything about it. The rod flew towards me, emitting a high-pitched whining noise. Visions of the blood-covered com station flashed before my eyes, which I reflexively shut.

Ethan saved me. Although I had been distracted, the kid had savvied onto what was happening. Somehow he managed to brace himself against the corridor wall, yank me back, and thumb the hatch shut before my head got turned into sausage. I flew backwards and ricocheted painfully off the opposite wall; reflexively I slapped the wall with my bim and commanded it to HOLD before I went flying off anywhere else.

"Thanks," I whispered after a breathless second. I looked at the door. "What is that thing?"

Ethan just shook his head.

"Well. I think I have an idea what happened to Chen–"

I was interrupted by a shrieking sound from the hatch. A sudden bulge bubbled out from the metal door, popping apart to reveal the... worm was the only word that sprang to mind. The creature squirmed through the hole and out into the corridor.

Small jets of vapor puffed out from its body as it oriented itself midair and darted straight towards me again.

Vaguely, I heard Xavier's voice from the com panel in the conditioner. "…out of containment! Some kinda drill or something!"

This time though, I was ready for the varmint. Releasing my hold on the wall, I reached out with my bim and grabbed the worm just behind its head. Through the bim I could feel hundreds of tiny spikes pulsing in a regular pattern against my hand; if I had tried this with my bare skin it could've ripped it to shreds.

The worm wriggled and writhed its way towards my face, trying to get out of my grasp. I hastily commanded the bim to HOLD and felt my implant's extrusions lock into the creature's surface. Its tri-winged mouth opened and closed with disturbingly mechanical regularity as it vainly strained to reach me.

"Dear God," said Ethan, clutching the cross at his neck.

Grimacing, I looked closer at the creature. "Let's get on back."

ଓଃ ଞ

"Holy hell," breathed Xavier. "This… thing… was in my lab!" Wheeling, he grabbed a large clamp and pushed towards me. "Keep it still, Cullen."

"Uh-uh." I held up my other hand. "Don't be hasty. Think about this: a xeno that lives in asteroids and waylays miners? We should probably get this bugger back planet side and let Tri-Star or somebody study it in case there are others out there. Speaking of which, how's it coming, Rath?"

"Almost there." Tongue stuck out; Rather fiddled with his bim. "Just need to patch in the fool proprietary... there we go." The vidscreen in his arm lit up with a feed of the conditioner room. "Looks clean there," he mused, swiping to the next feed, then the next. "Canteen, lock, hold... no sign of any more worms."

"Good." I relaxed just a mite. "Still, until the hopper gets here we're going to camp out in the med bay. We're all getting off this rock with Chen until Tri-Star can guarantee our safety."

"Too right," grumbled Xavier, still glaring at the worm.

"We'll need supplies, though," I continued. "It'll be a while, and Chen's med seals will need to be replaced. We could use some food, too."

Rather looked at me nervously. "Ah, I should probably stay here, right?" His voice trembled. "To keep an eye on things."

Ethan looked up. "I'll go," he said. Xavier muttered something under his breath.

"Okay, kid." I gave him a curious glance. "Portable rations are in the compartment back of the canteen."

He nodded. "I know where."

After he left, I looked over towards Xavier. "The kid's alright," I offered. "Probably saved my life back there."

He shrugged, looking a mite uncomfortable.

"You don't have to be best buds or anything. Just maybe give him a chance." He opened his mouth, then closed it, settling for a curt nod.

"Uh, g-guys?" said Rather, watching the vidscreen. "We got a serious problem."

I glided over to Rath, careful to keep the worm in my grasp and well away from everybody else. Onscreen, Ethan had an arm full of supplies and had just closed a large compartment in the wall of the canteen. Behind him, two – no, three more worms descended, mouths open, idly sweeping back and forth as though they were sniffing the air. Ethan turned around, saw them, and froze. With his free hand he scrabbled madly at the wall behind him but was unable to keep inertia from nosing him nearer to the worms. Breathing rapidly, he shut his eyes and grabbed the plassie cross around his neck.

"Frag me," I breathed. "He's praying." Sure enough, we could all see his lips moving rapidly, his eyes squeezed shut and his knuckles turning white around that fragging cross.

"I don't believe it," muttered Xavier. "Get out of there, boy!"

But Ethan just floated in place, mouth moving silently. Even more incredibly, the worms around him seemed completely oblivious to his presence, moving through the air in a surprisingly regular pattern through the drops of sweat coming off the kid as he drifted.

We were spellbound, waiting for the magic to break and the moment to end. When it finally did, it defied our expectations; the worms abruptly broke their pattern and moved towards the canteen hatch in near-unison, leaving Ethan alone.

"That's... no way!" Xavier said.

I knew how he felt. We had just seen something that defied belief – or bolstered it, depending on your perspective, I guess.

"Uh! Those things are comin' this way!" Rather lurched up, lost control of his momentum, and rebounded awkwardly off the med bay wall.

"Rather, hold up!" I yelled, but the fella was in a blind panic, repeatedly thumbing the hatch door until it opened. Gaining the corridor, he pushed frantically on the wall, heading for the hold as fast as he could.

He never made it. Three dull metallic flashes zipped right by us and chased him down, emitting high-pitched whines... but those three weren't what got him. Instead, as he reached the hold, a literal swarm of the worms erupted from the hatch and fastened themselves around his arm, obliterating skin and bone with those razor-sharp teeth. He screamed as his bim shattered, pieces of the vidscreen exploding into a sparkling cloud.

Swearing, I ducked back inside the med bay. "Grab Chen and move it!" By the time I got back out, I could tell that Rather was finished; the horde of worms plunged in, out, and through him with merciless regularity. I turned to see Ethan helping Xavier steady a thankfully still-unconscious Chen down the corridor, away from the worms.

I had forgotten about the creature I held in my bim until it suddenly vibrated, emitting an audible whine. At once, every worm that was swarming around Rath's body arced around, stopped itself midair with bursts of vapor, and started to whine in response.

"Oh, that's not good," I muttered, pushing myself towards Xavier and Ethan. I caught up with them at the lock, where Xavier was hurriedly trying to secure Chen.

"Figured we could make a last stand here," he said. "Escape into the asteroid if we need to." He didn't meet my eye; he knew as well as I did that we weren't headed into that infernal rock. There was no telling how many more of those things might be out there, waiting.

"Here they come!" cried Ethan. "Oh God save us now!"

"God? Xavier lost it. "You moron! What kind of god could possibly make something like that!?"

He had a point. The swarm had rounded the corner, individual worms stained with Rather's blood. Entrails and bits of organ clung to them, shedding particles of gore, bearing testimony to their horrific work. Tracing a regular geometric

pattern in the air, the worms' routes created a churning cloud that advanced steadily down the corridor towards us.
"God doesn't create evil," Ethan screamed right back.
"People create evil!"
Funny enough, that's when it clicked. Tri-Star. The worms. The holes. The lack of Vahan crystal. Chen.
"He's right!" I yelled.
"What?" Xavier glared at me.
"No, not like that... look!" Opening a gear locker, I grabbed a drill bit and smashed it repeatedly against the worm I held, breaking its head open... to reveal sparks and circuitry instead of alien anatomy.
"What is that?" yelled Ethan.
"That is a 'bot, created to mine Vahan." I said, grimly gesturing at the approaching swarm. "And so are all those."
"What the hell are you talking about?" said Xavier, eyes bloodshot.
"They aren't xenos – they're 'bots!"
Not that it did us any good to figure that out. The 'bots had turned down the lock, just a few feet from us and closing. Their pattern sent them through lockers, suits, and everything else inside the corridor; frags of metal and plassie flew in all directions as they eviscerated our mining equipment.
Snarling, Xavier leaned forward and seized the drill bit from my hand, thrashing back and forth at the metal worms. He managed to smash a couple or three before the bit snagged on a worm, yanking him forward. Hastily I grabbed him and pulled him back, but not before some of the 'bots bored through his hand and arm, spraying us with blood and muscle. His screams clashed with the high-pitched whine of the swarm.

I pushed back against the hatch, tempted to thumb it. Better to die in vacuum then to get ground up to shreds. Xavier huddled in the corner, alternately screaming and sobbing. Ethan held Chen tight. The fraggin' kid was praying again. "God, please deliver us now, in this our hour of need!" he yelled. "Please!"

ଓଃ ଚ୍ଚ

Now. I'm not one to make things up. When it comes to miracles and such, I tend to fall more on the skeptical side of things. But I'll never forget what happened next: While the kid was yelling, one of those cussed worms bored a hole into the pressurized canister that held the mining gel.

Boy howdy, that was a sight.

First, the canister spewed a stream of gel backwards, knocking it loose from the locker it rested in. Then, it started corkscrewing all kinds of direction, shooting gel all over the place. Thing was, for all of its random motions, it couldn't have been aimed better if a sharpshooter was steering it from inside.

First one sweep, then the next, then the next: every time it twisted it blasted another row of worms, violently driving them against the wall, then permanently sticking them there as the gel hardened.

At the same time, the gel managed to completely miss all of us. All I could do was sit there openmouthed, as the canister emptied itself, solidifying every single worm to the walls.

The canister emptied after a few seconds, momentum pushing it on in a silent, twirling dance. I stared at it for a bit, then looked down at Xavier, who looked even more shocked than I did. At the same time, both of us turned to look at Ethan.

His eyes were closed, lips moving in a prayer of thanks.

Soon after, we landed on the third of twelve planets revolving around the star Obsidens II. Purgatorie's perpetual winds blew around the office of the Tri-Star Mining Liaison, streams of fine sand continually threatening to bury any stray traveler.

Inside the office, the Chief Liaison looked like to be buried himself, in a manner of speaking. "I'm sorry, I don't quite understand…" he said, wrinkling his brow.

Xavier pounded his fist on the table, once. "It's simple." He pointed his finger about an inch from the Liaison's impeccably pressed shirt, just below his fancy-pants bow tie. "You pay all our medical expenses. You replace all of Chen's bims. Then, you buy out all of our contracts. Rath didn't have any kinfolk, so you donate his piece to…" he looked sideways.

"…Sisters of Hope Children's Home," Ethan supplied.

"Right, that," said Xavier. He sat back, arms crossed.

The Liaison shook his head. "No. I'm sorry the group of you ran into some sort of… astro-parasite or what have you…" the Liaison carried on, oblivious to Xavier's growl, "…but Tri-Star Mining is clearly not responsible for that sort of hazard." He sniffed. "It's all in your contract."

I put an arm on Xavier's shoulder. "Yeah, we know. We read it." I leaned forward, showing my teeth a bit. "I also read a few other things here recently. Say like, this old publicity piece about your upcoming TS-R mining 'bots." I tossed a printout on his desk. "Look, they've even got an artist's rendition. Funny, it sure looks familiar to me. What about you guys?" Xavier growled louder. Ethan somehow contrived to look both angry and disappointed.

My smile vanished. "That piece is from two years ago. So, I figure the 'bots didn't work out. Maybe some AI issues, maybe they couldn't track your homing beacons, maybe they even had trouble distinguishing Vahan inside a bim from Vahan in the rock. No worries, right? You can just send out a mass shutoff signal, collect them, and wait for your programmers to figure out the bugs. Hey, you can even stow them in the holds because they're all deactivated, huh?

"But then what happens if some of the 'bots don't get the shutoff signal? Or some of them start to reactivate themselves?" I slammed a hand on the desk. "We can tell you what happens because we were there when it did! So, you'll pay off our contracts, and what's more, you'll keep your miners off every single asteroid that might have those fraggin' TS-Rs on it. Because I'm known to a lot of miners, and you'll have the devil's own time getting anyone on your hoppers if I don't get a guarantee that this won't ever happen again!" I was shouting by the time I was done; I guess the memory of how close we came to dying had kind of hit me pretty hard right then.

The Liaison sighed and removed his spectacles, pinching the bridge of his nose. "You know, of course, that you can't prove any of this?"

Xavier smiled his wicked grin. "Well, that depends," he growled. "Did you know that the TS-Rs were all imprinted on the inside? 'Property of Tri-Star Mining', they say. It would be a shame if someone had one tucked away somewhere, maybe with bits of DNA all over it, maybe with a sworn affidavit and all kinds of fun things. Yep, a darn tootin' shame." He stood up. "Not that I'm confessin' to stealing anything, understand. I'm just saying… Well. You should have searched us right when we got off the hopper." He yawned, scratching his belly. "I'll expect that money transfer by tomorrow. You have our account info."

The Liaison put a palm to his own face, sighing even deeper. Ethan leaned over to him and patted his shoulder. "I'll pray for you," he said seriously. Then we walked out the door, leaving the poor man sitting at his desk, dismayed bewilderment all over his face.

⊗   ∽

Outside, we pulled our hats low against the wind. After we rounded the corner, I nudged Xavier. "Did you actually bring one of those things back with you?"

He shook his head. "Do I look stupid? Don't answer that."

We laughed and kept walking. After a minute, Ethan cleared his throat. "So, I'm picking up Chen on the way to the church house tomorrow. You guys want to trail along?"

Xavier sighed. "Look, kid. I know you think that God or whoever was looking out for you up there. But you gotta realize, those things were lookin' for Vahan crystal. The rest of us carry that in our bims, and it leaches out into our bodies, yeah? That's why that first one went for Chen, and that's the only reason they left you alone."

"Hmm," Ethan responded.

"And as far as that thing with the mining gel goes, well, the worms were flying in a regular pattern…" Xavier trailed off. "Anyhow, it's not proof of anything to me."

"Sure," said Ethan. "So do you want to come?"

Xavier sighed theatrically. "Ah, not this time."

The three of us scooted over to make room for a man leading a couple of lumms down the street. I watched them thoughtfully.

"Cully?" said Ethan.

"Maybe," I said. "By the by, have either of you fellas ever thought of taking up ranching?"

THE REGGAE POODLE

By Joseph Valorani

The little blue green creature floated in the air, in front of Captain Jodi Silverboots' face, "Ugh!" She thought with her eyes still closed. "The smell! It must be a Flit! How can something be so cute and smell that bad!" The fart smell increased near her nose as the flit continued to release gas in an effort to wake her.

The flit's little fin like wings moved the flit in a backward motion as it fanned more expulsed gas towards Jodi causing her to cough and swat at the persistent fish looking creature, "I'm awake!"

Her voice got the attention of her tiny dachshund who had just finished licking under her tail who came up and licked Jodi on the lips. "Chubba!" she addressed the dog, "I don't know which is worse, the flit or your breath!" She held the dog in her arms happy to hold her once again.

"Oh! Captain Silverboots, you're awake!" Came a deep voice from across the room. "How are you feeling?"

Jodi began coughing again, now experiencing the full effects of the damage from a caustic atmosphere she had experienced. "Uh! What happened?"

"Well Captain, seems the SexaZxans decided to board your ship. You had a 'discussion' with one called 'UxGnan' who likes to watch humans die slowly in their atmosphere. Your droid 'Too Many,' nice name by the way, sealed your suit while TuTu injected you with an antidote."

"And you are?"

"Oh, I am sorry, I'm Doctor Lorre," he stretched out his hand in salutations.

She took the hands in hers, "Where am I?"

Doctor Lorre chuckled. "Their atmosphere is still affecting you I see. You're on the Hospital ship Nyx. Your droid brought you over. The rest of your pilot ship is off the port bow. We are actually kind of slow right now, so we were able to dock alongside the space barge. Where were you headed?"

She rubbed her head trying to remember, "I was doing a cargo run to Lungecroft, Outpost Eight. Usual stuff, lights, heaters, food, medical. You know how it is, become a freighter captain, see the solar system!" she mocked.

Doctor Lorre rubbed his head, "well, hate to break it to you. The SexaZxans took a hundred containers."

Jodi rolled her eyes, "Well, there goes my bonus. Great, they should change the recruitment posters, see the galaxy, get the crap beat out of you, remain broke." She put the blonde dachshund on the floor as she stood up to get dressed. Jodi started walking across the room anxious to get back on her ship. "Come on Chubba!" she called. Chubba wagged her tail but refused to move.

Jodi walked over and picked her up, "You need a bath!" she announced, "Thanks doc!"

"Don't thank me yet! You haven't seen the bill!" The doctor handed her a piece of paper with instructions on it to finish her recovery.

"Worker's comp I hope!" Jodi commented as she exited the room and began walking down the corridor, she texted her droids to start warming up the engines. Too Many replied he was on the pilot boat and greeted her at the door. She put Chubby down, who walked over to her food dish, planted her rear-end and began to dine. Jodi smiled at Chubba's personality. The bridge was designed for a crew of six, but now that they were replaced with droids, she made it her living quarters as well. Her desire to live on a tropical island had influenced the décor in the bridge with fake palm trees, a viewer that played a moonrise over the ocean, and a hammock strung between support beams so she can relax as the droids did the work. Jodi didn't mind the lack of human companionship, she actually enjoyed.

Jodi set up mood lighting with waves as a background noise as the pilot boat connected with the space barge. Two of the three droids began to scurry around the pilot boat, eventually slaving it to the space barge. As this was going on, Jodi began looking over the manifest of what the SexaZxans took. A planetary year's supply of toilet paper and three thousand fingernail clippers. She read it again chuckling, "Well, it's going to be a crappy year on Lungecroft," she commented to herself. She looked over at her dog, "Maybe they'll learn to lick themselves like you do Chubba!"

She felt the final locks click in and the engines began to push the ship forward. As she began to drift to sleep her cell phone began to ring. 'You have got to be kidding me!' she thought to herself. She put on her best happy voice, "This is Captain Jodi Silverboots of the Reggae Poodle out of planet Seti. How can I help you on this lovely day?"

"Captain Silverboots, this is Ambassador Ali. I have a small shuttle headed towards you. Parliament would like you to transport six passengers and one hundred flits to Lungecroft."

Silverboots rolled her eyes. 'The ship is going to smell like a fart for months. Great. Parliament won't do a thing about the

SexaZxans, but I have to drop everything to transport their friends.' She mustered up a smile to prevent any sarcasm in her voice, "Why, yes. I would love to have the passengers. You do realize this is a freighter and they would have to remain in the crew areas? Also, I do not have provisions for them," she commented, hoping this would discourage them.

"We understand, they are bringing supplies and I understand you like chocolate?"

'Who doesn't?' she thought, "I have been known to enjoy it once in a while."

"They should be at your doorstep in about one hour. Thank you for your service," came the reply followed by a quick disconnect.

Jodi shook her head, 'well, at least he was polite.' She would be seven days late on her delivery. She reasoned it was still a seven-month trip. She looked at TuTu, "can we make up our time to Lungecroft?" The droid plugged into the computer system, beginning a series of calculations. A text came through her phone giving her a solution of using gravity off the sixth planet in the system to increasing their speed sufficiently. Bad thing is it took them too close by SexaZxan territory. She played with the numbers for a minute, since it would put them two days early at their destination, Jodi decided to risk it.

CR   SO

Jodi greeted the six passengers as they came on board all seeming to be couples, to her relief. She wouldn't have to deal with anyone trying to flirt with her. She led them directly to the 'old crew's quarters.' "I am going to have to ask you to remain in this area. The aft of the ship was inspected by the SexaZxans and their atmosphere is still there. It does not affect my droids and until we have finished with the run to Lungecroft, I do not have enough atmosphere to do an exchange." She pointed to her left, "Bunks are over there," she pointed to the right, "Kitchen is over there. You all have to police yourselves. My droids are busy doing maintenance and checking containers to make sure they are safely attached. Per Parliamentary code, no-one is allowed on the bridge. I will be on the bridge the entire time unless you need something." She smiled her disarming smile, even though it was fake, it was well rehearsed. Her big doe eyes and Rastafarian dark hair having a strange effect on the passengers as she spoke. "Who is taking care of the Flits?"

"I am Captain," a large muscular man stepped forward, "Doctor Dustin Meoff."

Jodi chuckled to herself, 'Dust Me Off!' "You will keep them over there in that room. I don't want to smell any of them on my ship!"

"No problem Captain. You do not have any on your ship?"

"No, I do not! Nor do I want one," she replied sharply.

"As you were quoting Parliamentary law, you are aware that you must carry one for every eight hundred cubic feet of human atmosphere because a fart is good for the heart, and it helps to counter the effects of SexaZxan atmosphere," the doctor said matter-of-factly.

"We are done here!" Jodi said dismissing doctor as he began to protest, "If Parliament would get off their collective asses and deal with the SexaZxans appropriately, we wouldn't have the problem and need Flits polluting our atmosphere. My ship will not smell like a fart, and if you do not like it, I will jettison you and your Flits and not shed a tear! I have spoken." Jodi walked off to her bridge, her heart racing from the slight disagreement. She wondered why everyone was out to disturb her calm.

It seemed like an excruciating amount of time before supplies were loaded and Jodi could bring the engines up to full power. She was glad to be underway as she adjusted the course towards the sixth planet Fersia. Fersia had been at war with the SexaZxans for centuries before "Human Intervention" struck a peace with them. SexaZxans found their atmosphere toxic, whereas to humans it acted like a drug along the lines of laughing gas. There was enough oxygen in the atmosphere to support human life for up to a week, then the atmosphere would begin to displace enough oxygen in the blood stream and a human would literally die laughing. Because of this, Fersia was also known as the suicide planet amongst humans who wanted to die peacefully from the atmosphere. Flits had no problems in the atmosphere and even smelled pleasant for a change. As for the Fersians, SexaZxan atmosphere was a very unpleasant way to die, just like humans. Yet Fersians the found the human atmosphere tolerable, but it lacked the sweet smell of their own planet. It wasn't until seventy years had passed that one of their scientists wanted to do a study of long-term effects in human atmosphere which eventually led to the discovery the two types of protein in Fersian blood, enabling one to live in human atmosphere and being able to return, and the other never being able to return after prolonged exposures.

As the ship began to get underway, Jodi looked longingly at the Hammock, but decided to stay awake until the maneuver was complete. However, she did put on her favorite Kimono and slip on her favorite sandals. She sat in the Captain's Chair watching as the droids made their course corrections when a bang at the hatch startled her. She opened it to find one of the male passengers standing there. "What?" she screamed.

He held up a small box, "Parliament, well, the Ambassador wanted to thank you for this favor."

She took the box from him and inside was an assortment of chocolates and a thank you note. She smiled. "Thank you. Sorry. This has been a rough trip."

He looked her over in her Kimono and slippers, he could see the frustration in her eyes, "You look like you're busy, so I will return to the crew quarters."

She offered him one of the chocolates, he accepted. They sat for a few moments and talked over Pina-Colada flavored tea, as the ship started to make its two-day long flight around Fersia. She explained to him that a two-mile-long cargo barge just doesn't turn quickly or accelerate very well. She was dreading the course, but thanks to Parliament, she was now in that situation. She asked what he did for a living which he responded that he was one of the Parliament delegates from Lungecroft. He had been at Parliament because of all the problems they have been having with supplies, the biggest being a total lack of toilet paper. Jodi laughed in response explaining the SexaZxans just took the supply of toilet paper she was bringing.

He shook his head, "Every time I brought it up, the SexaZxan delegates would laugh. It is a joke to them because they are getting away with it! I don't think they wipe their asses, so what do they do with it?" They let the question hang in the air as neither had an answer. Then he suggested, "Like the old High School Prank of toilet papering the house, maybe they toilet paper ships?"

Jodi didn't find it funny as she explained to him they are not even waiting the appropriate amount of time before putting their atmosphere into the ships before boarding, followed by the story of the violence that happened with her and how her suit was ripped. Jodi patted the top of Too Many, "and if it wasn't for my little heroes, we would not be having this conversation."

Too Many made a few noises as he responded with the text, "any time Captain."

"Would you be willing to testify about that in front of Parliament?"

"I would."

Satisfied with their conversation he excused himself, thanked her for the tea and returned to his quarters.

Left alone, Jodie watched the spinning atmosphere of Fersia as they passed by. She thought of the little romance she had there while on vacation. "Well, the bonus is gone from this trip. Maybe next time," she said to herself.

As the ship exited Fersia's gravity, she checked the hatch to make sure it was locked, then laid down in the hammock for a long nap with her faithful dog Chubby on her lap.

ଔ ຄଠ

Two began a check going down the service corridor that was still full of the SexaZxan atmosphere when the attack came. The energy beam came through the seven-cargo container high port side hitting the poor droid cutting him in half. The space barge was so massive that attack was not felt as the containers broke apart. Some containers had their own oxygen supply which began causing fires to break out.

It was Too Many that realized the ship was moving eight degrees off course from the damage caused by the energy weapon. He began to make course corrections, but the ship did not respond. He alerted Captain Jodi Silverboots and Tutu of the situation when the droid realized they had lost communication with Two.

TuTu began moving down the corridor looking for the cause, alerting Captain Silverboots and Too Many there was a bend in the ship halfway down the corridor.

Jodi took to the command chair opening up the view screen, adjusting it so she could see the aft part of the ship. As the screen switched to the aft view, Jodi could see several small ships headed towards the Reggae Poodle and the barge in tow. In pursuit was a Fersian Cruiser firing projectiles at the smaller ships. They hit one which crashed into the space barge severing it in half.

Jodi picked up the intercom, "Attention all passengers. This is an emergency. The ship has sustained severe damage. Everyone to the bridge immediately!" Jodi began to separate the pilot ship from the space barge, the entire time worried she would have to smell Flits flitting around the bridge.

The Flits came in first followed by the six passengers. Jodi could see the fuel exploding working its way up the main corridor dispersing cargo containers randomly into the void of space, as the two droids worked to sever the connections.

One of the attacking ships hit one of the cargo containers but the others kept firing. Several had broken off their attacks turning their attention toward the Fersian ship. Some of the projectiles from the Fersian ship began to hit cargo containers and the rear of the barge, with debris hitting the pilot ship's engines.

Jodi saw TuTu become fully engulfed in an explosion before he could make it back into the pilot ship. Her heart sank as she realized she had lost two of her droids that she has spent so many years with. "Too Many, sever the last connections!"

As the pilot ships remaining thrusters fired up, Jodi began to look for the emergency booster platform to get her to the nearest planet. As she was looking, her nose began to burn from the large amount of Flits near her in the enclosed area. Evidently, Flits become more gaseous when nervous. Finally, with tears in her eyes cause by Flit Farts, she moved the pilot ship forward when they felt a sudden stop in forward movement. She began to scan three hundred and sixty degrees around the pilot ship when Too Many piped up that it was coming from underneath. She switched viewers to see the largest SexaZxan ship she had ever seen. Jodi only had one suit. She put Chubba into her environment containment chamber then moved the passengers into three other environment containment chambers, each only designed for one person in the event of a SexaZxan "Investigation," or a hull breech. Each of the humans brought as many Flits in with them as they could into the chambers.

    The SexaZxan atmosphere began to flood the bridge without any warning. Jodi put on her suit as quickly as possible but enough of the atmosphere made it into the suit to cause suitable harm. She held her breath hoping to purge it at the last moment, but it was too late. She began to cough. Too Many came over and finished zipping up her suit as she sunk to the floor. Too Many stuck her with a needle in the buttocks, she didn't know if she should be thankful or offended. Too Many then took a hose and connected it to a small canister. She felt the air aerosolized with Flit farts enter the suit. She was still coughing when UxGnan entered the bridge.

    UxGnan was about five foot five, excluding the thick tail. Like all SexaZxans, he had six appendages, two short ones in the middle, the other four were arm like with six fingered hands. Jodi felt all three of his right arms pick her up. "Hmm…Jodi Silverboots," he said in his language as the cell phones in the room automatically started translating. He looked over the girl in the suit seeing her convulse and foam at the mouth. He laughed seeing the damage his atmosphere was causing and discarded the body thinking she would not live much longer. He walked over to the environment beds, stepping on piles of dying Flits. "So, Ambassador, too bad you're in there. It would have been so much more fun to watch your reaction as you watch your wife die. So, instead, you get to watch all these other criminals die first," he sneered.

The Ambassador hit record on his phone as UxGnan walked over to the first environment containment chamber. UxGnan began to state in a loud voice, "For crimes committed against the SexaZxan race, you will be sentenced to death." He opened the first tube letting the SexaZxan atmosphere slowly kill the Flits and the two people inside. UxGnan laughed watching them gasp for breath, their bodies twitching from hypoxia as the atmosphere dissolved their lungs.

To the Ambassador's horror, he could see UxGnan enjoying every moment of the "execution." UxGnan moved to the next tube cracking it open to watch its occupants slowly die trying to prolong their suffering. As they began coughing he was joined by several SexaZxans. They began pointing and making, what could only be assumed as rude comments, as they watched the humans slowly die.

Soon, the room was full of SexaZxans, some tripping over Captain Jodi Silverboots, as they started to play with the ambassador. UxGnan reached into the tube putting an oxygen mask on the Ambassador as other SexaZxans pulled the Ambassador's wife out of the tube. One SexaZxan squeezed her neck tightly hoping to keep the toxic atmosphere from entering her body when he heard her neck snap. He sneered in disappointment tossing her dead body aside. "Seems you humans are a bit more fragile than you appear. Look at the tears in your eyes. What? Are you going to…" he paused as if trying to find the right words, then finished with a sneer on his face, "Miss her?"

It was then when another SexaZxan enter the room. In their grumbled tongue he told UxGnan that the Fersians had several ships on the way. UxGnan laughed. "Ambassador, eventually you'll run out of oxygen. Too bad I can't enjoy the event with you." He then turned and left with the remaining SexaZxans.

ॐ ॐ

It was with much haste that Too Many moved. He grabbed Chubba and shoved her in the suit with Jodi and two Flits. He gave the suit another aerosol treatment and injected Jodi and Chubba with another antidote dose.

Too Many then switched his attention to the ambassador's wife. He put a lung resuscitator on her. He moved over to the Ambassador's environmental containment chamber. He injected a treatment in the chamber. With a quick analysis of the other chambers, he realized the other four humans and the Flits with them were unsalvageable. Too Many turned around, with a quick look, the lung resuscitator was functioning, she had good chest rise but no heartbeat. He attached a heart pacemaker to her.

The Ambassador removed his oxygen mask, with a hand on the chamber screamed at the droid, "she's gone. Let her go." He knew her neck was broken, even if she survived she would not have a good quality of life. He fell to the floor of the chamber. Too Many turned his attention to Jodi and Chubba as the battle waged on outside the drifting pilot ship.

After making sure he had done all he could for Jodi and Chubba, Too Many piloted the pilot ship away from the battle while purging the SexaZxan's atmosphere.

※ ☙

Almost a year had passed and Jodi was wheeled out in her wheelchair before Parliament. She was still on a lung resuscitator still while they grew her new lungs. Chubba was on her lap with a lung resuscitator also. She spoke out using a laptop, "the SexaZxans attack your supply ships. You do nothing!" the words rang out while she typed them with one hand. Frustration hitting her as she was finding it difficult to find the words that use to come so easy to her. "The SexaZxans kill and you do nothing. The SexaZxans attacked violently destroying ships, killing crews and political officials, and still you do nothing. How many Fresians died, and still, nothing. They almost killed my dog, almost killed me. Yet you do nothing. What are we supposed to do while we wait for you to do nothing?"

The SexaZxan delegation stood up, "She lies. Human Lies! And you wonder why we cannot trust them."

This was followed by the Fersians delegation, "She doesn't lie. We lost ships, we lost soldiers. The twelve planets know the SexaZxans did this! As for the Fersians we will no-longer tolerate it!" One of the Fersian Ambassadors pulled out a projectile weapon. He unleashed the wrath of the weapon on the SexaZxans with extreme prejudice leaving the SexaZxans nothing but a large pile of mush. He walked out of Parliament with disgust.

Jodi left quickly after.

※ ☙

Over the next year, she received new lungs, along with Chubba. She learned to walk with her dog by her side. She did not know of the revolution she had started, or the war being waged in the skies above, till the Fersian Ambassador approached her. "We fight for you!" he offered. "You have become the face of the revolution, of the war. Will you come fight with us?"

A Darrius Knightman Mystery: Murder Across a Sea of Stardust

Jorge E. Ortiz Marti

An unresponsive body has been discovered aboard the S.S. Starliner Nouvellia, on its long-lasting voyage to the farming planet of Ocrux V. Crewman Nichols, a short pale man with enough to worry about on his own plate, assists Darrius Knightman to the dreary scene, jogging down the passageways of the luxury starship post haste. Darrius, being the only Valthorian Security Bureau Agent onboard, has earned the task of bringing peace to the luxury starliner through the desolate Argelon Ring Cluster in outer space.

"Mr. Nichols, what can you tell me about the scene?" Darrius asked. He paced his breathing while making needed time during this urgency.

"There are guards posted at the room where they found the body, sir. Not much else happening. They won't even let us get close to it. And we dare not interfere with them for our own safety!" Nichols argued with anxiety in his voice on this incessant hallowed evening upon discovering said travesty.

"Have you identified the body, at least? I need to know who collapsed at this late hour of the night!"

"Not yet, sir. As I said before, the guards posted at the room won't let anyone inside to get a fix on the situation."

"I see. Do we know who the guards are associated with?"

"I believe high-ranking ACCESS Regime soldiers passing as security forces. They boarded the Starliner this morning, along with a General Ezekiel Hawker and another man, a Regulon Archveil. The General's guards discovered the body; they were the ones who called the emergency."

Just my luck, Darrius thought. Of all the 12 planets in the Monarch System, why did I have to find a forsaken Astrocratic Central Confederate Enclave of Star Systems (ACCESS) General and the billionaire magnate of the Technomachian Mercantile, here together?!

That can't be a good sign or a coincidence either!

He knew all too well those two men attributed to the mass murder of a few thousand men, women and children. One of the many atrocities they committed during the uprising rebellion on the twin planets of Mirros Ari and Mirros Uron. Both mining colonies that supply the Monarch Galaxy with the minerals necessary for faster than light space travel.

He carried on through the passageways of the ship like a madman on the hunt for his prey.

All the while, lingering in his waking mind, the facts remained:

The civil upheaval continues to this day, making these two individuals a pair of contributors of war crimes in this time of armistice and peace.

"Do we know if any medical personnel arrived at the scene to assess the situation?"

"That's just it, sir. We have no medical personnel aboard the S.S. Nouvellia. Only a holographic physician is registered in the Medical Bay. We would've taken the body there, but the soldiers won't permit us entry into the room. I wonder why they won't allow us the courtesy of aiding them?"

"I'm sure they have their reasons for not letting anyone inside, though they are a military presence travelling on a civilian Zeus-Class Starcruiser. They'll likely follow their S.S.P.P.s emergency situations such as this one."

"S.S.P.P.s, sir?", Crewman Nichols noted, while the buzzing sounds of the alarms going cornered every step of their trek.

"Strategic Standard Procedure Protocols, Nichols. The ACCESS will ensure any information on this matter never leaks to the public, especially around your precious luxury Starliner."

"No one should have any authority on board except us, sir. Unfortunately, Captain Korsair's hands are tied on this matter and suggested you handle the situation as delicately as possible."

"I'm aware the situation doesn't bode well for your people or your commodore for that matter. It can't be helped. It was bound to happen sooner or later when ACCESS are involved", Darrius shrewdly proclaimed, huffing and puffing from all the running. The alarms and hustle and bustle of the evening's ordeal didn't help his already tiresome state.

"Is it true what they say about you lot, Mr. Knightman?", Crewman Nichols perused his companion, his inquisitiveness surmounting, heading to their destination. Darrius raised his eyebrow curiously, looking back at his companion.

"How you Valthorian Security Bureau Agents are keepers of peace and stability, armed with ancient Neophian Technology at your disposal, granting superpowers beyond imagining and the like? If, so, then do you actually follow the regime's authority in such matters?"

"It's true we have 'access' to powers beyond imagining as you say and we are a peacekeeping force throughout the galaxy, sir. The Neophians were beings who previously inhabited the Monarch Galaxy. They were the ones who left the technology that enables us these superior ultimate feats. We few Members of the Valthorian Security Bureau are not in league with the ACCESS regime. We work solely for the inhabitants of our fair system, without cost or consequence. Even with power at our disposal, it is ultimately up to all of us to use that which has been left by our predecessors as responsibly as possible."

"I see. I thought as much. Though, I am still in a state of weariness. Mr. Knightman, have you ever encountered a situation like this one before?" Crewman Nichols questioned, out of breath from all the running.

Darrius took his time to answer, pacing himself to reach the body's whereabouts.

"I've dabbled on a few cases with veteran agents."

Although, this matter won't be any different, I'm sure.

Crewman Nichols' worries were dashed after being regaled of such manner.

Yet, the Valthorian Security Agent lied to his current company about such experienced earned.

This would be his first foray facing a case solo.

Darrius yearned to be a Prime Investigator from an early age. His love of detective stories fascinated him to no end. Deducing the plots made from others' fiendish ventures, distinguishing the truth between multiple suspects and following the clues to the utmost resolution to the many crimes he found to be the epitome of crime fiction. This made wanting to become a Prime Investigator all the more appealing to him. He joined the Peacekeeping Force for the sake of experiencing the endless, stellar frontier worlds of Monarch. To him, this was the opportunity he'd been waiting for to turn his dream into reality.

"This way, sir. The body is inside the premises, but as you can see..." Nichols said, pointing toward the room with the guards on watch, at least the few that were still conscious.

A rather large man in front of the men in uniform stood in furious frenzy mode. The hard-boiled bruiser was kicking and screaming like a wanton madman on a mission. All the while, playing the pointing-fingers-blame game at two of his men, both injured from the looks of it.

Of course, Darrius thought to himself again in spite, the ACCESS General is here, too. Just Perfect. I'm sure he's a barrel of laughs! May have to steer clear of this guy. Looks like he's in quite the frenzy.

Darrius grudgingly bemoaned the thought of crossing paths with this man. For him, this was a taxing ordeal not up for debate. He knew how dangerous ACCESS officials were if none of their schemes went their way.

Hmm, There's someone absent. Could it be the unresponsive body is that of the other gentlemen, Regulon Archveil? Darrius deduced. Opting to ponder a theory he hoped wasn't true. And could he be...?

He dismissed the notion, parting briefly with the thought. Putting it into the recesses of his mind for the time being.

The General, fury bound to no end, further confirmed his suspicions. The ACCESS Official ended his tirade, exhausted from blowing hot air at this point. He left in the opposite direction with a mess of soldiers behind him, like lost sheep herding to safety.

"Nichols, where does that hallway lead to? The one where the big brute just left towards?" Darrius questioned curiously, fidgeting with his glasses as he spoke, while pointing to the large hallway beyond where they stood..

"It is a nearby elevator chamber. It leads to the bridge, sir. Only VIP's and other high-ranking officials are permitted to use it for their convenience!" Nichols confirmed for him, nodding in said direction

"Good, then our raging General just left for the day, along with his goon squad."

"Maybe to speak with the Captain? He could be going up there to follow up on his so-called 'Standard Protocols' you mentioned before, Mr. Knightman!"

"Hopefully, that is his reason for his visit to the bridge. In any case, the guards standing guard should permit us to assess this predicament, and hopefully solve it once and all."

"I hope you're correct, sir. For both our sakes."

The two men walked toward the room nonchalantly, without a care in the world.

"No one is permitted at this point. Neither crew nor civilian currently. This is official ACCESS business. Please step away at once. Move along!" one of the guards said. His nameplate read 'Sgt. Kalinsky', he was bloodied and somewhat injured from the looks of it.

Both men stopped dead in their tracks by both guards.

Now, this could be a problem.

"What happened here, soldier?" Darrius pressed. His inquisitiveness running the usual gamut of questioning.

"Nothing to worry about, sir. This is official ACCESS business. None may enter!" Sgt. Kalinsky recited, regurgitating the usual military spiel.

"And what about you, soldier, the one next to Sgt. Kalinsky here?" Darrius asked, pointing at his face.

"No comment, sir. Please move along from the area. Official ACCESS business. Nothing to see here!" the soldier replied, who's nameplate read 'Private Serviceman Howell', firmly corroborating his partner's response.

The soldier, with a limping leg, sternly strutted back and forth across the room along the doorway.

"Mr. Knightman, I believe these gentlemen will not permit us entry at this time!" Nichols rigidly said.

"Obviously. At the very least, answer me this, soldier: Is there a VIP guest unconscious in that room?" Darrius interrogated the soldiers.

None uttered a word yet nodded in accord to his question.

"Have you examined the body?" Darrius urged rigorously, pressing on his curiosity and intrigue for the truth.

The soldiers stood silent and stopped moving about. A grim outlook strengthened Darrius' theory now.

For goodness sake! If no one goes in... Darrius told himself.

Time to take matters into my own...

He pushed past the soldiers, unexpectedly, making a clean break for the room to reveal the tragedy within.

The VIP Suite itself, an utter mess from the inside: Objects on the floor broken or busted up, with blood spatter adorning the walls and floors of the once graceful and luxurious palisade. Regulon Archveil's body lay there, his frail body cold turkey and lifeless. Darrius saw his eyes still open, pained from the horrifying end he met at the hands of his maker.

For such a decrepit old man, no one would've guessed that he was a tyrannical old fart. Darrius dropped to his knees to examine the body. He pressed two of his fingers to the man's chicken-ringed neck. No pulse. The Valthorian Security Agent felt aghast with fright, morbidity at the scene ensued. He closed his eyes and opened them once more; he knew what to do next.

"Mr. Nichols, please inform the Captain that Regulon Archveil is dead, immediately! Get some men here to take the body to the Medical Bay, now." Darrius rose to his stead and looked on at the entrance.

"This room is now a crime scene. No one enters or leaves the premises, that includes these soldiers, the ACCESS General, and anyone else who had any contact with the deceased!" Darrius had gone full-blown official business mode and wouldn't relent until the mystery of this man's death was solved.

With a flick of his wristband, a holo-menu opened up. Pressing a holographic button, Nichols called the Captain and some men to arrive at their location for the pick-up of the body. Darrius scanned the room with his wristband, picking up different things that felt out of the ordinary. Among those were: an empty file box cabinet, trails of blood that led towards another location entirely, Archveil, not showing any visible wound, save for a small needle-like puncture near his heart region, more blood spatter around the body, and finally a small toy figurine covered in blood, and a photo of a young woman, clutched in the hands of the deceased.

Moments later, a few of the crewmates arrived, cautiously picking up the body and taking it to the Med Bay for autopsy. Darrius slowly picked up and packaged the items he found, placing them inside a small black bag given to him by the crewmates that arrived, along with a sample of blood found at the scene. After the tool analyzed the data, Darrius neatly pieced together all the details of what might have transpired there. He stepped out of the room where the soldiers had stood, now gone after Darrius forced his way in without permission, to seek out their superior for an update. He analyzed an unnoticed blood trail that sped off toward another location of the ship. He opened a holographic map of the vessel on his wristband and slowly followed the video graphic of the blood on-screen.

"Nichols, what's this room, here on my holo-map?" Darrius pointed at the holo-image buzzing and bleeping in mid-air.

"Right here, sir?"

Nichols pointed to the same gap area on the holo-screen image.

"That would be the engine room, sir." Nichols answered.

Darrius scrambled from the crime scene to follow the holo-map to its location.

Suddenly, the ship came to an abrupt halt. Darrius' body flung stiffly forward with the pull of gravity decelerating to a crawl, stalling the vessel in anchoring fashion.

The ship stopped. Why now, of all times? Darrius thought. Could this be related to the murder as well?

He hurried back to Nichols. At the scene of the crime, they exchanged perplexed looks, while more alarms hollered beyond the VIP Suite floor, arriving at the same conclusion.

"The ship's anchor activated, Nichols. The ship is stopping in the thick of outer space. This is no mere imaginative concoction." Darrius deduced; the flickering of lights and flashes glowering among the distress didn't muster much assuage of the vessel and its supposed trained crew.

"Let me find out why we stopped." Nichols reacted rather squeamishly, sorting through the holo-menu for answers without reprieve.

Looks like the bloody trail ends cold there in the engine room, Darrius pondered some more, seeking the answers aimlessly in the dark.

No other blood traces were picked up by my scanners, aside from the one found in the room and outside of the suite. This won't be of much use unless we're able to identify whose blood it is redecorating the entire lower deck of this place; not until we gather and compare the samples back at Med Bay!

"Mr. Nichols, has the body reached Med Bay yet?" Darrius asked his compatriot, making his way inside the VIP suite.

"Yes. The crew sequestered the body through the service elevators quietly, as to not arouse any of the night's chaos to the other passengers, lest they be informed of such dreadful ire!"

"And what of the starliner dead in its tracks?"

"According to engineering, they've encountered a problem in need of manual actometry. Seems the ship's gravitonium brakes locked in at the last second. We may know more at the bridge if we hurry, sir!"

"That's good, Nichols. Excellent work! Time to present our findings to Captain Korsair in full detail, pronto!" Darrius addressed.

He and the crewmate soldiered on the first lift platform available to reach the bridge, while the ship languished in a proverbial standstill of its own making.

The lift platform sped up tremendously, reaching the vessel's bridge at record pace. In case of emergencies, the crew had control of its settings to safeguard their duties at a much quicker pace. The doors open revealing the room to be much large but compact enough for eight to ten people to manage. Captain Korsair stood by the security monitors, waiting for Darrius' arrival. The alarm system had been turned off by that point, giving Darrius some reprieve from the massive headache incurred in part of its distressing hollering.

"Captain, Mr. Knightman is here, as requested!" Nichols informed him.

"Thank you, Crewman. To your station, on the double!" the Captain ordered, without a moment's waste.

Nichols followed the skipper's orders, routing back to his seat to follow the ship's condition in the engine room.

"Am I glad to see your stick in the mud face here! Thanks again for coming. Normally, I'd handle the problems beset on my watch, however things have quickly spiraled out my control," Captain Korsair said, shaking Darrius' hand.

The Captain, a younger man in his twenty's, is tall, dark skin toned and heavily muscular underneath his white gold strung uniform. With dreadlocks for hair, he carried an exotic look to his conjecture, topping it off with a nautical hat placed on his shoulder hold for safe keeping.

"It's been quite a long time, how many years has it been, Keon?" Darrius asked, firmly shaking his hand, referring the Captain by his first name.

"Since college? Around five years or so. Anyhow, I appreciate you handling this matter, hush-hush. I didn't know who else to turn to. Figured you could help me out. We're the best luxury Starliner in the Galaxy. If word of this matter gets out, our credibility is gone!"

"I understand. I might be able to help you keep your credibility intact, old friend. I managed to get inside the victim's suite and found the unresponsive body. It turns out Regulon Archveil died some time ago."

"Makes sense. Saw those soldiers scurrying about back to their superior in a mess, limping and all."

"Guess, reporting to their superior was worth getting chewed out now rather than later."

"Looks like he's coming over to give you his opinion on the matter. Hopefully he doesn't hit your ego, too much, Darrius!" Captain Korsair said. Darrius braced himself, unprepared to handle an ACCESS General yet having no choice in the matter now.

General Hawker paused his rambling tirade to focus his animosity at a different target.

"YOU!", the General pointed his finger at Darrius, incredulous at the situation now. "Who in the Hellken's name are you and why in blazes are you here? No one gave you any permission to enter that room without my authority. You have no jurisdiction on this corner of the Galaxy. This is a private ACCESS military matter–" General Hawker demanded swiftly of the Valthorian Agent.

"–General Hawker, control yourself sir. Captain Korsair has asked Mr. Knightman, a Valthorian Security Agent, to investigate the events of tonight's unpleasantness" a crewmate intervened, one who was repairing a CYGOR Robot Unit, before it got ugly.

"It's alright, my good man. If the General thinks my expertise on this ship is invaluable–" Darrius stood up for himself.

The General responded in kind, with a pompous posture of strength, despite the intimidating show of force.

"–You're absolutely right, Lawman. No one here wants you or your opinion on this matter. I demand your removal from the bridge, at once!"

"General Hawker, Mr. Knightman stays. He's my guest and here to assist us. I suggest you wise up and let us handle this predicament on our own!" Captain Korsair pressed on the ACCESS Officer. General Hawker didn't budge, infuriated to no end by the Captain's intervention.

"You Valthorian Security screw-ups! A bunch of charlatans acting like cops is what you represent. You morons managed to make our lives a living Hellken when you let the Scylla Syndicate get away after that mess on Planet Alcyone." General Hawker confirmed. Darrius scoffed at such triviality with ease.

"I was never a part of that operation, General–" Darrius defended.

"–That's ACCESS General Hawker, to you, ValSec rookie. Because of you fools letting those gangsters escape that raid you interrupted, they've been cut loose on Caduceus Prime! I won't let you interfere here, too. Got that?"

"By my estimates, it wasn't our mistake that led to that conclusion, General. It was YOUR faulty information that led them to escape! The Valthorian Security Bureau couldn't confirm their whereabouts, as I recall."

"Oh, really? Kid, do you have any idea who I am and what I represent?"

"Yes, a lot of steam and hot air by my account!"

"Keep cracking jokes, Lawman. ACCESS Government will soon take over the entirety of the Monarch Galaxy."

"That's what you say, General. However, your little struggle against the rebellion on the twin colonies has had no bearing on your contingent warmongering. You've killed more people in this war than anyone else. Keeping casualties to a minimum was your department, if I'm not mistaken," Darrius called on his grandstanding.

The General shirked his stance, taken aback while grumbling petulantly as the conversation carried onward.

"Yes, I know all about the great General Hawker. I studied your tactics back at the Academy on Galaterra. You're just a bully who doesn't even comprehend the gravity of their own folly. Sooner or later, Valthorian Security Forces will take the fight to your doorstep and when that time comes–"

"–You'll do what, Lawman, play around with your badges and use your ancient Neophian weapons against us? You don't have the guts to pull that off. All you do is save people like a bunch of superheroes but, you're just as weak as the rest of this Galaxy." The General cajoled from his grandstanding now, bellowing heaves of pompous air into his own prideful lack of vision. "It needs a strong arm to guide into the future and you ValSec fools don't have what it takes to command life and death in your hands!"

"ENOUGH! I will not have authority figures fighting over who's the better man here. We get it, General. You don't like Valthorian Security Agents on your pretentious behind, but I can vouch for Agent Knightman. He can help solve this matter if you'll allow him the courtesy," Captain Korsair stated.

"Courtesy... COURTESY?! YOU IMBECILES! Allow him to do what? These two half-wit escorts for soldiers let our greatest benefactor's killer run loose on this ship! You think I care that some no name, rookie cop from Galaterra can find this killer? I want full authority on this matter now!" General Hawker rambled, his temper getting the better of him, in front of the Captain.

"Cool your jets, General."

"NO, you cool your jets, Captain! My people have a right to know what happens on this vessel."

"No, you don't General! STOP THIS NOW! This is my ship. I'm THE authority here; not you or your precious Regime. What I say on my command goes. And I say, Mr. Knightman stays to sort out YOUR mess. Do I make myself clear? Or do I have to escort you and your men back to your quarters, confining you for the rest of this voyage?" Captain Korsair argued, his temper exceeding his nonchalant, professional behavior.

"The Captain is right, General. The fact remains we have a serious problem on our hands and you're making things worse than they already are," Darrius reminded the General, disdain and annoyance blinding him to the truth at hand.

"HRRGH, CURSE YOU ALL TO HELLKEN, FOOLS! DAMN IT ALL!" General Hawker grumbled unintelligible words, cursing them under his breath.

The Captain retired to his ready room, a planning area on the bridge for charting and other ventures, while everyone waited for any news regarding Archveil's body. Darrius followed him, as did the General, hoping to get on the skipper's good side. The Captain sat in his chair at the end of a large rectangular table, littered with charts and maps, and a giant holo-screen in the middle. He slumped his exhausted soul on the weathered rocker, shamed by the night's events.

"My apologies for going off like that, old friend. It's been one of those nights, you know!" Captain Korsair explained while Darrius nodded in accord, what with General Hawker acting like he owns the place.

To make matters worse the ship is dead on arrival. It hadn't moved since they found the body, not even a slight crawl to its name. He took a seat next to the table, not knowing what to say or do.

"I can't believe this is happening," Captain Korsair said, his anxiety and despair creeping steadily into his voice.

"Don't be too hard on yourself, Keon. There's nothing we can do now but wait. I'm sure the Med Bay holo-physician will have an answer for us soon," Darrius reminded him, hoping he didn't fixate himself on the ordeals that plagued his commissioned quarry.

"That's not what worries me. Not only has a murder occurred on my watch, but two of Hawker's men were injured on my ship, while the other contingent of soldiers perished investigating the engine room explosion once the body was discovered. He should be more than grateful that some of his security survived, while the ship is still intact," Captain Korsair commented, which made Darrius unaware of such details in the matter.

"The engine room exploded?! Nichols never mentioned anything of the sort," Darrius reacted at the news.

"It didn't. The engine room is intact for the moment. When The engines went, the Pyronix crystals were destroyed, along with the engine fuel cells. Usually, Pyronix is a non-volatile component for the engine fuel cells to generate Hyperidium for the ship. However, when you add Zetrinium ore to the mix, well, you have this result."

"Serves you idiots right for keeping something as unstable as raw Zetrinium onboard. And you're the best Starliner in the Galaxy? What a joke! You can't afford the good stuff, so you spring yourself on the cheap!" General Hawker adding fuel to the literal fire.

"That's quite enough of that, General. You made your point. Please have some courtesy for our commanding officer!" Crewman Nichols defended, bringing his report back to the Captain.

Darrius ignored the General's outburst for the time being, while Captain Korsair continued to explain matters.

"We keep Zetrinium as a back-up in case we run out of Pyronix. The ore gets synthesized through the processing unit, and it transforms into Hyperidium energy. A good substitute but extremely volatile if not handled with care. In this case, according to Nichols' report, they found a piece of raw Zetrinium ore inside the engines, which may have caused the explosion to–" the Captain continued.

The General interrupted in a beguiling manner.

"–My men had nothing to do with that! They know better than to fidget with your machinery!" General Hawker interrupted again.

"I'd say you're right, General, what with them doing their job by following the supposed culprit to the engine room. But that isn't what worries me. It's what we received after that that has me quite disturbed with this business altogether." Captain Korsair glanced at the table.

"What do you mean, Captain?" Darrius questioned, pressing further for the truth to come to light.

"Around the time of Regulon Archveil's death, the fuel cells exploded. After the alarms went off, the crew in the communications office intercepted a message coming from inside the ship, that should have been broadcast throughout the P.A. System. Instead, they sent the message to the bridge to simulate it being broadcast throughout the ship. The recording is quite disturbing, even for my wild behavior. I wanted for you, Agent Knightman. I want to hear your thoughts on the matter. I'll play the message now!" Captain Korsair told Darrius, opening up a holographic menu in front of everyone and pressing play to listen in on the contents of the message.

"Attention, passengers and crew of the S.S. Starliner Nouvellia. I have ended the wretched life of Regulon Archveil, CEO of Veiltek Inc. The man has now accounted for his past sins and dealings with criminal organizations and warmongering entities. He created discord during our time of peace here in the Monarch Galaxy, by initiating a civil war, leaving many other citizens in a state of starvation and ultimately, death. Even now, Archveil continues to instigate harm by allowing 'other' guilty parties to walk free among the populace. I implore you to find this accomplice, presently on your esteemed passenger list, and bring him or her to the rightful authorities. As you are aware, the Starliner's engines have crippled your vessel, along with your tracking beacon. No ship will come to your aid at this crucial moment in time. You have been left marooned near a collapsing star and soon will be swallowed up by its gravitational forces, sending you all into oblivion. I beseech the Lawman travelling on your expressway to apprehend this 'other' guilty party, in the name of Justice and Peace. It is in your best interest to do so. You have less than 24 hours before you are swallowed up whole by the maelstrom just outside your reigns. That is all."

"Captain, the recording is correct. The tracking beacon's been damaged. It'll take at least three to four hours before we can fix it. On top of that, we're right in the middle of the Argelon Ring Cluster with a collapsing star just outside our purview. If we don't start those engines soon, the ship will be locked onto its gravitational pull!" Crewman Nichols informed. His face contorting with fear and despair, along with those in the room.

Whoever sent this message is also responsible for marooning us, too! Darrius thought, deciphering the meaning behind the voice's message.

There's no denying the facts. The Killer is among us!

"I'm putting two and two together and the timing matches with that of our current situation. This killer is being mighty gutsy for outing himself along with this accomplice to Archveil!" the Captain suggested. He pieced together what Darrius found and what they've shared with everyone so far.

"Yet, I highly doubt this voice, this supposed killer, would end up in our same predicament. Those last few words he said about us being swallowed up. The voice didn't include itself. Which means, the killer is not onboard the ship!" Darrius argued said conclusion. Skeptical in hindsight though, to the dismay of others, the theory was sound.

"That's preposterous, Lawman. The Captain said so himself, the message came from inside the ship. There's no way someone can send a message out here in the middle of nowhere. This area is a dead zone."

"No, but someone might be able to relay a message at the opportune moment and transmit across the ship."

"Darrius, are you suggesting that whoever transmitted the message is doing this from outside the ship's range? That can't be. We're in the middle of the Argelon Ring Cluster; there's no way to transmit this far off. Nothing but space rocks out there. Unless they're–" The Captain concluded.

"–Yes, they're transmitting from within the ring cluster, or closely to it. Masking their message signature, appearing as if they're onboard at all times."

"That still doesn't explain how two of my top men, who stayed behind, still got dropped by the killer," the General suggested, implying the obvious assumption by the onset of the voyage.

"That will be addressed in due time, as for the matter about the ship's engines–" "–Look, Darrius. I admit that using non-sanctioned fuel was an error on my part, but you must understand. I owe the head honchos of the Spacefarer's Guild a lot of money for this Starcruiser. I busted my sorry behind to raise enough funding, making ends meet to pay them back and buy off this rust bucket from them. Turns out the ship remodel would have cost me a ton. I pleaded with the head honchos of the Guild to take the ship off their hands, and they loaned me the money for it. Two years later, this is the top-of-the-line Starliner in the Galaxy. This next trip meets the last voyage of yours truly. Once I'm done with this trip to Ocrux V, I pay off the debt and my IOU's to them are done. I get to do whatever I want with the ship, that includes keeping her flying or selling it to the highest bidder. I had to start using some basic fuel and cut costs or else I wouldn't be able to even be in this situation.

Believe me, my reputation is shot if any of this mess gets out to the public!"

"I'm not here to judge you or your lack of decision-making, old friend. Heaven knows what you had to go through to become the man you are now. Nevertheless, we need to see this through to the end."

"With that said, I'm heading to Med Bay to examine the body. It might clear up a few things; questions that need answering the most. It might give us an objective view as to how Regulon Archveil died, and how it connects this matter with our present predicament. Inform me of any updates about the engine room. The safety of your passengers is at the utmost importance for you at this time." Darrius proclaimed.

"I understand." Captain Korsair rose from his chair, tidying himself up to officially speak to his crew.

The Captain left the ready room to attend the bridge, while Darrius fidgeted with his scanner. He examined the clues closely, searching for any discrepancies that may have escaped him while examining the crime scene, yet his thoughts went back to the photo held by the victim. He scanned his internal Valthorian Database and cross-referenced with any known sources for the woman in the picture.

"I spoke to my crew. They'll have the ship ready to fly by morning. Just make sure you find the culprit!" Captain Korsair told him, a few moments later, while Darrius reviewed his findings.

"Here's hoping for more than luck with my investigation than anything else. Mr. Nichols, please join me at the Med Bay. I will require your assistance in this matter. You don't mind, do you, Captain?" Darrius asked.

"By all means, he's the best man on my ship."

Yes, and he might have been the one to sabotage the ship, Darrius thought. In fact, half of these ACCESS soldiers, along with General Hawker, Captain Korsair and some of the engineers might be in on this matter. But, who among them would gain more from ending the life of Regulon Archveil and stranding everyone in the middle of the Argelon Ring Cluster; for what reason would there be for this situation to occur? I must be wary of everyone here, especially those troublesome ACCESS soldiers. Who knows what they're capable of at this point in the investigation? The ongoing civil unrest on the twin planets of Mirros Ari and Mirros Uron is also a disputable topic of contention in this murder; an excellent catalyst for such an endeavor of its caliber. The Voice in the P.A. system acknowledged as much. What else could the old magnate been hiding? That picture of the young woman still haunts me. Who is she and would she be involved in all of this? And what is the deal with the toy figurine found on the deceased's body? So many questions and yet few answers factor into this case even more. I just hope and pray I find the manner the old man perished; that is what concerns me the most!

The Valthorian Agent pondered this theory, being the only person with the means to solve such an intricate deceit of web and lies.

Not only was his friend the Captain lying to him about using unauthorized materials on his ship, but the fact that the crew and the ACCESS passengers have a lot more to hide, worried Darrius even more so than his pleasant evening on this luxury, upscale ride.

"Very well, Mr. Nichols. Firstly, we'll need to examine Archveil's body immediately and determine the cause of death; that way we can at least figure out a timeline between the attack and how an accomplice would fit into this predicament!" Darrius proclaimed.

"Where do you think you're headed off to, Lawman?" the General demanded, blocking his path to the elevator platform.

"I'm going to Archveil's room; is there a problem that I can address for you at this time, General, if not I must be on my way–" Darrius answered.

"You're not authorized to see that body; Archveil himself is littered with sensitive military secrets not privy to public eyes, Lawman! I should be the one to be there in case anything of value is uncovered!" General Hawker demanded.

His alcohol-fueled breath brushing down on Darrius face, smelling the tenuous spirits emanating from his person like leprosy on skin.

Seems the General had been drinking earlier in the evening; his angering complexion tarnishing his reputation even further.

"I admire your initiative, General. I wish all you ACCESS men and women in uniform would be so forward and open with your dispositions. However, I need to examine the body myself thoroughly to determine the cause of death. I believe it would be best if you would wait for my investigation to be over before you muddy your hands all over this mess of yours and contaminate the crime scene even further than it already is." Darrius reminded the General, still in his drunken stupor.

"You didn't hear a word I said, Lawman: You are NOT allowed to go into that sick room. I won't allow you to pick apart our asset to your liking!"

"General, it's in your best interest to let Mr. Knightman do his job." Captain Korsair ordered. He pushed him aside allowing Darrius and Nichols to proceed to the elevator lift, reaching Regulon Archveil's final humble abode.

The elevator opened its doors to a wide hallway with circular windows passing by to the end of the corridor. A large, gated doorway revealed the Medical Bay area with four large empty beds, a small cryo-morgue area on a wall near them and at the center, a medical table base used for complicated healthcare procedures.

A holographic model of a woman materialized next to them when they entered the bewildered medical hall. Interesting, a tall brunette, slender and very young for her age; a fitting visage of youth and care beyond that of a typical female in the Galaxy." Darrius commented, examining the life-like features on the holographic figure.

"Greetings, passengers. I am Dr. Celia Sana, your holographic physician/healthcare provider. I am fluent in all languages possible in the Monarch Galaxy as well as knowing all types of conditions, diseases and treatments suited to your needs. How may I be of service to you, today?" the holographic physician said. The 3-D model heartily welcomed them.

"Intriguing. I've heard of these life-like holographic models before but never seen one. Galaterra mostly has beautiful woman, but she is quite the looker. She could be as real as anyone here. I wonder if there is someone like her there?" Darrius said surprised.

Crewman Nichols laughed.

"Mr. Knightman, Dr. Sana is a real person, though she is no longer with us. We've checked the information of her systems. Her model is based on a beautiful actress and singer of the 20th century back from Planet Earth in the Solar System. Naturally, she was created to ease in the patients that come through her halls."

"I can't fathom the beauty that she portends. Alas, we're here on business. Shame, had she been real, I would've asked her out for a common drink."

Darrius approached the table in the center. Dr. Sana materialized there for convenience sake. "Hello, how can I be of service, Mr. Knightman?"

"Dr. Sana, I would like to see the body of Regulon Archveil. He was transferred here a few hours ago," Darrius ordered.

"Yes, Mr. Knightman. You have been granted full access to this deceased passenger. My condolences for his untimely demise."

"Agreed. We can only hope that this man is in a better place. Assuming that the body has been exhumed, have you found any abnormalities that can ascertain his death?"

"Yes." Dr. Sana exclaimed.

The medical table turned into a large rotating holographic image of Regulon Archveil's body. It scanned the body from when it arrived using 3-D imagery to explain its process.

"After a thorough medical autopsy of his body, I have assessed small traces of various substances lingering within his heart chambers, including semi-large shards of a metal casing as well. They have attempted to exit throughout his body but to no avail."

The holographic image expanded, showing the large, fragmented objects passing through the body, attempting to meld with the host body to no avail.

"His heart gave way soon after one of these substances was absorbed within his heart muscles. A small needle-like puncture can be seen traversing through the right atrium. It rotted his entire circulatory system, flooding it with a metallic mineral that can only be known as Tyrantallum!" the holographic physician explained.

"Tyrantallum? Isn't that deadly to our bodies, Mr. Knightman?" Nichols said.

Darrius studied his expression, making sure Nichols would be ruled out as a suspect. His reaction to the news was natural, honest to a fault.

"Yes. An unusual mineral to be found in the body, specifically it is found on the twin planets." Darrius commented.

"So, the murderer did have a grudge against him for the civil war erupting in the twin colonies." Nichols remarked.

"Or it was injected in his body to make it look like that way. I suspected as much. And assuming we can identify the other substances in his body at the time, those would logically be Nyrihil and Alcohol mixed in. Nyrihil being the counteragent to Tyrantallum, and Alcohol because he was drinking in his room. There was a bottle of Cognac there. General Hawker was half-drunk, and his breath fumigated the room with Cognac."

"The General might have killed him."

Darrius disagreed with the crewmate's observation.

"No, it would be too obvious and convenient for the murderer to be him. This feels like a larger scheme altogether. There are too many variables to consider and contend with at this time."

The holographic doctor closed out the imagery and asked, "How can I be of service?" Dr. Sana redacted, repeating her prerogative again.

"I would like to examine the body now, if you will, please?" Darrius asked Dr. Sana.

The holographic physician acknowledged, and the body was transported from the cryo-morgue unit near their them directly to the center table. The center table opened up with an assortment of instruments and medical equipment at their disposal, among them plastic surgical gloves. After placing the gloves on, Darrius carefully examined the body, with Nichols assisting. He reached the area where the needle-like puncture was made and cross-referenced with his scanner what they already knew.

"This puncture was not done with a normal syringe. I doubt anyone else on the ship had access to these instruments, but better be safe than sorry."

"Mr. Nichols, who else has access to this Med Bay besides the crew and the Captain?" Darrius demanded.

"Everyone, sir. The room is accessed when passengers or crew are injured. The Med Bay is open to anyone but only the holographic doctor is able to dispense any and all materials to our guests, should their needs be met at the time of visit." Nichols remarked.

"Could anyone have access to surgical equipment?"

"The Captain and the Quartermaster are the only ones who can override any materials given. Our Quartermaster did not make it this trip. The Captain took over those duties and only assigns one of us in case of emergencies."

"Any materials missing at this time?"

"I checked the logs as soon as we took Mr. Archveil's body to the Med Bay. Nothing has gone missing in our storeroom."

Darrius pondered the facts further. He continued to observe the wound carefully.

"The puncture is very hollow, not very distinct and unseen by the naked eye. It was a surgical and precise motion when the needle-like appendage entered his heart. To that degree, only a skilled physician could have made this wound aesthetically as possible. Unless…" Darrius reacted.

He recalled his thoughts on the bridge, remembering something else. "Nichols, at the bridge, I saw one of the crewmates repairing a CYGOR Robot Unit. What happened to it?"

"The Andromecha Unit was found near Archveil's suite. It was not functioning, so we brought it to the bridge to jolt it back online. Why do you ask?"

"It's just a thought; I wonder if it could be possible..." Darrius pondered, still thinking of the events that occurred throughout the evening.

Nichol's holo-band sirens blared alarming the whole room; its deafening sound made Darrius jump back to reality.

"Yes, come in, this is Nichols."

"Nichols, Captain Korsair wants you and Mr. Knightman to return to the bridge at once. We have another pressing matter..." the comms on the scanner reported.

Darrius heard and scanned the rest of the body, taking his findings back to the bridge; Nichols following suit.

Darrius and Nichols returned to the bridge, now at an uproar again, adding a new wrinkle to the already mountain of problems plaguing the ship. Aside from the crewmates still working on the CYGOR Unit, Darrius' gaze caught sight of a woman in her late twenties sitting at the far corner of the planning room. Her complexion, solemn with sadness and grief, crying shamelessly without thought or care for her own peace of mind, foretold a tragedy unfurled earlier this evening.

"Captain, what's going on?" Darrius questioned, his mind still reeling from the Med Bay's discoveries.

"Another complication has come to our doorstep, so to speak. One of the passengers has gone missing from their quarters. One Jacen Lightbourne, an eleven-year-old boy from the looks of it. His mother, Sarah Lightbourne, sitting across from us, reached out to one of crew members about the disappearance. My men have searched all over the ship to no avail. Between the engine problems and the murder victim, on top of the ACCESS soldiers hampering our efforts, we're shorthanded as it is; this might be up your alley as well, so I'm asking for another favor!" Captain Korsair proclaimed, hopping his friend was not out of courtesy at this point.

Darrius looked over to the woman in her frail state of mind. His memory shifted into that of the picture he found.

Wait, this woman, Darrius thought to himself, recalling far back a few hours ago to when he remembered this woman and her young child. I've seen her before. I think we've even met. But I saw her earlier today as well, but where?

Yes, I do remember her, from the elevator to go to my room, Darrius recanting his thoughts again, pinpointing the exact moment when they met. The boy was with her as well. He was awfully curious about my belt and who I was…Let me see…

"I noticed you like my belt. It has all sorts of things, though some are dangerous; others not quite so much, and some are just like…" Darrius told him closely as his hands revealed bluish energy forming the shape of a toy figurine, materializing in the palm of his right hand, on the spot. "…Magic!" The boy was floored with excitement, while Darrius gave him the figurine.

"Mommy, look, he knows magic, I told you. He's some kind of wizard, or maybe you're a spy, or even better, a superhero, like my favorite holo-comix superhero and space fighter, Spark Guardius!" the boy commented frantically to his mother, showing her the toy and now annoyed that he bothered a total stranger to boot.

"I apologize for my boy's behavior. It has been quite some time since he's had any interaction with other children or excitement for that matter. He seems to like you a lot. He hasn't stopped pestering me since he saw you walk into the ship's lobby." The boy's mother explained.

"I don't mind the attention. Being in uniform has that sort of effect on everyone I meet, even schoolboys."

"Is that what you are, mister, a Secret Agent? That's sounds intergalacticool." The boy asked of Darrius, thrilled by the discovery.

"I'm what you call a Vathorian Security Bureau Agent! We protect the Galaxy from all manner of things and evil doers. I just graduated from the academy in Galaterra and am heading back home to Ocrux V. Might I ask where you both are berthing from?" Darrius proclaimed, while trying to learn more about the duo in tow.

"We're originally from Ionica. We're headed for Ocrux V, to be farmers. Mommy says we can find work out there and then we can meet Daddy there as well–", the boy's mother, interjected.

"–Jacen, hush now, we shouldn't be bothering the nice young man. He has far better things to think of than us poor citizens looking for a new place to go home to. That's why we want to go to Ocrux V."

"Oh, madam, I'm sorry. It's no trouble at all and believe me, just wanting to make some conversation since the lift has been rather slow."

"I beg your pardon sir. I should introduce myself and my boy, I'm Sarah Lightbourne and this here is…"

"I'm Jacen Lightbourne, and I love outer space, but nothing beats anything like meeting a real-life superhero Mr. Valsec Agent."

"It's Knightman, Darrius Knightman, at your service, should you need any help!" Darrius assured them.

The lift made a sudden dead stop and opened its protective glass coverings, letting the boy and his mother out.

"Well, I hope we get to see each other again, Mr. Knightman and thank you for the toy figurine!" Jacen told him waving back as he left the platform, jumping with joy.

"Yes, Agent Knightman, I appreciate the kind gesture, but we must be on our way now. Have a pleasant evening!" Sarah told him.

"Both of you as well!" Darrius told them as he key logged the floor where his room was located and headed there to relax before departing.

"Yes, Sarah Lightbourne and her son, Jacen. I gave him the toy figurine. The same one found in Archveil's room. The picture...It's her. It all makes sense now!" Darrius said.

His eyes now fixed on the woman crying her heart out for her missing offspring. He turned to Nichols.

"Mr. Nichols, how long until the crewmates repair the CYGOR Unit?" Darrius asked

"It shouldn't be much longer now, why?" Nichols replied, perplexed.

"Take the unit back to the Med Bay. I need you to assess something for me."

After explaining in detail what he had to do, Nichols took the robot unit and the blood samples back to the Med Bay for analysis. Instead of interrogating the woman, Darrius spoke to the Captain in private, in his chambers. Captain Korsair's room was small with no visible decorations to be had, yet he had a window to view outside the premises of his Starcruiser.

The collapsing star visually stunning in brilliance marked their very deathbed in which they stood. The Captain ignored it and held steadfast that his crew would come through for him at the last possible moment.

"So, what's so urgent that you need to speak to me in private?" Captain Korsair asked, his gaze fixed on Darrius and his shifty nature.

"I need an update on the engine room and the boy's disappearance. Also, where are the ACCESS soldiers along with our favorite military General?" Darrius demanded of his friend.

"Like I said an hour ago, the engines will be fixed by morning. We're still on schedule. General Hawker and his men returned to their quarters, with armed guards, apparently. As for the boy…"

"Did you find him? I gave Nichols the means on how to do it while he goes to the Med Bay to assess more clues on the matter at hand."

"Yes, my men found him inside the vents on the first floor. They used the scanner frequency you gave Nichols. Apparently, he crawled all the way there. Said he saw bits and pieces of what took place inside Archveil's room and mentioned something about the CYGOR Unit being there at the time, as well. He's heading back up here to be reunited with his mother. Why do you ask?"

"Keon, I may have solved this mystery, and everything related to what happened here in the first place. I need you to take everyone involved to the lobby, immediately; that includes General Hawker, his two subordinates, along with the boy."

"Wait, why? You think the kid killed the old man?"

"I'm not sure yet, that's why I sent Nichols ahead to examine the body again. I have a working theory, but it won't pan out unless you do exactly as I've asked."

"Listen, I've known you a long time, and I know when you're reaching and when you're right and I'm looking at you right now; you're reaching!"

"Not true, Keon. This will all make sense, I promise."

"And what about the boy's mother?"

"Bring her as well, however I prefer the boy be in your custody if this gets messy." "Darrius, you're not suggesting…"

"…God no, man. I'm not a savage, but I think this woman, Sarah Lightbourne, is not who she says she is. She's hiding the truth and the key to all of this is Regulon Archveil himself."

"All right, I'll contact my men to get to the lobby before they get here, and to bring the rest of the people involved in this mess. Are you sure this woman has something to do with this matter? With everything, I mean?"

"Trust me, she'll spill the beans when I get her to sing!"

Darrius left the Captain's room, ready to end this, once and for all.

A few moments later, Captain Korsair gathered the suspects, leading them to the lobby of the Starliner. Darrius arrived from the elevator on a whim and a prayer, hoping what he discovered would resolve itself during this crucial moment of acrimonious revelation. Nichols arrived soon after him. And now, the case would be solved.

"Thank you for meeting me at such short notice, everyone. After conducting my investigation inside the room of the deceased Regulon Archveil, while cross referencing every single detail, I can ascertain for a fact that the killer and accomplice are one in the same. Yet, they are also, not!" Darrius explained.

"What's that supposed to mean, Lawman? What are you getting at?" General Hawker barked.

"Since, you've been quite outspoken all evening, General, let's start with you!" Darrius smirked; his gaze fixed entirely on the General.

"What in blazes are you rambling on about, you rookie? I have nothing to hide—"

"—Oh, but you do, General. In fact, you're meeting at Ocrux V with Regulon Archveil compels you to be involved in this mess."

"...Okay. I'm game. What was I going to do there, Lawman?"

"For starters, let's talk about that top-secret file box Archveil had in his room. What are those files for?"

"I'm not at liberty to say..." General Hawker said.

"General, please sir, it's time to come clean. Just this once!" Sgt Kalinsky said; his voice timbered with regret as the words left his body wholeheartedly.

"I'll have you court-martialed for speaking out of term, Sergeant!" the General threatened.

"It doesn't matter, General. The truth will come out eventually, when the ACCESS realize that Archveil died on your watch. Your entire career will be in question and the one to answer for all of this, will be you. The time for you to purge yourself is at hand. I ask you again, what are the files that Archveil had on him?" Darrius continued with his questioning.

With pressure mounting, the General sat down in one of the chairs at the bar, located next to the elevators and took a glass of cognac that was on the table, pouring himself a drink.

"FINE! You want the truth? Here's the truth! The files Archveil was carrying, are for a top-secret weapon to fight against the coming uprising. There, happy now?"

"So, the plans were those files, assuming you were going to Ocrux V to build such a weapon. The planet is full of farming communities; the perfect cover to place such a project. Which means, Archveil was going there to negotiate how much the ACCESS would pay for such a thing to build." Darrius argued.

"You're wrong, son!" General Hawker revealed. Darrius looked at him quizzically, waiting for his response. "Archveil wanted to go to Ocrux V not just for business but to save his daughter's life. He found out that someone had threatened her life, so he demanded a trade: the plans of his secret weapon project for his daughter's safety. But, as things are now, that wasn't the case. In truth, Archveil was dying and only his daughter would have become heir to his vast fortune. Well, her and her son."

The room felt aghast as they all gazed at the single mother and her son. Darrius fidgeted with his glasses, walking slowly toward the young mother and her ward.

"Which brings us to you two, Miss Lightbourne and young Jacen Lightbourne. I'm Darrius Knightman, the Valthorian Security Agent. You and I met yesterday on the elevators; we both hopped on to reach our rooms, if you recall," Darrius reminded the single mother.

She raised her head, sobbing still; tears rolling down from her eyes, meeting Darrius' when she spoke timidly, in a weak, meek voice,

"Yes, I do, Mr. Knightman. My boy, Jacen, went missing and I didn't know where he was. One minute he's with me and the next he's gone!"

"Well, I'm sure you're happy to be reunited with him. The crew found his whereabouts on the first floor."

"Thank heavens! I thought I'd lost him forever; he's the only thing I have now!"

"Interesting that you would say that because I was under the impression that you were to meet his Father, your husband, on Ocrux V"

"Yes, but..."

"Intriguingly enough, my scanners found a picture of a young woman bearing your resemblance in the hands of Mr. Regulon Archveil. Using my scanner tool, I cross-referenced the photo with your recent identification card, and you are an exact match with the picture! Let me show you!"

With the push of a button, a holographic screen appeared in mid-air showing both likenesses of the woman in question.

"I don't look anything like her. She's too young! You must be mistaking me for someone else!" she told Darrius, in front of their esteemed audience.

"Yes, except I cross referenced the picture with a more recent one and it matches the timeline in which this young woman in the picture disappeared. It's you, my dear. No question about it. Might as well come clean now, Mrs. Sarah Lightbourne or should I call you, Selene Archveil!"

Sarah began to laugh instead of cry, cackles assaulted the ready room, even scaring her boy, Jacen.

"My, my. You really are quite the detective, Mr. Knightman. I guess the jig is up. Yes, I am Selene Archveil. Tell me, when did you figure it out?"

"I didn't. It came to me when I saw the picture and our conversation in the elevator just happened to justify your likeness. I scanned the picture and began to search information about the woman and that's when I found out that Archveil had a daughter; one that had disappeared for a decade, before reappearing today, and with a child in tow. You were going to Ocrux V to kill your father, weren't you, so you did it before we even berthed there!"

"No, I had no part in his death! You have to believe me. Yes, I am on my way to Ocrux V but not to kill my father but to stop him from trying to save my life, but in the end, he died. The man had it coming. He was a bad man, to be honest, but rest assured I never killed him. He was to meet my late husband, Rossieu Lightbourne, the Voice in the P.A. System, or so he would think. He died helping my father until he was betrayed by him, so you won't be able to contact him in any way. The transmission came from me. I was to collect the weapon plans to give to the rebellion, putting them on equal footing against the ACCESS Regime. That was the deal. I guess my father wanted to do the right thing in the end."

"So, the Voice in the P.A. System came from you, inside the ship? This is all starting to make sense now!" Darrius proclaimed.

"Still, it doesn't explain how Archveil died or how the engines exploded," Keon questioned inquisitively.

"I'll come to that in a minute, but before we can clarify the rest of this ordeal, Jacen, you were in the room when Archveil, your grandfather, was still alive, correct?" Darrius acknowledged. He returned the toy to the young boy.

He smiled and answered politely.

"Yeah, Mr. Knightman. He tried talking to me and wanted to know more about me. That's when someone knocked on his door. He hid me inside one of the small vents and gave me this weird, little square-looking device, he traded my toy for it. He told me to give it to Mom in case I never saw him again."

"Exactly, which brings us to the actuality of his death. We know that Archveil had shady dealings with not just ACCESS military or the Miners of Mirros Ari and Mirros Uron. He also had ties to the Scylla Syndicate. The voice in the P.A. System, a.k.a. Rossieu Lightbourne, confirmed as much."

Darrius turned off his scanner and walked to the middle of the lobby readying to resolve this case.

"As to how our victim died, Archveil knew too much for his own good: secrets of his company and that of the ACCESS military. As with any good asset, ACCESS assured their secrets would die with him if any other entity would get ahold of them, so they implanted a Tyrantallum capsule in his heart, in case he ever threatened or close was to revealing their dirty laundry, so to speak. And he was, last night, when he had no alternative and activated the capsule to end his life, but not before the CYGOR Unit came to its rescue."

Darrius pointed at the robotic unit, fully repaired and wavering about an assortment of gadgets, including a needle that resembled the puncture wound on the body.

"Yes, this little Andromecha Unit tried in vain to save the old fart by injecting Nyrihil to save his life, but by then it was too late. The real murderer, the one who was inside the room threatening Archveil and seeking those files, was attacked by the CYGOR Unit which was deactivated at the last second by the same person. He led a trail of blood to the engine room where, to make sure he could get the files that were missing, sabotaged the ship, leaving us stranded in the middle of nowhere to lead to our deaths. The other soldiers were given orders to investigate the engine room that led to their deaths." He looked at the General but instead turned his gaze to his remaining men.

"General Hawker never gave that order; someone close to him did. Per Mr. Nichols' valued assistance, he and the onboard holographic physician, Dr. Celia Sana, have analyzed the blood samples that were found in both Archveil's room and the trail leading to the engine room. The only person injured here was Private Serviceman Colton Howell. Sgt. Maxwell Kalinsky was unconscious during the attack. Which means the 'other' guilty party and member to the Scylla Syndicate is Colton Howell!" Darrius concluded.

The others shot their gaze back at the only injured soldier, whose blood seeped through his injuries now.

The jig was up. Howell knew it. He homed in on Sarah and the boy, and thrust at them without mercy, taking them hostage, injured and all. Sarah and her son were frightened and surprised. Howell took a pistol from his jacket and shot Sgt. Kalinsky. The injury was not lethal though, it did put him out of commission again though. "What the Hellken you doing, Howell?" General Hawker yelled, while erratically finishing his drink.

Howell shot the bottle of cognac. It spilled all over the General.

"That's enough out of you, ACCESS fool. As for you, wench: give me the files or I'll blast you to smithereens. And don't think you're off the hook, Valthorian Security punk. I knew you were bad news from the start. Should've killed you when I had the chance, but had to settle for marooning the ship, instead."

Darrius stood defiant against the immediate threat. Sarah had no choice, while still being a captive, along with her son. She gave the device to Howell,

"Indeed, in your current state, you can't do a single thing. The ship is halted from your little stunt and the escape pods won't work unless the bridge activates them. There's no way out of this mess. It's over, Howell!"

"Oh yeah? Think again. Once I get those files and take my leave with these hostages, Don Zegario will make me his right-hand man and with that weapon, Scylla Syndicate will take over ACCESS HQ and rule the Monarch Galaxy instead. How's that grab you, ValSec pig?"

"Nothing surprises me in the slightest from scum like you!" Darrius replied, pressing on his badge.

He turned to Jacen.

"Jacen, buddy, remember how the magic affected you? Use it now!" Jacen understood and threw the toy figurine to the ground.

It shattered instantly, causing a flash in the entire lobby, blinding Howell long enough for Nichols to reach both hostages and jettisoning them to safety.

Darrius transformed his body into an armor-like form, becoming more superhero than mere actual human, with the help of his Valthorian Security Badge. He glowed ominously at his enemy, showing no mercy to the threat at hand. He lunged at Howell, attacking him at a speed no human is able to detect.

Howell shot back at Darrius; the blaster's fire didn't even scratch a surface on our hero's armored persona. The ValSec Agent stepped forward and took the blaster from the villain's hands. The weapon's hinges broke into pieces, disintegrating instantly. Howell backed away, knowing he had no way of winning, but instead ran toward a nearby airlock. He pried it open and threw a bomb inside it.

"Everyone, get away from the lobby now!" Darrius warned the room.

The blast opened a hole that sucked out everything in its path. The ship's alarm system sounded off. The entire ship woke up from its blaring horns. Darrius had no choice; the suction pulled the people around its peripheral area with the force of a hurricane. General Hawker gripped tightly to Kalinsky who was up the staircase, holding on for dear life. Darrius saw his prey and went straight to Howell. The Scylla Syndicate crone reached for the files; reached for Sarah and the boy, while still holding on for his very life.

"Give up those files, or else you'll know what it's like to live in outer space!" Howell demanded angrily, with Jacen in his clutches.

"In your dreams, old fart!" Jacen said, pushing him back with all his might, and getting in Darrius' path. He pushed Howell through the airlock, sending him into the collapsing star, oblivion and all. Darrius used his powers to create an invisible wall around the gaping orifice.

"This is Captain Keon Korsair. Activate protocol Singular Echo Annex Luna!" Keon order through his wristband to bring out the shutters and close off the hole.

Mechanical panels swarmed the lobby, engulfing the room in a blanket of darkness, while the shutter lights blinked on. The threat was done with and the case solved, at last. Now Jacen could admire Darrius in all his heroic glory.

A few hours later, the ship was repaired, escaping the collapsing star and shuttled back on its voyage to Ocrux V, making it on time; all thanks to the efforts of the S.S. Nouvellia Crew.

Once they arrived on the farming planet, ACCESS soldiers boarded the ship, took Archveil's belongings and departed back to Caduceus Prime. General Hawker, along with an injured Sgt. Kalinsky, departed to make amends for their part in the upcoming rebellion, forging a new path to end the uprising peacefully, though no absolution ever came of it.

Sarah Lightbourne, renounced her name of Archveil, decided to help those affected by her father and sold the company in pieces in order to live with her son on the farming planet; free of any detriment her father's past upheld in the process. They visited Jacen's father, at his grave, every day.

Captain Keon Korsair decided to retire the S.S. Nouvellia from a luxury liner and turn it into a mercenary ship, seeing as though the tourism part wasn't really his thing and adventure was the name of the game.

As for Darrius Knightman, he arrived on Ocrux V to visit his family and report the incident on the Starliner to his superiors. For his accomplishment in solving Archveil's murder, Darrius was given the new title of Prime Investigator 1st Rank and a new post on the farming planet. Content with his new standing among the Valthorian Security Bureau, he relishes in the thought of his next adventure only for it to drop on his lap, literally.

Another case arrived; another mystery to solve, one about a young upriser rebel from the twin planet colonies who managed to unfurl ancient Neophian technology at her beck and call, summoning a golem of energy to fight back against her oppressors; a case he would tackle and report another time altogether.

A Darrius Knightman Mystery: Murder Across a Sea of Stardust

Mustangs

Art Lasky

"I can't believe they left me alone," said Lieutenant Jennifer Duffy.

"Well, you did draw the short straw, and you're not alone; you've got me."

"Sparky, don't take this the wrong way, but you're just the AI Omni-crew unit, so I am alone."

"Hey, I've got feelings, you know. You named me Sparky, we chat, we kid around. I even know most of your secrets."

"Alright, sorry. I'm not alone; we are alone. "Mustang Five" you, me, and our IS-287 Interceptor are on our lonesome. They expect us to protect an entire 12-planet system. Ha!"

Duff shook her head in a show of disgust, belayed by the set of her jaw and the confident smile.

"Hey Duff, we've got a visitor," said Sparky.

"Thanks, Sparky. Where?"

"They're in sector J320 North. About an hour out, if they maintain their current rate and course. I'll put it up on the screen, magnification thirty."

"Hmmm, we can't get much detail at this range, it doesn't look natural. Could it just be junk?"

"No, Duff, Its trajectory is all wrong and it's accelerating. It's got to be under power."

"Maybe it's Josh returning early from his scouting mission. He could be putting out a false image. You know how he likes to yank my chain."

"I don't think so, Duff; there's no telemetry at all. Even he's not that reckless."

"Okay, we'd better investigate. Plot an intercept course."

"Shall I try to hail them?

"No, Sparky, hold off on that until we're closer. You'd best give the Aldane mining colony a heads up, though."

◌ ◌

"Shoot! Son of a Bi–"

"Sparky! You know how I feel about cursing."

"Duff, it's a Trang cruiser."

"Damn! Son of a Bi– uhm, Sonofagun! Time to earn our pay; open up a comm-channel."

"Unidentified vessel, this is Lieutenant Jennifer Duff, commander of Mustang Five, the Aldane Defensive Service. You have entered a restricted zone, under the control of Terran Central Command. You are ordered to immediately withdraw from this planetary system."

"I am Battle Commander Third Rank (untranslatable) of the Trang Fifth fleet. I am sure you have identified my vessel. You must also know why we are here. I have no reason to comply." Though filtered thru the translator unit, there was still an alien quality to the voice.

"I am in a generous mood," Duff replied. "I will give you one last chance to withdraw, before we are forced to destroy you."

Sparky, spoke off Comm, "Uhm, Duff you do know we're over-matched and alone out here don't you?"

"No wonder you're such a poor poker player, my digital friend."

"I believe that your threat is what you humans call a bluff. Your one-man interceptor is no match for my cruiser," said the Trang.

"If you think I'm alone, keep on coming. You'll find out the hard way," said Duff, trying to keep the quaver out of her voice.

"I am inclined to take my chances. Mustang, is that not a Terran animal?"

The Trang liked to talk, a trait they shared with humankind. Most space-faring species used communication purely to transmit critical information. The translator somehow managed to convey the enemy's arrogance along with his words.

Duff cut the radio, and whispered musingly,

"he's an arrogant piece of work, isn't he?"

"The Trang Commonwealth had a lot to be arrogant about. They'd decimated Nebula Fleet and driven us entirely out of the Procyon quadrant," Sparky replied.

"Thanks for reminding me, Mister Glass-is-half-empty. Is there anything else that you'd like to depress me with?"

"Well, they've occupied three Terran systems, and brutally put down a rebellion on Centuri-5. Also–"

"My question was rhetorical!" Duff interrupted Sparky. "Don't bother reminding me that our resources are stretched thin; which explained why, we're here alone. Just a single Interceptor left to defend the entire Aldane system.

Duff keyed the radio and spoke to the Trang commander. "Yeah, Mustangs are like your Narfbeasts, only stronger, smarter, and better looking. Kind of like me and you, slag face."

The translator returned a sound that might have been a laugh.

"My computer informs me that Mustang is an Earth animal. A horse; a beast of burden." The laugh sound again, "very appropriate for your future position as a slave of the Trang Empire."

Duff cut the comm, and spoke, "Ready weapons, Sparky; we're going in."

She slammed Mustang Five into a high-v sprint toward the bigger, more powerful enemy. Sparky fired their full complement of anti-matter missiles, just before Duff veered off sharply. Mustang Five shuddered as disruptor beams raked her stem to stern.

"Duff, we've lost our long-range communication array, the pulse cannon targeting is out, there's minimal engine damage, and shielding is down to seventy-eight percent. We didn't even scratch the cruiser."

"Well, let's see if we can't buy some time for the colony. Take us out of the system, for now. I think it's time for plan-B."

"I don't have a plan-B in my data pool."

"That's because, I haven't thought of it yet."

"Duff, you'd better think fast, the Trang are coming about."

"Okay, how about this for starters? We're going to be the hare, and hope the Trang decides to be the hound. Can you speed up?"

"We're moving out at full speed, Duff."

"Give me a little more, red line it! We can't let them get in range."

"Roger, that."

"Thanks, Sparky. Now let's start the plan. Give me a course to Selene IV."

"Are we going to hide behind it?"

"I don't know, I'm still working out the rest of the plan. At the least it will draw the Trang away from Aldane."

Duff keyed in her acceptance of Sparky's plot, and Mustang Five altered course toward the fourth Aldane moon.

Getting back on the comm, Duff spoke to the enemy, "Mustangs are not beasts of burden, they are wild and free."

"Free to run away," taunted the Trang commander.

Duff raced toward the distant satellite. The Trang pursued and within half an hour, was drawing into weapons range.

"They are too damn close. That drive damage is limiting our options. Is long-range comm still out."

"Yes."

"So, what do you think, Sparky?"

"Given the parameters of our mission and how well I know you, I've figured out what the rest of plan-B is. We have no choice."

Without further conversation, Duff dove straight toward the moon's surface; its gravity boosting her speed. Using the moon as a sling, she whipped Mustang Five around the far side and emerged at an unsustainable and self-destructive velocity. With what little control she had left, Duff guided her doomed craft toward the enemy.

The Trang cruiser didn't have time to avoid the collision. Its defensive fire managed to turn Mustang Five into a spectacular fireball, which nonetheless slammed into it, inflicting crippling damage.

The Trang cruiser drifted helplessly, it would take hours, perhaps days, to restore maneuvering and weapons capability.

A new voice, a Terran voice, spoke to the Trang commander. "There's one more thing you need to know about Mustangs; they are herd animals. Mustang squadron here, back on station. I sure hope you don't want to surrender."

Mustangs

BIG DREAMS

Patricia Spradley

"Ladies and gentlemen be prepared to be amazed for I am the great magi Velho, and this is my talented, energetic assistant, Ayana." Ayana prances in front of Velho on the street. Velho is a young man with brunette hair that goes just past his ears, olive green eyes, and is an average height of around five feet.

A child stops, points, and asks, "Is that a ferret or a porcupine?"

Velho replies proudly, "That is Ayana she is an albino *saltu ericius*. Her quills can produce music. Would you like to hear it?"

The child claps. "Yes!"

"Then let the show begin! Ayana, music please."

Ayana's quills vibrate. The vibration sounds like chimes playing an old human folk song from the planet Nazavah.

Good, I'm getting a crowd now. A small crowd from Nazavah, but it's a start.

The small crowd claps as Ayana finishes the song.

"Now, Ayana can play ten different songs. Would you like to hear one more?"

The small crowd softly claps. That was pitiful.

"I SAID! WOULD YOU LIKE TO HEAR ANOTHER SONG?"

The children clap and scream, "YES!"

"Ayana, please play us another delightful tune."

Ayana's quills vibrate and chime an old folk song from the planet Giorgio.

Various anthropomorphic animals approach. Good, now I have the attention of some of the Giorgioans.

The song ends. Velho exclaims, "Now it is time for the real show to begin!"

Ok, think light ring. Hold closed left hand up. Open left hand. Touch left ring figure with right hand. A rainbow hoop appeared in front of him. It worked; of course, this is the easy one.

"Ayana, jump." Ayana jumped through the hoop twice. Let's go higher.

"Ayana, jump." Ayana jumped through the hoop twice again.

A gruff voice in the crowd commented "Is that all you can do?"

Great, a critic. I hate critics. They have no idea how many hours it takes to teach Ayana and learn spells. Take a deep breath, smile, and be nice.

"Ayana must warm up before getting to the amazing stunts; in fact, the more you cheer the more daring and spectacular the tricks will be. So, let me hear you cheer." A few kids cheer. "You can do better than that!" The kids scream, but the adults say nothing.

I love kids. Time for some tricky jumps. Velho pats the top of the hoop. "High." Ayana jumps over the hoop twice. Velho pats the top of the hoop again. "Bigger." Ayana jumps over the hoop flipping twice. The crowd claps more. Velho had Ayana do a few more fancy flips and for a little flare Ayana's quills chime. The crowd grows more interested in the show.

The gruff voice complains, "I thought you said that you were a magi, all I see is a pet doing cheap tricks."

Cheap tricks! This is a family show. Kids love Ayana. Take a deep breath, smile, and be nice.

"I am a great magi, but just like Ayana the more you cheer the more daring the show."

Time for a new spell. Think ball. Use both hands to from a circle. A medium sized rainbow ball bounced in front of him. Perfect! Ayana automatically jumps onto the ball. All four of Ayana's paws move the ball around weaving in and out of the crowd. She's so cute. She really likes doing the ball tricks. The kids seem to also like it since their faces always light up. Kids make this job so much fun.

"Ayana, stand." Ayana stands on her back paws on the ball and continues to move around. "Bounce." Ayana begins to bounce the ball while weaving through the crowd.

The gruff voice complains again, "My dog can do that. What kind of a show is this?"

I doubt that his dog can do this trick. But it is time to get ready for the finale.

"Prepare." Ayana brought the ball in front of Velho, still bouncing. "Ok, now."

Think stairs; use left hand to mimic walking up five steps. Ayana does a back flip. The ball turns into a set of stairs with five steps on each side. Ayana lands on the top step doing a handstand. The crowd claps and cheers. The children's eyes light up with delight.

Yes, she cleared the landing, and the crowd loved it.

"It is time for the grand finale!" The crowd cheers. "Ayana, let's dance." Ayana's quills vibrate chiming an upbeat tune. Ayana then flips, prances, twirls, and handstands up and down the steps.

Time for the spell that doesn't always work. Think sound; point to left ear. The steps hum in tune with Ayana's chimes as she dances. Yes! It worked.

The crowd claps and stomps while children laugh and dance to the beat.

"Big finish." Ayana made her way back to the top of the steps; there she did a back flip.

Time for my favorite spell. Think fireworks; alternate left and right hand opening and closing them as I move them. The steps burst into what looked like fireworks. Ayana landed on top of Velho's head. The crowd cheered and clapped. Take a bow. Ayana settles down on Velho's shoulders.

"Thank you, thank you it has been a pleasure to put this show on for such a lovely crowd; and please if you enjoyed the show…"

Think bucket; have left hand open facing down; then clasp it and pull it up. A rainbow bucket appeared in front of him.

"Place some money in the bucket so Ayana can eat tonight." Some of the people in the crowd walk away while others put money into the bucket. "Thank you." One person puts an apple core into the bucket. "Thank you."

"It's not a complement," the person gruffly says.

"But the apple core has seeds so that means you enjoyed the show so much that you believe that I should always have food to eat."

"I'm from Nazavah not Giorgio which means I think you should find yourself a job!" The person storms away.

What a jerk, I bet he was the one complaining throughout the show. Ayana chirped. Velho strokes her. I still can't get over how soft Ayana's quills are.

"We have three more locations which means three more shows today. Are you ready?" Ayana chirps. "Ok, let's go."

⋘   ⋙

At the end of the last show, Velho asks, "Ready to go home?"

Ayana chirps.

"I'll take that as a yes."

Velho walks to the edge of the resort and toward the apartments that houses the workers. Velho comes to a rundown shack behind the apartments. The shack is one room with a few blankets on the floor and one box storing breakfast bars. "We're home," Velho claims. There was no answer. "Maybe we should do some work on this shack. It looks like it's going to cave in."

Ayana jumps off of Velho's shoulder and bounces to a blanket in the right corner to lie down. "You're right, we worked hard today, and need our rest. I need to put our earnings away first. Please get up for one minute." Ayana yawns, stretches and jumps onto Velho's shoulder. "Thank you, it will only take a minute." Velho moves the blanket, lifts a loose board under it, picks up a bag, and puts the money inside. "I wonder if there is enough for a ship yet." Ayana paws Velho's cheek. "Ok, Ok, I'll count it later." Velho puts the bag under the board and adjusts the blanket. Ayana jumps down and settles onto the cloth. "You're so soft. You would think that quills would be sharp, but yours are covered in thin fur." He hears a quiet rumble. "I'm getting hungry. I wonder what Makoa will bring home to eat. He's going to be mad that I didn't eat lunch again. It's just hard to remember to eat when there's so much to do." Velho folds his hands behind his head and lay back on the floor. He sees the fading light of the sun shining through the holes in the ceiling. "Maybe, I should add more spells to the show; like walking through a wall, moving objects, teleporting.

Those spells are hard, but it would bring in a bigger crowd. Of course, I did promise The Lady that those spells would only be used in a time of need. After all, no one thinks that such spells can be done. People can be so narrow minded. But one day you, Makoa, and I will go to other planets, and we'll open their minds to the possibilities. I'll become a famous entertainer; everyone will want to see our show."

A gentle nudge in his side preceded a harsh, "Our show; I don't want to be in your show."

Velho sits up. "I was talking to Anaya." Makoa got a new metal right leg, and his left arm is missing again. Maybe he trashed it again. Makoa is tan, muscular, has thick bones, and long black dreadlocks pulled back in a ponytail. Makoa looks to be about forty, but he has never had facial hair. None of his people do.

"Did you eat lunch?" Makoa inquired.

"That new leg looks good on you; where did you get it?"

"You are young; you need to eat."

"I'm saving my money to buy us a ship."

"You need to get your head out of the clouds. People like you and me are at the bottom of society. Our dreams don't come true." Makoa drops the bag he had in Velho's lap. Ayana jumps onto Velho's shoulder who gives her a piece of fruit. "Besides, Melisam is the best planet to be on, some people like the Isambardans enslave magi like you."

"But some, like the Hopi Motu, worship magi."

Makoa frowns.

Ooops, I opened my mouth without thinking. Makoa doesn't like talking about his home world. I know–

"I would like to go to Aniani, they say that the planet is covered in crystals."

"Things don't usually turn out the way people want them to; look at me."

He always says that, but he never tells me what happened to his leg and arm. At least I assume that is what he is talking about.

"Are you going to tell me what happened?"

"When you're older."

"I'm 19; how much older do I need to be?"

Makoa groans.

Time to change the subject. Makoa talked about how he was going to train someone today.

"So how did the training go today?"

Makoa jesters to his missing limb. "If my leg wasn't already gone, I would have lost it today. That kid thought that he knew everything about how to cut scrap metal. Tomorrow I'm going back to fixing ships instead of scrapping them. What about you?"

"About the same. What about your arm?"

"You know that I hate the prosthetic arm. It doesn't move the way I need it to, so it just gets in the way."

"Maybe one day a prosthetic arm will move just like a real one."

"That will never happen. Although I never thought they would discover a new fuel source."

"What new fuel source?"

"More and more people are talking about how a new fuel source has been found. This fuel is supposed to last longer, cost less, make ships faster, and help ships fly out of this system. Of course, dreamers have always dreamed about finding new fuel, but the Hopi Motu and Eldoris won't let that happen." An unconfutable silence followed. Makoa yawns and rubs the back of his neck. "It's getting late. Good night." He laid up against the right wall to go to sleep.

A fuel source that could allow us to explore new worlds would be great. Hopi Motu and Eldoris wouldn't have a monopoly on fuel anymore either. Dreams can come true. You just can't give up when things get hard. I wonder what dream Makoa had. He must have had one at one time then something happened, and he gave up. It must have something to do with his missing arm and leg. Maybe, one day he will tell me. Velho hears Makoa snoring. Time for bed.

03   80

Velho stretches and enjoys the warm sun coming in through the cracks in the wall. The morning birds sing melodious songs. This music inspires musicians, poets, and artists throughout the system. Velho gratefully relishes the harmonic melodies every morning. "It is time to perform in front of a roaring crowd."

"Do you have to be so loud in the morning?" Makoa moans.

"I'm an optimistic person."

"You're a dreamer, and what does that have to do with being loud in the morning?"

"How long do you think we will be at this resort?"

"Who knows? You know I could get a more permanent job here this time, and we could rent an apartment, and have a better life."

"Then one day you will want to move to the next resort here on Melisam just like you did when I was a kid."

"You're still a kid."

Velho walks to the box to get a breakfast bar. "I'm going to go meet my fans and preform wonderful feats of magic." Ayana

chirps and jumps onto Velho's shoulder. He breaks a bar in half and gives it to Ayana.
"Your magic is unique; but you don't have any fans."
"You never know. I might have lots of fans out there. And one day everyone will know my name and I will go down in history as the greatest entertainer of his day."
Makoa shakes his head. "One day you're going to wake up and see that life isn't about making your dreams come true; it's about people like us barely surviving while the rulers of the different planets take advantage of others."
Velho gives Makao a breakfast bar. "I need to go. I want to get to Anne's Breakfast and Café when the breakfast crowd gets there."
"Be careful. And don't forget to eat lunch today"
"I'll be careful. I'll take a deep breathe, smile, and be nice. I hope you are careful fixing those ships today. Bye."
I'll show Makoa that there are lots of wonderful things in life and lots of wonderful people out there to enjoy it with.

ଓଃ   ଚ୦

Velho felt the afternoon sun beaming down on him. This is the largest crowd we've had all week! I think I see someone with wings in the crowd. She doesn't look like she's form Giorgio. The winged person stood about eight feet high and looked human besides the wings. Shouldn't she be at the Fly High Resort for the people of Zephyrine. The show ends and he takes his bows. "Please if you've enjoyed the show place some money into the bucket so Ayana can eat tonight."
The Zephyrinian lady walks up to Velho and puts money into the bucket.
"Thank you."

She inquires "I am looking for entertainers to perform at the Royal Resort; would you be interested?"

The Royal Resort! Every entertainer on Melisam wants to perform there, but very few get to go.

"Yes."

She gives him some papers and says, "I can't promise that you will be paid; each representative of each planet that will be at the meeting will choose to pay you what they believe you are worth."

"I understand. But why are you inviting me?"

"I saw your show last year at Fly High Resort and found it quite entertaining. How do you make objects appear?"

"Any magi can use their source magic to form objects, but most magi just stick to the basics and never explore what else they can do."

"Interesting. Your ticket to Royal Resort is in the papers along with when you are expected to be there."

"I won't be late."

He looks over the papers as she leaves. These papers say that I need to be at the Royal Resort in two weeks. My dreams are in reach. The diplomats at that meeting will be so impressed that I'll get plenty of money for a ship. Maybe, one of the diplomats will even offer me a job. Or, the manager at Royal Resort will want me work there full time. I'm going to be famous. I can't wait to tell Makoa.

೧೩   ೫೦

The fading light of the sun shines through the holes in the shack. Velho paces in the shack. "When is Makoa coming home?" Ayana chirped. "As soon as he gets here, I'll show him the papers and tell him about that Zephyrine lady."

"What Zephyrine lady?"

"Makoa!" Velho shoves the papers into Makoa's hands. "I'm doing a show at the Royal Resort in two weeks! Isn't this great!"

Makoa rustles the papers. "I can't go to the Royal Resort."

"Why not?"

"I'll just stay here and continue repairing ships."

"But I thought that it would be great if you could come too. You could see it as a vacation."

"I can't go. Besides the people of Zephyrine see magi as servants or lower-class citizens. This invite could be so they can make fun of you."

"She was impressed with my show. She said that she saw it last year."

"Look you are the only magi I know that uses their magic for entertainment. You do spells that no one has ever seen done. She probably sees you as an anomaly and wants to show her boss what you can do. That boss will look down on you and may want you as a 'pet', I mean servant, to preform anytime he or she wants. You will lose the freedom that you have now."

"But what if she just wants to show her boss that magi are more then they appear to be. Maybe, she thinks that there is more to life than what one sees on the surface. How about you come with me so you can see for yourself?"

"Ok, I think it's time I tell you how I lost my arm and leg."

He's really going to tell me. This has to be one of his "The world isn't fair, the higher class look down on everyone, the little people don't have a choice in who they will be, and dreams don't come true" speeches.

"I'm serious. Maybe, after you know, you will understand that dreams don't come true and people like us don't get to choose our paths. The people in power get to choose for us."

I knew it. But he really is going to tell me. After knowing him for ten years, I will know how he lost his leg and arm.

"As you know I'm from the planet Kauhoe. My people the Hopi Motu who live on the islands and the Eldoris who live in the ocean believe that magi are gods. We worship them and obey them. I dreamed of working on a ship for the 'gods' and becoming one of the best well-known followers and speakers for the 'gods'."

"You. I can't see you worshiping magi."

"That's because I don't anymore. But at one time, I studied the ways of the 'gods' and ship building. When I was 19 almost 20, I got my big break. I was hired as one of the engineers for Kaimana the god of the sea. My parents were so proud of me they hosted my tattoo ceremony, and I promised them that one day I will be the speaker for the 'Elder god'."

"Elder god?"

"The Elder god is the ruler of all. Basically, he or she is a king or queen."

"Tattoo ceremony?"

"As a Hopi Motu move up in society, they get a corresponding tattoo and there is even a ceremony."

"Oh."

"I was happy to work on the ship. The chief engineer told the engineer crew that we were going to the Royal Resort on planet Melisam. Kaimana had important business there, but the planet is full of non-believers and demons that would test our beliefs, but we must stand strong and follow the ways of the 'gods'. I couldn't imagine anything that would shake my belief. We landed at the Royal Resort. The crew was told to stay with the ship. I was young, I wanted to explore. So, me and a friend I made on the ship went to explore the resort. I saw for the first-time people from Giorgio. It was strange to see people with fur, some with scales, large paws and claws. My friend and I watched them for a minute. A cat child noticed us and walked over to us. I can't remember the details of the conversation only that she laughed when we said that magi were 'gods. She showed us that she was a magi and that she was just a person like anyone else. My friend said that we needed to go back to our ship, and he told me that that must be a demon trying to confuse us. I agreed with him, but I couldn't stop thinking about it. So, I went off by myself to try and find out if that little girl was a demon in disguise. I came across the Isambardians. They were about half my size. I saw a magi repairing the outside of the ship, a regular Isambardian was cracking a whip and yelling at the magi to hurry up. I asked her why she was treating a 'god' with such disrespect. She replied that magi were born to serve their masters and they aren't 'gods' and you Hopi Motu are so naive and weak to let the magi control you. I couldn't help but wonder if this was another demon or maybe she was right, I was naive. Over the next two days I would talk to different people among the Giorgian, Isambardian, Daedalus, and Nazayah. The Daedalus would say that magi were useless. The Nazayah and Giorgian agreed that magi were just people like anyone else, but their talents were best suited for farming. Isambardian would say that I had been brainwashed and I need to stop following the magi. I started thinking about how the magi among my people treated us; they controlled the food, fresh water, daily schedule, jobs, marriage, how many children we could have. That's when I realized that I was just as much a slave as the Isambardian magi. My people couldn't truly make our own decisions without the so called 'blessing of the gods'. I talked to my friend about it. He seemed to be really listening and understanding; however, he reported me as a heretic to the chief engineer and an investigation ensued. I was brought before Kaimana. He talked to me in private asking me many questions, threatened me, and insulted me. I had never seen any of the 'gods' act like that before and all my doubts about where I stood went away. I know that magi were people some good, some bad just like anyone else and I told Kaimana just that and that he was one of the bad ones. He called all the crew of the ship to a meeting and said that I had lost my way and that I had two choices: first when they returned to Kauhoe I could go to a monastery where I could devote myself to the 'gods' and seek forgiveness for the rest of my life, or I could be labeled a traitor and receive the great punishment, living in misery. I again told him that he was just a person like anyone else; not a 'god'; and that the Hopi Motu and Eldoris who weren't magi were treated like slaves. He said that it saddened him that one of his children had fallen into darkness and refused to see the light, so I would receive the great punishment, and to spare my parents the shame they would be told that I died. I know from our private conversation that he wanted me to receive the great punishment from the beginning. So, my right leg was cut off so I couldn't walk to heaven after death and my left arm was cut off because I had no place in society. I was told that if I return to Kauhoe or to the Royal Resort or to the Island Paradise Resort for the people of Kauhoe I would be executed so my lies could not spread. I learned that day that life is cruel, that those in power use others, and the little people like me don't have a say. I can't go to the Royal Resort but just know that your dreams may meet a tragic end, and if they do, I'll still be here for you like I always have."

"You mean since I tried to pick your pocket when I was nine."

"Yes."

"We are here, Ayana. The Royal Resort." In the center of the resort is a building that looks like a castle. The castle has twelve towers circling the center and a thirteenth tower in the center of the circle. "So much for thirteen being a bad number."

"Are you the magi Velho?"

Velho turned to see who was talking. He saw a person that had metallic looking skin, was about five feet high, and wearing a suit. He must be from Daedalus. "Yes."

"Please follow me."

Velho follows him out of the station and to a black hover car that had no roof. The Daedalus motions to the car. Velho gets in it. As the Daedalus gets in the car, Velho sees that the driver is also from Daedalus and wearing a suit.

"Please put the seat belt on," says the driver.

Velho buckles the seat belt. Ayana jumps off of Velho's shoulder and into his lap. The driver speeds down the road. The buildings go by in a colorful, vibrant blur. This hover car is going faster than they normally do. Of course, we're not sightseeing.

The hover car stopped behind the castle. It looks like we are going to go in the castle through a back door.

The Daedalus man got out of the hover car. "Please follow me inside and don't wander off."

Ayana jumps onto Velho's shoulders as he gets out of the car. "Why does this castle have thirteen towers?"

"There is one tower for each of the twelve cultural diplomats that come here. The thirteenth tower is where the meetings are held."

"Wouldn't it be better to have eleven towers then. One for each planet that has sentient life and one for the meetings?"

"When this resort was built the people of Hunapo were in the middle of a civil war and the people of Kauhoe each wanted their own tower if the people of Hunapo each had one."

"Ok, when do I put on my show? And where do I go?"

"That is not my department."

"So, who do I talk to?"

"They will come to you. Now please follow me to your room."

Velho follows him into the building. The walls are perfectly white. The bronze doors have silver plaques with symbols such as trees, a stove, bathroom, electric current, hazard, x, and numbers. This is your room. Please stay here until you are given further instructions." The Daedalus man left. The silver plaque on the door has a bed and male symbol on it.

Velho opened the door to the room indicated. The room had four bunkbeds against the wall. There were four other guys in the room. Two were from Giorgio. One looked similar to a red panda and was about 4 feet tall, the other looked similar to a muscular black panther and about 6 feet tall. One was from Nazayah with dark skin, and was tunning a guitar. The other was from Zephyrine. "Hi, I'm Velho and this is Ayana. Are all of you performers?"

"Yes," says the red panda, "I'm Sheng and this is..." Sheng jesters to the muscular black panther.

"I'm Ajit," the panther states. "We are part of an acrobatic group."

Sheng adds, "We have two girls in our group, but the sleeping arrangements are that boys sleep in one room and girls in another."

The Zephyrine states, "My name is Joaquin. My wife and I are dancers."

Velho inquires, "You can't stay in the same room as your wife?"

Joaquin says, "No, only two rooms are reserved for performers, but when my wife and I are not performing here we stay at our apartment at the edge of the Royal Resort."

The human states, "I'm Azibo. I sing and play the guitar. What do you do?"

Velho says, "I'm a magi, and Ayana does tricks."

Azibo responds, "I've never heard of a magi being an entertainer before."

Joaquin challenges, "Are you sure you're a magi? Or do you do tricks that make it look like you're a magi?"

Velho replies, "I know it isn't normal, but I am a magi."

Sheng asks, "Shouldn't you be taking care of a family farm?"

Velho replies, "I'm an orphan. I don't know who my parents were, and I have lived on Melisam for as long as I can remember."

Ajit states, "You were invited here because your act entertained one of the talent scouts for Royal Resort, so all of us should see you as one of us."

The Zephyrine lady that invited Velho entered the room. "Velho, I just wanted to go over a few rules with you."

Velho says, "Of course."

The Zephyrine lady says, "I am Elissa. I am in charge of all entertainment. One of the diplomats had an odd request for an entertainer and you fit the request. Now, you will be sleeping in this room, there is a room for you to practice your act, and a room where you will eat. Your fellow entertainers can show you where these rooms are. You can only be in one of these three rooms."

Velho asks, "But when and where do I perform?"

Elissa says, "Your act is scheduled for day three of the meeting. You will be escorted to the dining room the diplomats eat at on that day. If you wander you will be arrested and could face the death penalty. So, please stay in the rooms I mentioned and go nowhere without an escort. Do you understand?"

Velho answers, "Yes."

Elissa says, "Good, if you have any questions ask one of your fellow entertainers. They have all performed here before. Enjoy your stay." Elissa leaves the room.

Velho comments, "The rules are strict here."

Joaquin states, "They have to be."

Sheng adds, "It's because they have to protect all the diplomats and rulers. If something happens to one of them and you're not where you were supposed to be you can be blamed."

Ajit says, "We promised to meet the girls for practice, so if you're not too tired from your journey you can follow us to the practice room."

Velho strokes Ayana saying, "I'd like that. It would be good for me and Ayana to practice as well."

Sheng says, "Right this way."

Azibo asks, "Do you mind if I join, I'd like to see what you can do."

Velho says, "I don't mind."

Joaquin adds, "I would like to see your magic as well."

Velho followed Ajit and Sheng to the practice room. Joaquin and Azibo walked behind him. Occasionally, pictures of Melisam frame the walls. The pictures show the forests, waterfalls, flowers, and various animals. The pictures of Melisam are nice too. I wish I could explore, but I don't want to get arrested or executed. They enter a large open room. Velho saw a grey fox a little taller than Sheng and a grey and white cat a little shorter than Ajit doing some stretches.

Sheng gestures to the grey fox, "This is Querida," he gestures to the grey and black cat, "This is Niviarsiaq."

Niviarsiaq says, "Most people just call me Nivi, or Medium-rare."

Velho puzzles, "Medium-rare?"

Querida replies, "That's her stage name. We each have one. I'm Medium."

Sheng says, "I'm Rare."

Ajit says, "I'm Well Done."

Velho laughs. "I'm sorry."

Nivi says, "It's fine. It's supposed to be funny."

Querida inquires, "What's your name and what's your act?"

"I'm Velho and this is Ayana. I'm a magi."

Joaquin states, "Let us see some magic."

"What would you like to see?"

Ajit says, "Just do your show and we'll be your audience."

Velho says, "Ok." He went through his whole performance. The group was an excellent audience clapping and cheering throughout. Joaquin's wife came in and joined the group along with two other girls from Daedalus who looked like twins. The performance ends. "Thank you."

Sheng says, "Ayana, is a great acrobat."

Nivi says, "That jump onto the stairs was a difficult one, but your timing was perfect."

One of the Daedalus girls says, "It's good that you found a use for your magic."

Joaquin's wife comments, "I have never seen a magi make objects appear."

Joaquin adds, "Or that magic be a rainbow."

Velho says, "My source magic is light. When I cast a spell, I shine my light through the water particles in the air, so the object becomes a rainbow."

Querida says, "I hope you don't mind, but we need to practice our act. We are supposed to perform tomorrow."

Velho says, "I would love to see your act."

Sheng, Querida, Nivi, and Ajit put on their acrobatic act in front of the group. They balanced on each other. Ajit always on the bottom. They were juggling, cracking jokes, and doing flips. Velho admired their talent.

Velho enjoyed talking to everyone during dinner. He found out that Joaquin's wife's name is Bonita. The Daedalus twins' names are Calla and Despina. Calla and Despina are comedians. Everyone in the group except Velho had performed in Royal Resort before and had all moved here from different resorts after their first invite. I don't want to live here. I want to travel and show everyone that there is more to being a magi then what everyone thinks.

ଔ   ฅ

The day came for Velho's performance. He had a good time with the other performers; however, they did warn him that his performance may cause an argument. Right before dinner Velho is escorted to a small room. He is told to wait in the room until Elissa introduces him to the diplomats. The room is the same white color Velho has seen in all the other rooms. Velho is setting on a chair and Ayana is on his shoulder. Sheng told me that the diplomats were extra stressed. Nivi told me that it is because the Daedalusian scientists found a new fuel source on Timbisha. But Timbisha is a desert planet, no one lives there. Anyone who crash lands on Timbisha die in just a few days. Those scientists must have worn special equipment to survive there. Joaquin says that the diplomats from Isambard are here which means that I will have critics. But I know how to handle critics. I'll just take a beep breathe, smile, and be nice. Bonita seems to think that there will be a war and my performance won't help matters. But I want people to see what magi can be capable of. Everyone thinks that magi should just be farmers, servants, or slaves. Magi are capable of so much more. We can help build a better future and we should be allowed to choose our own path.

Elissa walks into the room, "Velho, it is time for your performance. Please follow me."

Velho follows Elissa to a banquet hall. The walls of the room are brightly colored with animals and plants from the eleven inhabited planets. Along the wall in front of Velho is a row of tables. The tables each have a cloth that is embroidered with gold and crystals. On top of the cloth is an array of food. Velho has never seen so much food in his life. Sitting at the tables Velho sees that there are three diplomats from each of the cultures from Zephyrine, Daedalus, Isambard, and Kauhoe. I was hoping to see what an Eldoris looks like, but with a metallic environmental suit I can't see their faces.

Elissa announces, "As requested by Mahpiya the representative of Zephyrine, I present to you an act you have never seen before. This is Velho." She whispers in Velho's ear, "Bow."

Velho bows and Elissa walks away. "Ladies and gentlemen be prepared to be amazed for I am the great magi Velho, and this is my talented, energetic assistant Ayana!"

An Isambardian says, "Magi!?! Are you some kind of clown?"

Take a deep breathe, smile, and be nice. "I do feats of magic never before seen and Ayana does tricks."

A Daedalusian says, "Magi are useless."

A Hopi Motu says, "We are not useless. Besides you said that only a magi can collect this so-called new fuel source. This so-called fuel is useless."

The metallic voice of an Eldoris says, "Kaimana makes an excellent point."

Kaimana! That's the Hopi Motu that had Makoa's leg and arm cut off.

A Zephyrine says, "Please let us watch the show as we eat and continue the debates later."

I wonder if that is Mahpiya.

The Zephyrine gestures to Velho, "Please proceed."

Velho continues. Throughout his performance the Isambardians glare at him. Take a beep breathe, smile, and be nice. The Daedalusian, Eldoris, and Hopi Motu seem to find the performance interesting. Two of the Zephyrine seem to look down on Velho, but one is so interested that he barley eats. The performance ends and Velho bows. "Thank you."

Kaimana comments, "This is why magi should rule over everyone!"

An Eldoris says, "Kaimana is right. You Isambardians should show more respect for magi!"

An Isambardian yells, "You magi are not responsible enough to rule! All you want to do is have fun." Gesturing to Velho she continues, "This magi was left to do what he wants and what does he do? He plays around with that animal all day. He doesn't know anything about how to take care of himself or others!"

A Daedalusian comments, "At least he found something to do with his magic. Magi have very little use and are limited in what they can do."

Kaimana yells, "We are not limited! We control elements like water, earth, and wind! Without us crops on many planets don't grow!"

A Zephyrine says, "Magi do have their uses, and they do need guidance. If magi are the only ones who can collect this new fuel source, then it is yet another useful talent."

Kaimana yells, "You don't need a new fuel source! We Hopi Motu and Eldoris provide all the needed fuel!"

A Daedalusian comments, "But this new fuel will last longer and help ships leave this system and explore new worlds. Think of the discoveries that could be made on new worlds."

An Isambardian says, "New slaves."

A Zephyrine says, "Cures for cancers."

A Daedalusian says, "Improved technology."

Velho says, "Equal rights to all no matter who they are or where they come from."

All the diplomats glare at Velho except one Zephyrine. He gazes with interest.

Elissa comes up behind Velho, sternly grasps his arm, and says "Come with me, and don't say anything."

Reluctantly Velho walks with Elissa. She's not giving me a choice. Elissa takes him to the small room he was waiting in right before his performance.

Elissa sternly states, "Stay here. In a few minutes, maybe hours, one diplomat from each culture represented will come in and pay you what they think you are worth. However, after that remark you will be lucky to get out of Royal Resort alive." Elissa slams the door behind her.

What was wrong with my statement? I was just contributing to the debate. I didn't insult anyone.

Two hours later, Kaimana and one of the Eldoris enter the room. Kaimana says, "You have quite the talent."

Velho says, "Thank you."

The Eldoris gives Velho money and asks "How about you join us? You would be called a 'god'."

Kaimana adds, "You could help us unite magi from all cultures so that the magi could rule over all planets; and be worshiped."

Velho says, "No thank you; I just want to be a great entertainer."

The Eldoris says, "But you would have servants; you wouldn't need to do any work; and all your needs and wishes would be met; you would have it made."

These are the people who hurt Makoa. Why in the universe would I join them? Take a deep breath, smile, and be nice. Velho says, "The offer is tempting; so just let me think about it."

Kaimana says, "If you want to be a 'god' you can come to my ship; I'll be here for three more days maybe a week at the rate this meeting is going."

Velho says, "I'll keep it in mind. Thank you". Kaimana and the Eldoris leave the room.

It is wrong to call yourself a 'god' just because you were born a magi. The Hopi Motu and Eldoris should be ashamed of themselves for taking advantage of others like that.

An Isambard diplomate comes in, spits on Velho, and yells "If you were my slave I would have you flogged! A magi should never speak!"

Velho wipes the spit off and says, "The Hopi Motu and Eldoris who are here are magi."

This infuriates the Isambardian, and she hollers, "You should be kissing my feet and begging for mercy! I'm going to report this insult and have you arrested!"

Take a beep breathe, smile, and be nice.

Velho calmly remarks, "I'm sorry you feel that way. Do you have any suggestions that could help me improve my show?"

The Isambardian was so mad that her skin and hair turned even darker. Her veins along her arms were pulsing. She balled up her fist and stormed out of the room. The door slammed with such force that the doorframe cracked.

There was no need for her to get that mad. You just can't please some people.

A Daedalusian enters the room next. She says, "I always thought that magi were useless. But lately I have learned that magi have some uses."

Velho says, "Thank you."

The Daedalusian asks, "Would you like to help mine the new fuel?"

Velho says, "No, thank you. I would prefer to continue entertaining."

The Daedalusain argues, "But we could help guide your talent, and make it more useful. Right now, your talent is being wasted."

Velho says, "I'm doing something that I enjoy."

The Daedalusain says, "Very well." She begins to walk away.

She didn't pay me. Although it seems she enjoyed my show.

She turns back around at the door and says, "We did not appreciate your comment. You are an entertainer and nothing more." She closes the door behind her.

I just want people to see that there is more to this world, and that everyone should be given an opportunity to better their lives.

The Zephyrine enters the room, gives Velho money, and says, "I am Mahpiya. I have never seen anyone use magic the way you do."

Velho says, "Thank you."

Mahpiya asks, "How did you do it? I did not think that magic could be used in such a way."

"Everyone puts too many limits on magic and don't use their imagination to see how far they can take it."

"But magic is limited, one can only us the element they were born to, for example a wind magi can adjust wind currents, and an earth magi can help seeds to grow."

"A fire magi can't make seeds grow; and a crystal magi can't move fire. However, all magi can make rings, balls, or steps out of their respective element if they want too. They don't do it because they have been taught only the basic levels of their powers and what will help their society most. It is good to know the basics; but different cultures put different pressure and expectations on magi and limit their abilities; the only true limits are one's stamina, knowledge, and imagination."

"That is interesting." He pauses then asks, "Would you be interested to taking your show to my home planet?"

"You mean perform on your planet?"

"Yes; you could do the show in front of our leaders; I would like them to see it; you could also do a performance in the theater for the commoners if you would like too."

"I would love too."

I don't have a ship; and what about Makoa?

Velho asks, "Would I be given a ride there?"

Mahpiya says "Yes, I can provide transportation."

"I have a friend; well, he's like my dad; can he come too?"

"If it is important to you; yes; if he wants to."

"He is banned from the Royal Resort; he's a Hopi Motu."

"Then we can meet you at the harbor of the resort he is staying at."

"We are currently staying at the Farmers Paradise."

"We will give you two weeks to get your things together and talk about it with him."

"Thanks."

I can't believe it I got my big break!

☙ ❧

The next day, Velho is eating breakfast, laughing and talking to the other entertainers. Elissa storms over and says, "Velho, you are to leave as soon as you finish breakfast."

Velho asks "Why?"

Elissa informs, "After your statement yesterday the Isambardians, Daedalusian, and two of the Zephyrinians wanted you to be arrested for immoral conduct. However; you did agree to work for Mahpiya. Mahpiya promised the delegates that you will leave Royal Resort and will only return here after you have had a proper education on how to conduct yourself. Thus, you are to leave the Royal Resort and wait for Mahpiya. If you do not leave you will be arrest. Do you understand?"

"I don't understand what was wrong with my statement, but I will leave and wait for Mahpiya."

"Good." Elissa walks away.

Querida asks, "What did you say?"

Velho replies, "I just said how everyone should have equal rights."

All the entertainers give him shocked looks.

Azibo says, "That was stupid, and bold."

Joaquin says, "Your statement goes against how magi are treated in all cultures."

Calla says, "Only on Melisam do you have the freedom to be who you are."

Bonita says, "Someone could have taken you in as a child and brought you to their home planet to be a slave, servant, or farmer."

Nivi comments, "She's right. You're lucky."

Sheng says, "You got to choose your path."

Ajit adds, "You're the only magi who got to do that."

Despina says, "That's all over now. You're going to be working for a Zephyrinian which means that you are now a servant."

Velho says, "I'm opening his eyes to the possibilities, and one day my show will inspire other magi to pursue their dreams and expand their abilities."

Azibo says, "You are a dreamer, but one person can't change how things have been done for hundreds upon thousands of years."

Velho says, "You never know."

Joaquin says, "Only war can help you get the change you want."

Velho says, "I don't want war."

Bonita says, "War is coming, and it will be about fuel and how magi should be treated."

Velho didn't know what else to say. I don't want war. Surly there is a way for everyone to just get together and talk about it. But the diplomats were arguing and refusing to compromise. No! I can't think like that. I'm going to Zephyrine. There I can talk to the leaders and open their eyes. Maybe, they will see reason and be willing to compromise with the other cultures. I'm sure that there is a peaceful solution. Velho finishes his breakfast and tells the other performers bye. The performers wish him well.

Velho lies on the floor of the shack and Ayana is on her blanket as they wait for Makoa to come home. I wonder if Makoa will come with us. I hope he does. He did say he would always be here for me.

Velho feels a gentle nudge in his side. He sits up.

Makoa asks, "So how did it go? Was it everything you dreamed it to be?"

Velho smiles, "It was great! One of the diplomats offered me a job."

"Which one?"

"His name is Mahpiya. His a Zephyrinian."

"Please tell me you turned him down."

"I accepted."

"Why would you give up your freedom like that?"

"He said that he would like for me to perform for the leaders of Zephyrine and the commoners too."

Makoa shakes his head.

"He said that you could come too. If you want too that is."

Makoa doesn't say anything at first. He's thinking about it. I can tell that he wants to come so he can look after me. But he doesn't want to come because he enjoys going from one resort to the next fixing ships.

Makoa finally says, "For the past twenty years I've done what I wanted to do when I wanted to do it. For ten of those years, I have tried to teach you and look after you. I have enjoyed my freedom. However, if I don't go with you, I will spend the rest of my life wondering what happened to you, and if you are taking the time to take care of yourself." Makoa pauses. "I will regret it if I don't go with you even though it means giving up my freedom to do so."

Velho jumps up and hugs him. "Thank you. You won't regret it. And you're not giving up your freedom. You're opening up a new chapter in your life. One full of adventure and possibilities!" Ayana chirps in agreement. "All you need to do is–take a deep breathe, smile, and be nice."

Acknowledgments

Special thanks to the many talented authors who devoted their energy to this project. Thank you. As well, to the editors and proof-readers for their valuable time.

The proceeds of this book will be donated to charities on behalf of the authors represented in these pages.

Other exciting titles from
Jumpmaster Press™

Chronicles of Stephen — Book Four
Kenyon T. Henry
The Road to Darkness

Philip Ligon
This Strange Engine

Art Lasky
Camelot's Last Heroes

Jeanne Hardt
Regenerates — Death Has a New Purpose